THE JUNIOR UNDERTAKER

DREAMS BECOME...

THOMAS KILCOURSE

EDITED BY **ALEXA TÉIDE**

EDITED BY **WILLIAM LINUS**

PHOTOGRAPHY BY **STEVEN GASKIN**

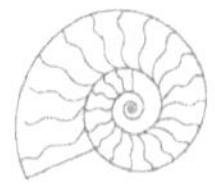

Nineteen eighty-two was quite a year! The memories of the summer and fall months I spent in SoCal are still vivid in my mind. As a kid, I was just like any other youngster from a small town with unforgiving weather who daydreamed after watching a show or movie filmed in California. I dreamed of going to The Golden State often, to visit its amusement parks, to see the Lakers or the Dodgers play. Then I reached puberty, and after having watched the Rose Parade every year of my young life during those freezing New Year's mornings, I fantasized about walking along the beach on a summer day or any day of the year. I imagined all the fun activities I could do because it seemed the weather in Southern California was always perfect. If you add that by my teenage years one or two adult magazines had gone through my hands, my adolescent feverish mind concocted dreams about Los Angeles as the place where models with bunny ears were running free. At least that was my fantasy. But let's go back to the weather.

Every Rose Parade morning, my siblings and I watched with envy the lack of snow on the streets. We wondered what it was like to be there. Feeling the warm morning sun on our skin, seeing the cheerleaders wearing miniskirts go by, and we as spectators not being wrapped up in heavy coats, scarfs, hats and gloves, looking like the Michelin man or the Pillsbury Doughboy. We wondered what it would be like to wear shorts on a winter day. Instead, we were all bundled up, sitting on the couch watching the sun shining brightly through the TV, while outside our windows the snow was piled up knee-high and icicles hung from the edge of the roof. Yes, I had dreamed of going to SoCal since I could remember, and my wish was made true in an unforgettable way.

Before I start recounting those days in Manhattan Beach from when it was a regular coastal town without the glamour that it now has, tell me, have you had a day, a week, a season that became pivotal in your existence? A period where the days went fast, and you lost track of what was going on? A period you will always remember for the good, the bad, and the ugliness that sometimes life dished out to you at once, when you were not expecting it.

For eighteen years my life had been simple, and you can stay monotonous. My childhood and teenage years were uneventful, but everything changed in an instant. One call, and 1982 became the year I will always remember for the memories made under the golden light of the California sky.

My aspirations after graduating high school were zero, there is not harm in saying it. After receiving the diploma my only goal was to enjoy the summer as much as my father would allow me. I was eighteen years old. I had time to figure things out, at least that's what I thought.

In 1982 I learned two very important lessons: the first, that things can change in an instant; and secondly, there is so much to explore—that is if you can hold on to life. Here are some memories from my days in a Southern California town by the beach, Manhattan Beach.

CHAPTER 1

MEMORIAL DAY AND MOM'S BIRTHDAY

MONDAY, MAY 31, 1982

WHEN YOU LIVE on a farm there is no eight to five, and holidays may be observed with a special dinner or a modified schedule, but if you expect to just sit down, kick your chair back, and put your feet up on the porch banister, you are mistaken.

Yes, I remember clearly Memorial Day of 1982, I had been helping Pa since the crack of dawn. The list of chores was endless: clean the stalls and animal pens, feed the animals (chickens, turkeys, pigs, cows, horses and rabbits), go to the fields and check that there are no issues with the irrigation system, do whatever needed to done for the crops depending on the growing cycle, plus any handyman work required for the house, barn, or any of the farm structures. There was always something breaking and you were the carpenter, plumber, and electrician. The list of daily activities had been ingrained in my brain since I was almost a toddler. No, my parents didn't send me wearing a diaper to dig trenches or unload hay, but as a young child you start to realize that there is a schedule that cannot be altered because guess what, the fields and the farm animals are not going to wait for you to get motivated to get out and do the job; neither is the bank going to wait because you were not inspired or didn't feel like getting the land ready for the new crops. I learned what bad weather meant for the farm just by looking at my father's face after making the rounds of the fields after a storm. He came back to the house wet, muddy and with an expression of sadness, rage, and despair. Before he could say a word, my mother would tell him that everything was going to be all right. Sometimes it was all right, other times it wasn't. Those were tough times.

Our farm was a working farm and not one of those idyllic ranches in the movies or a TV series where everything is spotless, and the rancher never looks dirty or tired. Nope, that was not our life; cuts, sweaty foreheads, dirt under the nails and worn-out clothes were our daily existence. Our tools and equipment had seen decades, and if we were fortunate, only years of use. You knew you had used something enough when the handle of your ax needed to be repaired or when it found its match in a stubborn piece of wood and broke, almost screaming *enough is enough.* You could hear it screaming at you "I cannot do it anymore, go and buy yourself something new." But we didn't have money for something new. My dad bought what somebody else didn't want when *they* bought the shiny new tools. Those were the days when things didn't make it to the landfill half used just because the new model was on the store's shelves. Oh no, in our household we only sent pieces of tools and unrepairable items to the landfill; we were recycling and up-cycling before those two words became fashionable.

But I have derailed my story and wound up telling you the condition of the farm tools. Let's go back to Memorial Day of 1982. Pa had promised Ma that we were going to take the rest of the day off after lunch, and yes, we were. Because the plan was to do everything that we regularly did in the day by the time we sat down to have lunch. No sir, there were not going to be any tasks left undone for the next day, not under my father's supervision. I am pretty sure if Mom had been in charge of the farm, she would have been OK with leaving a few things for the next day, but Mr. Joe E. Smith Jr. could never leave something for the next day. The old man's favorite refrain was "Do not leave anything undone today because tomorrow nature will not forgive you." He couldn't get over the memory of his childhood when his family lost a fifth of the crops because they didn't start early harvesting the fields and an unexpected storm arrived on the last day. They were able to use the grain, but they could not sell it, not at the price they wanted.

I don't remember Paul working as hard as I did. He got lucky—he went to school around the time we started having unexpected expenses. He never had to experience when our financial situation was precarious. Back then when Paul was in high school, Pa could afford to hire a few extra hands to help him with the farm, but during my high school years those extra hands were mine and sometimes even Daisy's. She had to put some gloves on and help, even if Ma had a list of things for her to help with around the house. Poor Daisy, she never complained when she needed to change her dress and put on her old beat-up denim jeans, her cowboy long sleeve shirt and her working boots. She was working as hard as Pa and myself—all while her girlfriends were doing their nails or going to the café and getting an ice cream sundae.

Yes, Paul was the lucky one, he convinced my father to let him go to college after getting several acceptance letters from schools offering him athletic scholarships. He finished his degree in accounting with honors and got married right away to his soulmate Gracie. He never had to come back to the farm to help full time like Daisy and I did. Sometimes, I wonder if my Pa made me work hard to motivate me to figure out what I wanted to do in life, but then I knew times

were hard and he was getting old. It didn't matter if I graduated from high school or not. He still could not afford to hire
more help and he could not afford to send me to college. Plus,
I was not getting any athletic scholarship, that was for sure,
and I was an average student that never had dreamed of
graduating with honors or obtaining an academic scholarship. I was just happy I was graduating. I used to think I was
destined to see the sunrise every day for the rest of my life
even if I had preferred to wake up one or two hours after the
crack of dawn and ignore the rooster singing in the morning.

Working on the farm was not my aspiration in life, but I
wasn't ready to join the army like my father did. That was my
last option. I was clueless. There is no shame in accepting that
at eighteen years old you are dreaming, making up stuff,
thinking you know what you want, and trying to sound all
grown up. But inside you are just a kid, a kid without diapers.
Your height and tone of voice doesn't determine your level of
maturity, I found out. I thought back then that I was mature
for my age, but I discovered in those few months in
Manhattan Beach that I was naïve, and I was a dreamer.
Reality has an interesting way in crashing into your dreams.

———

My mother had been working all morning in the kitchen
preparing the special lunch she had been planning for days
and that we had been anticipating. You see, besides Memorial Day, it was my mom's birthday. There was no way my
father could take her out for a fancy dinner, not even to the
modest diner we had in town. During those lean years my
mother seemed happy preparing her celebratory birthday
feast. She liked to cook, but most of the days she had to
settle for something simple, due to time and money
constraints. Not every day could she afford to prepare a
wonderful lunch and dinner. As on most of her birthdays,

she had decided to make barbecued ribs; she had spent all the morning preparing the ribs, using the secret recipe from her great grandmother, a recipe that includes honey. A recipe that my mother has not divulged to this day, and says it is included in the will for Daisy and I. As for Paul, after he graduated, he started to care less and less for country cooking, and more for fine white tablecloth restaurants than quaint small town eating establishments with red checkered linens.

I still remember how the tender meat came off the bone almost without touching it. Ma always liked to have as many side dishes for the ribs as she could cook—corn on the cob, potato salad with celery, scallions, carrots and bacon, macaroni and cheese, green beans, and for dessert she would bake an apple pie. Because it was her birthday, she also prepared an exquisite chocolate cake.

The days were getting warmer, and she planned something special for herself and Dad—a pitcher of mint juleps to be enjoyed on the porch later in the day. Just to relax and have some quiet time and enjoy the scenery. Daisy and I would be lucky if before dinner she would give us just a little of the mint julep. She would pour it into these crystal champagne cups that her mother gave her as a wedding gift; they were small with a silver border. While our family was not the champagne drinking type, my mother liked to use them to serve the only two cocktails that were prepared at home occasionally: old fashioned and sidecar. She cherished those little glasses so much and they were used sparingly. My parents drank their mint juleps in proper tall glasses with crushed ice.

Mother had just finished setting the table with a festive checkered red tablecloth when my dad and I walked in. She was standing at the end of the dining room, next to Dad's chair at the head of the table. She was quietly observing the table which was ready for her birthday and the Memorial Day food extravaganza. The natural light was trickling in and made the vase with white carnations sparkle. Mom looked happy.

"Rosie, you have made the last half hour difficult for us to work. We could smell those ribs all the way from the barn. We are ready to eat," Father said as he started to walk toward his usual spot at the table. I followed behind Pa, ready to take my place.

"Not so fast boys, first you need to go and take a shower. Today you are not sitting down with dirty clothes to have lunch," Mom said.

Mother knew that Father may wind up working after lunch if he still was wearing his working clothes. I was ravenous and ready to eat a double portion of those mouth-watering ribs hidden somewhere in the kitchen, but I knew better. And Mom was not going make an exception even if I was fainting from hunger. The quicker we showered and put on our Sunday best, the quicker we could get our hands on those ribs.

"Mom I will go and get ready; I will shower down here, while Dad uses the shower upstairs." I turned around and ran upstairs to get my towel and clean clothes. While the shower downstairs was functional, in the winter was an icebox and it was seldom used; we preferred to use the upstairs shower. Summer was just few weeks away. The weather was warm and using the downstair shower was fine. I would have taken a shower outside if that meant I could start eating.

"Why are you running?" Daisy asked as I almost collided with her in the hallway upstairs.

"I need to shower," I said.

"That's a first," she snarled, and turned around heading downstairs.

I could hear Dad and Mom telling her she looked lovely in the dress she had finished sewing over the weekend. Daisy was sweet when she was younger. She became a teenager and all of a sudden was moody—you never knew which Daisy you were going to get.

———

"Honey, thank you for this wonderful meal," Dad said as he was reaching for one more piece of corn to eat.

"You are welcome, I am happy we are together. If Paul was here, it would be perfect."

Mother got a little sentimental every time we were having a good time. After years of Paul being gone, you would think she was over it. It was not like Paul was dead or lived on the other side of the world. I guess he was the first born and he always was going to be her baby.

"Rosie, you should call him after lunch," Dad suggested, hoping to get my mom out of her momentary funk.

But I understood it wasn't the same to call your son on your birthday rather than your eldest son calling you to congratulate you. My mother had been waiting for a birthday card. The days before her birthday she went through the mail, slowly hoping to see an envelope addressed to her with Paul's writing. There wasn't and she had a frown on her face when she put the mail down on the little table next to the entrance. That was her routine not only for her birthday, but also when she expected a Christmas card or Easter card, which were sent by Paul's wife; too late for my mom's liking.

"I may call but I don't want to interrupt their day off," Mother responded.

I couldn't understand my mother sometimes, one minute she was missing her son so much and the next she was concerned about interrupting the day of her absentminded son Paul.

"Well, Rosie if you don't call him, I will," Dad said as he took a bite of a biscuit, putting an end to the Paul discussion.

"Joe you may want to save room for dessert."

"I already did," my dad replied with a big smile, and he rubbed his belly. Daisy and I chuckled, as my mother moved the basket with the biscuits away from my father's reach.

The phone rang and Mom turned to see the phone sitting on one of the tables in the living room. My father had a rule—meals should not be interrupted by phone calls or anything else. If somebody needed to talk to you, they would call you back. With every ring of the phone my mother became more anxious, looking towards where the phone was, wondering if Paul was calling. I thought my brother knew better than to interrupt our feast, but then again, maybe he had forgotten. After all, it had been almost six years since he had left home.

"Rosie, whoever is calling will call back."

"Yes, just I thought it may be our son."

"Well, either he calls back later or we call him," Dad stated.

Mother took a sip at her glass of lemonade.

"Mom and Dad, can I go to Emily's house after lunch for a few hours?" Daisy asked. My baby sister was fifteen years old and as she was getting closer to sixteen, my parents were becoming more protective of her. I was wondering if they weren't going to let her out of the house except to go to school after her sweet sixteen. She may not even want to turn sixteen if my parents were going to keep monitoring her every move like hawks.

"Yes, just be back before six," Mom said.

"And stay away from Johnny," Dad added.

Johnny was a year older than me, nineteen. He was Emily's oldest brother, the black sheep of her family as Dad liked to refer to him. He had a reputation of being a trouble-maker and bad boy—a reputation that had every parent with teenager daughters concerned because his looks and bad boy status made him a teenage girls' magnet. He was the rock star of our small community.

"Yes, I will be back at six, and Johnny most likely will not even be home. Don't worry, I will stay away from him," Daisy replied as she lowered her gaze to her plate. I thought she may secretly be one of Johnny's many followers. My parents would have grounded her for eternity if she was.

"How about you Dan? What are you planning to do for the rest of the day?" Mom asked. I knew she didn't literally mean the rest of the day, she just wanted to know what I was planning to do between lunch and dinner.

"I want to catch up with some reading and then Carson and Matt are picking me up to go to the creek," I omitted that half of my senior class was going to be there and some of the guys were planning to bring beer bought by their older siblings after having paid a hefty cost. I knew Mom and Dad would be OK if I drank one beer because I wasn't driving and because they felt that if I wasn't allowed to have a beer occasionally then I would be getting drunk behind their backs.

"Be careful and be back for dinner."

"I will Mom."

"Why does he get to be here at 7:00 and I have to be here at 6:00?" Daisy pressed my mother.

"Because you are only fifteen, young lady and because you need to help your mother to prepare dinner," Dad said in a tone of voice that we knew it meant he had spoken the last word. No point in arguing.

As usual, after having a slice of pie, we thanked Mom for lunch. The chocolate cake was for dinner when we would give Mother her presents. Each one of us got up and took our dirty dishes to the kitchen. Father usually took Mom's dishes. Daisy was excused that day from washing the dishes and even Mom didn't start washing them right away, after all it was her birthday.

She went and sat in the living room. She kept her knitting basket next to the chair with the best natural light. Mom loved to knit. If she had her way, she would be knitting all day long and we would have more sweaters, scarves, mittens, and hats.

Father grabbed the local newspaper and right away he started commenting on the local news.

"Can you believe it? They haven't given up on trying to re-build that hideous bridge nearby the Benson's farm." Mom listened to him and occasionally said a word or two, but she knew he was just thinking out loud while he read the paper. Daisy ran upstairs to change because she would be riding her bicycle to Emily's. I went to my room and instead of reading the book I had borrowed from the library, I started looking through the February issue of *Popular Mechanics* that my friend Fred had lent me. His dad had gotten him a subscription to the magazine, and he was nice to let me read the old issues. I used to dream that one day I would get to drive one of the fast cars in the magazine, while Fred's dream was to be an engineer and work for NASA. The issue I was reading had an article about deep sea exploration. Yeah right, I only could dream. We lived far from the ocean, and I was sure that a degree was needed in order to do that type of research, or any other type of research. Most likely I was not going to go to college. Nevertheless, I enjoyed reading the magazine, even if there were articles I didn't understand completely. I was daydreaming about the deep-sea exploration when the phone rang. I was sure Mom was going to run to answer it.

"Daddy, I will get it."

I could hear Mom walking to the phone to answer it. Our wood floor made a lot of noise which was expected in old farmhouses like ours.

"Hello this is Rosie," Mom cheerfully answered the phone, hoping that her first born was calling.

"Oh! Tony what a surprise! How have you been? How are the girls?"

Tony Westfield was Dad's friend, and buddy from his

years in the army. I could hear my dad's footsteps as soon as Mom said Tony.

"Please give my regards to Pam, hope you guys come to this side of the country soon, here is Joe."

"Hey Tony, how are you?" Dad took over the conversation with Mr. Westfield. Tony and Dad usually talked around Christmas or New Years, on the anniversary of D-day and a few more random times. I tried not to listen to what my father was saying, but I couldn't avoid paying attention to his words when he said my name. "Daniel graduated from high school last week, no he does not have plans to go to college anytime soon." There was a long pause, Dad was silently listening to whatever Mr. Westfield was saying and then he said, "Gosh Tony that is a generous offer, but first I need to talk it over with Rosie. You see Tony, Daniel has been helping me a lot, and now that he is out of school, I was planning to repair the barn and take care of some deferred maintenance."

I wished I could have listened to what Mr. Westfield just said to Dad.

"Tony if it is okay with you, I will call you later tonight after I discuss it with Rosie. I am sure Daniel would be happy to help." A quick silence and my dad ended the call and hung up.

"Joe, what did Tony want?" My mother was quick to ask.

"Pam convinced Tony to take them to Europe on a two-week summer vacation. They need somebody to take care of the two dogs they have. They just remodeled the house, from the back fence to the front yard and they don't want any strangers in the house. He was asking if Daniel could go and take care of the dogs and the place."

Tony lived in California. That meant he was asking my father if I could travel to California. Wow!!! The day was looking better, the summer was looking better. But my parents' conversation got interrupted by a knock on the door.

With all the excitement I had not paid attention of the sound of the car parking in front of the house.

"Good afternoon Mrs. Smith! And happy birthday!" I heard Carson saying through the screen door. Of all days, that day Carson and Matt arrived early to pick me up. They were always late. Never on time. Carson wishing happy birthday to my mom only meant he wanted a slice of any sweets my mother had prepared; I shouldn't say that he always hadn't been nice and polite to my parents, but I also knew about his sweet tooth and how he could work his way into getting slices of pies or fresh baked cookies.

"Hello Carson, how are you doing? Come in!"

"Doing well ma'am. Hi Mr. Smith!"

"Hi Carson, where are you guys going?" Dad knew we were heading to the creek, but he just had to ask in case that I had told him a version of our outing or had not told them the truth which until then I never had lied to him.

"We are going to the creek to meet some of our former classmates," Carson replied.

"Do not get in any trouble."

"No, sir we will not."

Carson knew that getting out of the car and saying hi to my parents went a long way. He and Matt took turns when they came to pick me up.

"Dad, Mom, I will be back by 7:00," I said, wishing to stay there and find out what my parents were going to decide regarding Mr. Westfield's request. I could be going to California soon, a trip I never thought about in my wildest dreams. But I had to wait. For all I knew they could say no to him, and I would never be told.

———

After a short drive we reached the unpaved country road leading us to the spot on the creek where the Memorial Day fun was going to take place. I had been looking forward to this, but I wanted to go back home and ask my parents about Mr. Westfield's call. The prospect of going to sunny California had stolen the enthusiasm of getting together with former classmates, the beers, plunging into the creek, and of course the girls.

"Hey, I think Betty Ferguson is here with her girl-friends," Matt said and pointed to the old green pickup truck parked under a mature birch tree. I had liked Betty since freshman year but every time I tried to get close to her and just make small talk, one of her friends showed up and took her away. The first week in my senior year I came close to inviting her for a soda, but Burt Kilroy came from nowhere and got in front of me, just as I was ready to say her name. She went out with Burt for a while. It didn't last. Some said because Burt was just collecting dates. Then she went out with Tim Reynolds for a month or two, but her parents put an end to it because he was eight years her senior and they were more protective than my parents, if that was possible.

"Are you afraid that old Ferguson will show up at your house with his shotgun if you talk with Betty?" Carson said as he chuckled. He took immense joy in my lack of luck with girls; not that he had a lot, but somehow, he liked to gloat over my misery while ignoring or masking his own.

"Nope, I am not afraid. I will talk with her today."

"Matt, did you listen to that? Dan is going to propose to Betty today!"

"I didn't say that I was going to propose, I only said I will talk to her. You know, just talk."

"Come on Carson leave Dan alone, I am sure he will talk to her." Matt was mellower than Carson, but I was concerned because he had a grin on his face.

We parked and walked to where everybody was. Matt took the lead, and we followed him. I was not paying attention and all of a sudden we were right in front of Betty and her girlfriends.

"Hey ladies, do you mind if we join you?" Matt asked.

"No, we don't. Right girls?" Theresa Olsen replied. She was the most outgoing of the group.

I sat on a rock that was opposite to Betty.

"Hello Betty, are you not getting in the water today?" Those were the only words that I could come up with. She was wearing denim shorts and a pink top with ruffled straps.

"Hi Dan, no I'm not. Pete and I will be leaving shortly, we're going to the city with Mom and Dad to do some shopping. Mom does not want to miss out on the Memorial Day sales." Pete was Betty's twin brother who was splashing in the creek like a salmon swimming upstream.

"Do you think the stores will still be open by the time you get there?" I asked.

"Good point, but nobody will dare mention to Mom the possibility of the stores closing early," Betty replied.

Betty was sitting on a small crocheted brown blanket over a patch of grass. She was hugging her legs and when she stopped talking, she rested her chin on her knees. Just as she had said, in less than fifteen minutes Pete was out of the water trying to get dry before getting in the old pickup truck and driving away the girl of my dreams. I was left counting the minutes to get back home for dinner. It's interesting when you want time to fly by, it just passes like a snail over the grass.

––––––––

That night dinner was delicious and quiet. Mom had baked a chicken with potatoes and carrots; she even saved some mint juleps for Daisy and me, the watered-down version from the pitcher that had been in the refrigerator earlier in the day. By the time the dinner was over, Mom had lost the cheerfulness she had earlier. I thought she was just tired, or she was sad that they tried calling Paul and nobody answered, and he had forgotten Mom's birthday. There were three important days for Mom that meant a lot for her and should not be forgotten: her birthday, my parents' wedding anniversary and Christmas. But soon I understood the reason why Mom was not her usual self.

After eating the chocolate cake and Mom opening her birthday gifts, we helped clear the table. Daisy started washing the dishes right away. I went to my room and Dad went to check on the chickens after hearing a sound and a little commotion coming from the chicken pen. There had been sightings of a red fox. After Dad went to check on the chickens, he came to my room.

"Daniel, you left the grain bucket on the roof of the chicken pen and the wind tipped it over, the sound got the chickens all rattled."

"Sorry, I will be more careful," I replied. I didn't consider my absent-minded incident to be an event for my father to come up to my room and tell me the emotional state of the chickens. It was nothing compared to the time I forgot to close the door of one of the horse stalls and we found Roger wandering in the front yard. He didn't reprimand me for that besides just telling me to be more careful and walk the horse back to his stall.

"Daniel, my friend Tony called earlier, and he asked for a favor. He will be out of the country with his family for two weeks and he would like for you to take care of their dogs and house. After giving it a lot of thought, your mother and I agreed that it will be a good opportunity for you. There are so many things we need to start working on now that you are out of school, but those projects can wait until you come back. What is a few more weeks after the months we have waited. It will be more tiring to work in the summer months, but this is an opportunity to see a different part of the country."

A trip to California!!! I played it cool, I wanted to jump up and down, but I restrained myself.

"Dad, why does Mr. Westfield want *me* to take care of his dogs and house?" I was curious, I was sure there were plenty of people who could do it that lived in Los Angeles.

"Son, I don't completely understand why he doesn't ask somebody in his neighborhood. But remember a few summers ago when he came and visited on his way to Chicago? Well, you made a good impression on him. Tony doesn't have relatives in the area, and he doesn't want to ask one of his employees to take care of the house. So, he figured you may want to go and spend two weeks in sunny California."

Sure, I wanted to spend some days anywhere but on the farm—some place that I would not be working from sunrise to sunset.

"Is Mom OK with me going to California?" I asked. Even if she was not OK with me going, I knew that ultimately it was up to my father, because he was going to be losing a pair of hands.

"She is now, after talking with Tony. She knows we cannot afford to travel as a family to a part of the country as far as California. If one day you go to college, this is a good opportunity to see what it's like to live away from home and in a big city like Los Angeles. She doesn't like it that you will be gone for almost three weeks, but she also knows that she cannot keep you in the house forever. One day you will leave the house and maybe the town or even the state."

I thought Mr. Westfield must be a great salesman if he had convinced my mother in letting me go.

"When do I need to be there?"

"He wants you to get there by June 19th to be able to spend at least three days with them, to go through what you will need to do, show you the town and get the dogs used to your presence."

"Am I taking the bus there or the train?"

"You will be flying."

I only had flown once when we had to fly to see my grandma for the last time because she was dying in the hospital. She was getting weaker by the hour and my father thought this was the only way to make it. He was right. We arrived by early afternoon and the next day Grandma was gone. There was enough time for my dad to say his goodbyes and hold my grandma's hand one last time. My father was in the room with her when she closed her eyes, not to open them again.

"Wow, I can't wait!"

I couldn't contain my excitement anymore. Going to California, no working on the farm, flying, being alone for the first time in my life. The summer was looking pretty good.

"Well Dan, have a good night."

"Goodnight Dad."

As soon as Dad left my bedroom, I searched my closet for my old atlas of the United States; I wanted to see which states I was going to be flying over. In the following days I couldn't think about anything else but my upcoming trip to California. Matt and Carson asked ad nauseam to send them postcards; Daisy was happy for me, but she told me not to get any ideas of staying longer than the weeks Dad had agreed to with Tony. She didn't want to be stuck with being the only one helping Dad and Mom forever. Two days before my departure, Mom entrusted me with her Kodak 110 camera, she even gave me two cartridges of film. Soon I was packing for my first solo trip!

CHAPTER 2
THE ENDLESS WAIT

SATURDAY, JUNE 19, 1982

EVERY OTHER DAY I had to drag myself from bed to get ready for the day, but not on that day, the day I was embarking on the unexpected summer adventure. I remembered jumping out of bed, like a jack-in-the- box, quickly making my bed, then sitting there for a good hour waiting patiently for my parents to wake up. A small suitcase was by the door. I read a book, trying to calm my mind and stop looking at the clock wanting the dial to go faster so I could get to the airport and get aboard the plane to my connecting flight and cross the country on my way to Los Angeles. Finally, I could hear the steps of my parents getting ready to leave their room. Their door opened. Soon I could hear Daisy complaining it was too early to get up when my mother went to wake her up. Within thirty minutes everybody was in the car ready to take me to Chicago where I was going to get my flight to Los Angeles.

Mother was not happy or sad. She had not smiled and was silent on our way to the airport. Father tried to start conversation, but it didn't last. As soon as we reached the outskirts of

Chicago, he stopped talking; he needed to concentrate on navigating the city traffic. Daisy fell asleep minutes after we left town. She could sleep anywhere, and having woken up so early just made it easier for her to doze off in the car. She had wrapped herself in a blanket she dragged out of the house.

There we were, Mother was not too happy about me leaving for three weeks, Daisy didn't want to be there and be left behind, and Dad was content that I was going to have a working vacation in a place we could not afford to travel to. Finally, we were at the gate.

"Remember son, you will be taking care of somebody else's property and pets. Do not do anything stupid. I don't want to get a call from Tony upon his return," Dad said as he put his right hand on my shoulder. That was as much of a hug as I was going to get from the old man.

"Don't worry Dad."

"Dan, please be careful in the city. Be cautious at the beach; you are not used to swimming in the ocean," Mom said as she gave me a big hug.

"Daniel, be back soon. I don't want to be left taking care of your chores forever. Bring me something from Los Angeles," Daisy said as she hit me on the arm.

"I will be back, sis," I said as I returned the hit.

"OK Son, it is time for you to get going."

"Yes, Sir."

I took my backpack and I proceeded to board the plane. I turned around one last time to see my family and I saw Mom hugging Dad and Daisy holding my mom's arm. I turned back and kept walking.

I remembered the pilot informing us we were within an hour from arriving to Los Angeles. Shortly after that there were houses, buildings, and streets as far as you could see. The open land that we flew over for the last few hours had vanished and only buildings, highways, and streets were visible for miles. The small towns and cities scattered over the land connected by roads that from the air looked like threads were gone, and now there was this enormous city. My father always said California was beautiful, but what I was looking at was grey. Then there was a layer of brownish fog, it seemed that in no time we were going to be engulfed by it. There was a little bumpy patch before landing. The lady next to me was nervous, the same lady who told me before we took off that flying was the safest form of transportation and there was no reason to be nervous. This was after I told her it was my first long flight. She screamed when we hit turbulence and drank two small bottles of whisky to calm her nerves. I didn't think too much about the turbulence, it reminded me of driving on one of the country roads after a good rainstorm when the potholes just got bigger.

Finally, we landed and taxied for a while to our gate. I never had seen so many planes, and big planes, 747s in so many colors with logos of airlines I didn't even know existed. I was wondering from which part of the world those planes had come from, and what was their next destination. Were the seats bigger because the plane was bigger? We reached the gate and the lady next to me wished me a nice time in Manhattan Beach and told me I was going to love it.

I only had seen Tony once in person when he had stopped by to visit us. I had seen his younger self in old pictures from World War II that my father kept in an envelope in the desk in the living room. I remembered he was tall, had a mustache and a small diagonal scar on his face, a reminder from the war. I came out of the gate, to a sea of people, there was so much commotion, families welcoming loved ones, travelers making their way through and running to other gates to catch their next flight. I slowly scanned the area and I saw Mr. Westfield holding a piece of paper with my name.

"Good afternoon, Mr. Westfield!" I stood in front of him and extended my hand. I remember he was taller, but I had what my mom called my last growth spurt, and by that summer I reached six two.

"Hi Dan, welcome to Los Angeles! How was your flight?"

"It was a calm flight. I never have travelled this far, and it was interesting to fly over different terrain."

"Well son, I am happy you could make it. We sure appreciate it that you will be taking care of the house and the two spoiled dogs that belong to my daughters. Did they feed you? Are you hungry?"

I was starving, even after the little tray of food that had been given to me midway. I could have eaten the tray of the lady next to me. She was too nervous to eat, she just opened the little dish and put the cover back, I was going to ask if she was going to eat it, but I could hear my mother telling me no.

"They gave us a small snack," I said. I didn't want to tell my host that I could devour a sandwich or two.

"I'm sure you could eat a stack of pancakes. At your age I was always hungry, maybe the smell of bacon and maple syrup will wake up your appetite."

I smiled and we started walking through the terminal. Soon we were taking a tunnel and driving on a street that ran parallel to the airport, later I learned that its name was Imperial Highway. Mr. Westfield was giving me information as we drove; the town next to the airport was El Segundo and next to it was Manhattan Beach where he lived. On the other side of the airport was Marina del Rey. The main industry in the area was aerospace—satellites, planes, radar systems and defense stuff. We reached the end of Imperial Highway and turned onto Vista del Mar (View of the Sea); it was the most beautiful view I had seen in my life. There it was, the Pacific Ocean that I had seen in so many movies and shows, I was finally in front of it, and I couldn't wait to get my feet in the sand and touch the water.

"Isn't it beautiful?" Mr. Westfield asked, taking me out of my contemplation.

"Yes, it is."

The beach was wide, and the water was blue, a dark blue. I could see at a distance a plane flying over the ocean. The car windows were down, and a whiff of rotten air came in. I thought, how can something that beautiful stink so bad.

"Dan, this distinct aroma is the price we need to pay to see this view. This faintly rancid smell is delivered to you thanks to the sewage treatment plant, or as some of the locals call it— the 'Poo-Poo Factory'—that we just went by. It is a shock to visitors who are not used to the smell of wastewater being treated."

"It is good to know that the smell is not coming from the ocean. The stench reminds me of the smell of an outhouse on a warm summer day," I said without thinking. My comment would not have been approved by my mother as part of the first conversation with my host.

"Ha ha ha! No, no Dan!" Tony chortled. "The ocean breeze is salty. You are lucky, today the marine layer cleared early, sometimes during this time of the year we do not get to see the sun until after lunch. Well son, this is Manhattan Beach."

The houses were small and hemmed in against each other. From every intersection you could see the shimmering ocean. We stopped several times to let girls in their bikinis or guys barefoot and with shaggy hair cross the streets. I was told that with everybody out of school, the beaches were busy with people playing volleyball, sunbathing, surfing and just hanging out. I was speculating if I was going to be able to meet some of the locals during my short stay in Manhattan Beach.

We parked on a side street and walked two short blocks to a small building with blue roof and trim that turned out to be a pancake house and breakfast place. There were people waiting, but we were assured that it was going to be only a five-minute wait. The smell of the pancakes and bacon made the wait longer. It was a small place with no more than ten tables jammed inside. We sat next to a window and between bites of bacon, pancakes, hash browns and fruit salad, Mr. Westfield told me how he met my father during army training.

My dad and Mr. Westfield were only seventeen years old when they enlisted. Their first day during boot camp the sergeant in charge of their group asked who Joseph Earl Smith and Anthony Westfield were. After identifying themselves, the sergeant said he was not running a f… nursery school and didn't know what he had done to be assigned not just one, but two seventeen-year-old kids to his unit. Since that day my father and Mr. Westfield became friends, and they trained the hardest to show the sergeant they were not babies. After training they were sent to Europe, but the war ended within a month of their arrival. One day they were driving a jeep when a drunken guy that had been in the war since Normandy hit them. Dad was injured and sent back home. Mr. Westfield was sent to the Pacific where he saw combat in the Philippines, and a Japanese soldier gave him the scar on his face, but the Japanese soldier paid with his life. Mr. Westfield went to Japan during the occupation and then in 1951 came back to the United States.

"It's nice finally to have breakfast with somebody that will eat. I need to twist my daughters' arms to come for a weekend brunch to this place. Leslie and Megan as soon as they turned twelve or thirteen years old started eating like rabbits. They used to love to come with their old man to have some good pancakes. This was cheaper for me. Now they love to go shopping with their mom and spend as much money as possible. Dan, let's go and meet the ladies of my life," Mr. Westfield said as he put some dollars and coins on the check tray.

"Thank you for the breakfast." I told him.

"You are welcome, Daniel."

I followed my host out of the small quaint place and headed back to the car. We left behind the main street that we had be driving on, on our way from the airport.

"Dan, do you see that church tower with the dome on top of it? We live just two blocks away from it."

I noted that it was an easy landmark that would serve me as reference in case I went to the beach while taking care of the Westfield's house. We started driving uphill and turned left and right a few times. We pulled into a driveway of this impeccable white, two-story house, with red and pink rose bushes in the front yard and well-maintained green grass.

"Son, we are here. I thought you could meet the girls before their excursion to the shopping center. Too bad we missed them. Knowing how they go from store to store, I am sure they won't be back until almost dinner. We are going to be gone only two weeks and they are acting like it's going to be for months, and as if we will be rubbing elbows with the royal families of Europe. You would think they have nothing in their closets."

Mr. Westfield had this rapid-fire way of talking; he sounded like a salesman trying to convince you to buy an old jalopy. This was interesting because in his business, a funeral home, there was not too much selling. The customers fall at your feet. They would find you, you do not need to find them.

We entered the house. My host took his shoes off and I followed. The sound of a vacuum filled the entry way. At the left there was a dining room and to the right the living room where a petite lady was vacuuming furiously. She passed the vacuum in the same spot more than once and yanked the cable like a cowboy pulling the rope of a horse.

"Dolores, Dolores we are home." Dolores didn't turn around. "Dolores would not even know if somebody broke in. You cannot take away that little radio from her. If I had known, I would not have given it to her when we got the Walkman."

Mr. Tony went and tapped on Dolores' shoulder. She jumped in the air. She was petite but stocky. She turned around and faced him.

"Ay Dios mío! Mr. Tony, you want to kill me? Stop doing that," Dolores said, removing her little headset.

"Dolores, I called you several times. You didn't hear the car parking in the driveway, the door opening, nor us walking inside the house. I sure hope nobody ever breaks in because they could come and go without you knowing it," Tony exclaimed.

"Mr. Tony, I can feel bad energy when it is around. You have good energy, then I do not feel fear."

My host looked at me and smiled. He didn't respond to Dolores' energy comment.

"Dolores, this is Daniel Smith, he will be staying here until we come back from the trip."

"Hello, Danny. I am Dolores, I take care of the house and cook. You need a good sandwich, you look like you need one, you need more meat on those bones. I will make sure you eat properly while you are here. I will go and make you a sandwich right now," Dolores declared as she was ready to leave the vacuum lying lifeless on the carpet.

"Thank you, Miss Dolores, but Mr. Westfield took me to breakfast on the way from the airport."

"Well, if you get hungry, just let me know and I can prepare for you a sandwich."

"Thank you, Miss Dolores."

"Oh, Mr. Tony, this kid is so polite. Nice kid, nice kid," Dolores said as she turned around, put her head set on and turned on the noisy vacuum.

"Dan, let me show you to your room so you can unpack. If you need anything else just let us know. I will be in my studio making some calls after Dolores is done going around the house rolling that vacuum."

Mr. Westfield pointed to a door next to the living room, then we started going up the stairs to the second floor with the two teenagers' bedrooms, a family room, and a guest bedroom. The master bedroom was downstairs. My room was going to be the one next to the street. We had just entered the room when two dogs came up the stairs barking. They made a tremendous noise. The barking was inversely proportional to their size. The two puffy lap dogs came into the room, one was brown and the other one white. Tony told them to get out of the room while ushering them out. They knew Tony was the master of the house because they went down the stairs quickly, but they didn't stop barking.

"Darn dogs, the two balls of barking fur that you just saw are my daughters' dogs. For some reason they like to spend the day in the master bedroom until my daughters come home from school. If they come back and start barking, just ignore them, otherwise they will keep barking. They are smart enough to realize they need to change their behavior if they want attention and affection."

"OK, I will."

"Dan, we are thankful your parents let you come to help with the dogs and the house. Now make yourself at home."

Mr. Tony turned around and almost walked out the door. He stopped by the threshold, and putting one hand on the door frame he said, "You know Consuelo usually is not that talkative with visitors, you made a good impression on her, and that is half the battle."

I just smiled. What did he mean *"half the battle"*?

———

I didn't realize how tired I was. After looking around the room that was going to be my bedroom for my stay, I unpacked. The bedroom had its own private bathroom and there was a small shower stall. Everything looked new, like it had never been used. The room had an aroma like the one from department stores, where everything is new. The beige linoleum didn't have a tear nor a mark, the color was uniform from the corners to the door, there was no sign of wear. The shower and sink faucets were so shiny that you would have thought that they had been polished, or you were in a show-room. My mom would have loved to have this 3/4 bathroom where our icy downstairs bath was. The furniture was new wood furniture. I knew it was new because in one of the drawers of the dresser there was a yellow tag that said SOLD with red letters. There was a chair in one of the corners and an empty small closet. Back home all our closets had some-thing in them, they were not bursting with things, but they were full. The bed was a queen size bed. I never had slept in a bed that big. All my life I had slept in a single bed. The carpet in the room was a plush brown carpet. There was no dust in the room, not a total surprise after seeing Consuelo vacuum.

I took in all the details because I was sure my mother was going to ask me to describe the Westfield's house. I emptied the contents of my backpack and suitcase, took off my shoes and then laid on the bed. It was so comfortable, and I was so tired that without trying, I dozed off.

I was awakened by a commotion in the hallway. Voices of women talking non-stop. Dogs barking, but not with an angry bark. With my eyes half opened I could see that the sun had lost its mid-morning splendor, the light had changed and there was fog in the street and the aroma of meatloaf impreg-nated the house. I sat on the bed and started to listen to the words of the conversation down the hallway, it was difficult not to.

"Girls, please stop it. What is our guest going to think," said the mother.

"That Megan is a loudmouth!" bellowed Leslie.

"Little sister, stop being sore that I got the last sweater in your favorite color," insisted Megan.

"I looked at it first," Leslie said.

"You did, but I took it off of the rack first," countered Megan. The spirited conversation was coming from the bedroom down the hallway from mine.

"Leslie, tomorrow we will go back to the mall, and we will find you a beautiful sweater," their mother counseled.

"But Mom, I looked everywhere, and I didn't see anything I liked."

"I will take you to Torrance, to Del Amo. We will look there," their mother assured Leslie.

"Torrance? Mom that is not fair, I want to go," Megan cried.

"No, you are not going."

"Leslie, I am not talking to you."

"Girls, get ready for dinner and stop this nonsense."

I sat on the bed and was ready to get up when Mrs. Westfield knocked on the door that was partially closed. When I went to bed the door was open, Consuelo may have closed it while she was going around vacuuming.

"Hello Daniel, I am Pam, Tony's wife, and mother of the two screaming teenagers that must have woken you up with their nonstop shopping drama. How was your flight?"

Mrs. Westfield was tall and dressed in a vibrant blue dress with shoulder pads rivaling the pads of some of my friends from the high school football team. She had blonde hair styled in a modern look that my mother would not dare to wear. Her makeup was on the heavier side but then I was used to seeing my mother wearing no makeup at all, unless we were going to church or to a family barbecue, when Mother would apply some pastel rose lipstick. But my hostess was generous when applying her makeup, it seemed her eyeshadow matched the blue on her dress.

"No, they didn't wake me up. My flight was fine," I

replied. No more words came to my mouth. I was tired, all the anticipation of the trip and then the long day to get there had caught up with me.

"Daniel we are happy you are here. Freshen up and come to the dining room to have dinner and meet the girls. We usually have dinner at 7:00, but we lost track of time while shopping. Come out when you are ready."

Mrs. Westfield moved her hand signaling me to come and join them. Her wrist had three white plastic bracelets that clanked away with every move of her hand.

———

"Hey Dan, how was your nap? I wanted to ask you to join me in a walk around the neighborhood, but I saw that you were sleeping soundly even with Consuelo vacuuming. God, that woman loves to vacuum." Tony asked as soon as I arrived in the dining room. Tony was seated at the head of the table with a martini in front of him. Pam was bringing the food from the kitchen.

"It was good, I was tired. Mrs. Westfield, may I help you with anything?" I volunteered. My mother would not be happy if I didn't ask if I could be of some help.

"Oh, Daniel please call me Pam. Thank you for offering to help, that is something I do not get too much from my daughters. Please sit here."

My hostess pulled the second chair from Tony's left. I was wondering who would be sitting next to me.

"Where are the princesses?" Tony inquired and got up to fetch his two daughters.

Pam rolled her eyes and went to the kitchen for the rest of the food. On the table there were already bowls with salad, a platter with asparagus, a bowl of mashed potatoes, and a gravy boat.

"Hello, my name is Megan," Tony's oldest daughter said as she sat next to me.

"I am Daniel." I turned and smiled. She had the hair of her mother but the eyes of Tony. She turned, smiled, and gave me an inquisitive look.

"How old are you?" Megan asked.

"I am eighteen years old, and you?"

"You never ask a lady her age, it is not polite," she said, and she looked at me in all seriousness, just bursting into a laugh when she saw my perplexed expression.

"You can ask her age because my sister is not a lady."

A younger version of Megan took her seat across from me. The only difference between the two sisters was that Megan had long hair and the youngest had hair to her shoulders and braces.

"Daniel, may I introduce to you Leslie, my baby sister?"

"I am not a baby. I am fifteen years old."

"Then stop acting like a baby and crying about everything."

"You two girls stop it. We are going to have dinner, and it is the first day of Dan with us. This is not the way to carry on in front of our guest." Tony's tone was clear that no more kibitzing was going to be allowed at dinner time.

The sisters gave each other a look signaling that they were not done. Just at that moment Pam arrived with a platter of meatloaf already sliced in one hand, and a basket of fresh baked biscuits in the other. She gave the platter to Tony and took her seat. They didn't say grace like we did, they just started passing the bowls and platters around and taking what they wanted.

"OK, let's eat," Tony commanded.

"Dan, tell us what your plans are after high school," Pam asked. "What schools did you apply to?"

"Pam, let the boy eat, you can interrogate him later," Tony said.

I didn't reply to my hostess. I learned that the Westfields didn't talk during most part the dinner, they waited until the moment that coffee and desert were served.

"Daniel do you like chocolate?" our plates were almost empty when Pam asked.

"Yes." I replied.

"Perfect. We are having homemade chocolate pie that Consuelo prepared based on my grandmother's recipe."

Pam got up and took her empty dish and also Tony's. Before Megan and Leslie could get up, I stood and helped to clear the dirty dishes. Megan decided that she also was going to help and took care of the leftovers while Leslie just sat there still brooding over the pink sweater snatched away from her hands hours ago by Megan.

"Leslie, help set the table for dessert," Tony instructed his youngest daughter. She reluctantly obeyed.

I only could imagine what was it going to be like traveling with those two for fifteen days. I had the feeling that they were always finding something to disagree about. I was thankful that I only had my sister Daisy to deal with and she never carried on like the Westfield girls. Also, if Daisy was dramatic and wanted to be moody, it wasn't going to be tolerated by my mother nor father. It was clear in our family that moodiness was a passing moment and not something you stewed over for hours.

The pie arrived at the table. Pam skillfully cut it. Mr. and Mrs. Westfield sure knew how to keep teenagers at the table to start the daily interrogation. Desert time was the time the Westfield family talked about the day. Tony asked about their day and Pam shared any of the gossip she had learned recently. But tonight, the focus of the interrogation and conversation was going to be about my family and myself.

"Tell us Dan, what school you are going to go to?" Pam asked. She had not forgotten the school question. It seemed I was destined to be reminded about my lack of college plans.

"I didn't apply to one yet," I said. "I do not know what I want to do, and I need to help my father with the farm and figure things out."

"I am going to USC," Megan was quick to say.

"Yes of course you are going to USC. UCLA didn't want you!" Leslie blurted.

"Leslie that is not a nice thing to say. Your sister was accepted at UCLA but decided to go to USC. You know Neil Armstrong and George Lucas are graduates from USC. USC is a good school." Pam was trying to put an end to the latest rant of her youngest daughter.

"Leslie what do you want to study?" I asked trying to steer the conversation away from my lack of college plans.

"I want to be an interior designer. You know, somebody that finds colors and nice things to go in your home." Leslie showed some liveliness for the first time during dinner.

I didn't know that people could be paid for that, or that somebody could be occupied for hours doing that. I had so much to learn. I thought the folks in the city had a little more complex lifestyle, but did they really need somebody to tell them which color to paint their houses? Later in life I learned it wasn't that life was complex; if you have the resources, you can have a professional advising you in how to decorate your home and make your living space as nice as you want it, and some people can afford it. Also, I learned that designers really like to spend money on your behalf.

"Megan is going to study engineering," Tony said with in a proud tone.

"Yes, and someday I'm going to work for NASA," she added.

What was it about NASA? First my friend Fred, and now Megan wanting to work for NASA.

"Oh dear, you don't want to go to swampy Florida," Pam said.

"Mom, not all the state is a swamp," Megan countered.

"Tell us Daniel which other states you have been to," Pam inquired.

"Illinois, Texas, Minnesota, Iowa and Indiana."

"Which countries have you visited?" Leslie inquired.

"I have never been outside of the United States. Once we were going to Canada, but our car broke down and then we got busy on the farm." I told her.

Leslie just gave me this look that to this day I don't know if it was one of pity or amusement.

"Do you have brothers or sisters?" Megan asked.

"I have one brother, the oldest; he went to college to study accounting, and a younger sister that is almost sixteen."

"Is she going to have a sweet sixteen party? I am going to have the biggest sweet sixteen party on the block," Leslie said with exuberance.

The thought of the sweet sixteen party had diminished her moodiness, she finally looked like a lively fifteen-year-old. Megan breathed deeply signaling her annoyance with the topic, and her expression said, "Here we go again."

"I do not know," I responded. "I am sure Mother will prepare a cake and Daisy's friends will be invited." I didn't know if there was going to be a big to-do for Daisy's sixteenth birthday.

"Leslie you will have a party, but I don't know if it's going to be the biggest on the block. Some of your friends, frankly they have overdone the whole sweet sixteen thing," Tony uttered.

"But Dad, Lauren's parents rented the hall down the street and had a live band for hers," Leslie said.

"Do you want a party or to go to college?" Tony asked her, and before she could answer Pam intervened.

"Sweetie, I am sure we can throw you a lovely birthday party. It doesn't need to be like the rest of your friends, it will be unique and memorable. Your father and I will discuss our options and then you and I can start planning it when we are back from Europe."

"Yes, one thing at the time," Tony said so as to end the conversation about the sweet sixteen party.

"Tony, tomorrow we are going to go back to the mall, we need to go to Del Amo in Torrance to find a sweater for Leslie."

"Again?" Tony was surprised and a bit annoyed.

"Yes, only Mom and I." Leslie said maliciously, eager to annoy Megan.

"If you are going to the mall tomorrow, the three of you should go. You ladies need to start packing and stop going to the mall. Tonight, make sure that you check the items you are bringing on the trip and start packing. If you are missing anything else, you buy it tomorrow because this is going to be your last shopping excursion. I want your luggage by the door on Wednesday morning. The plane is not going to be waiting for us. This is not a road trip where we can have the luxury of a late start. Understood?" Tony gave a stern look to his wife and two daughters. They were leaving Thursday morning, and he wanted the luggage by the door 24 hours before they left the house.

"Yes dear, the girls will be ready," Pam said.

The rest of dessert went quickly, everybody focused on finishing their slice of pie. The sisters asked to be excused. I was going to do the same, but Tony asked me to stay because he and Pam wanted to tell me what exactly they wanted me to take care of. Tony went to grab a pad of yellow paper and a pen.

"Here Son, it will be better if you write what you need you to do."

"Daniel, please water the plants in the back and front yard every other day. But if there happens to be a heat wave and the plants look wilted, water them even if is not a watering day," Pam told me.

"Should I water them tomorrow?" I was eager to start with my chores before they left on their trip and make sure that I was taking care of things just like they wanted.

"Yes, please," Pam answered.

"Get the mail from the mailbox and put it on the desk in my studio," Tony added.

"The dogs need to be fed in the morning, a snack midday and one more feeding at night. I will show you where the dog food is in the morning. Make sure their water bowls have water and please change it every day. Wash the bowls. Please clean any mess they make," Pam noted.

Mess? I was wondering what my hostess meant about mess. Were those two little puff balls having accidents inside the house or just running around the house leaving a trail of destruction? I couldn't imagine the two small dogs being that complicated to take care of. Sure, they could bark, but they were lap dogs.

"Pam, I am sure Dan knows how to take care of dogs," Tony said.

"Consuelo will be coming every day. To clean the house and cook," offered Pam.

"I can cook my own meals Mrs. Westfield."

"Dan, it is best if we don't disrupt Consuelo's routine. She likes cooking; just let her know if you don't like something and she will prepare you something else. She also will do the grocery shopping," Tony said.

"It is difficult to find as good a housekeeper as Consuelo. We like to keep her happy," Pam added half smiling.

I felt as if I was going to need to walk on eggshells around Miss Consuelo.

"Dan, I will need you to pay some bills in my absence. You just need to put them in the mailbox for the mailman to pick them up, or if you want to take a break from the house, you can walk and take them to the post office. Tomorrow, I can show you where I am leaving the bills. Dear, what else should Dan take care of?"

"I can't think about anything else. Let me see what you wrote." Pam looked at me and took the notepad from my hands. She followed down the list with the tip of her index finger as she read it in silence. "Your handwriting is nice," she said as she returned the notepad to me.

"Dan, I am sure you are tired, after all you started your day early back home. See you tomorrow morning. I want you to join me at 7:00 to walk the dogs."

"Yes sir, I will be ready."

I got up and I was going to tear the sheet of paper from the notepad when Tony said, "Just keep it Son, you may want to write."

"Okay thank you, good night."

"Good night, Daniel, thank you for helping with the dogs," Pam said, and she went to the kitchen.

"Good night, Son," Tony added.

CHAPTER 3
SHOPPING

SUNDAY, JUNE 20, 1982

THE DARKNESS of the night was leaving the area when I opened my eyes and looked through the curtain to the deserted street. My alarm clock hadn't rung. I turned it off. There was no need to let it ring, a short three minutes to six. It was time for me to get ready for my first day in Manhattan. I was looking forward to walking the dogs with Tony, and hoping we would go down to the beach on our walk. I was ready to explore the neighborhood that I was calling home for the next two weeks. It didn't matter that I had daily chores; the tasks assigned by Tony and Pam were nothing compared to the list of things I did during one of my days at the farm. In my mind, the days at the Westfield's house were a vacation. There was no work from sunrise to sunset, nor any heavy labor involved.

I made the bed, took a shower, and then waited until it was ten minutes to seven to go to the kitchen and get some orange juice.

"Good morning, sir," I greeted Tony who was standing near the coffee maker with a steaming cup in hand.

"Good morning Son, did you have a good night?"

"Oh yes, I slept soundly."

"I just made a fresh pot of coffee," Tony offered.

"Thank you. I was thinking of drinking a glass of orange juice."

"Go ahead, the OJ is somewhere in the refrigerator," Tony noted.

I opened the refrigerator, and I never had seen so much food stuffed in an ice box. I didn't need to dig in, the bottle of orange juice was in the front row. Tony pointed to the cabinet with the glasses.

"Dan if I didn't say it yesterday, I will say it today—make yourself at home."

"Thank you, sir."

"While you finish your juice, I am going to get the newspaper and then we can take those dogs to walk."

I was left alone in the kitchen. Everything was new, the stove looked like it never had been used, all the appliances were brand new. On the counter there was a fancy blender, a mixer, and a toaster. There was a big window over the kitchen sink, overlooking the backyard with the pool. It was a big house. Tony came back with the newspaper under his arm.

"Dan while we are away, please bring the newspaper in. You can read it or just put in the garage. We collect them until I take them to recycle."

"Yes, sir," I responded.

"OK, let's get those two dogs to walk." Tony opened a drawer and took two leashes out. Then he started shaking a box of cereal.

"Bella and Ginger, Bella and Ginger!" He called as he kept shaking the box of cereal. The two dogs came down from upstairs and rushed into the kitchen. I had not seen them since yesterday when I arrived. They had disappeared for the rest of the evening.

"Come you two, let's go for a walk," Tony said. "Son,

these dogs are the reflection of a moment of weakness that I had when Leslie asked if she could have a dog and I said yes. Megan then demanded to have one too. She still remembers that at Leslie's age, she had asked me for a pet, and I said NO. Their mom promised me that they were going to take care of the two animals. I believed her. Now I am the one taking them to walk in the morning because my daughters go to school or are late risers just like their mom."

Late risers? At the farm we didn't have the luxury to be late risers. Every day it was rise and shine, even on the winter days when there was no shine.

"I see," I commented. I could tell Tony liked the animals even if he appeared to be annoyed by the daily task.

With the dogs on their leashes, a paper bag and an old newspaper in hand, we left the house. Our morning excursion couldn't have been more than half an hour. We walked down the hill, passed by the church, turned right a few times and then we were back on the street. I learned that the main reason I was there was because Consuelo didn't take care of dogs. She had been vocal about getting the dogs. She told Tony that having a pet required discipline and she didn't see it in the young Leslie. Then when Leslie got the dog and Megan wanted one for herself, Consuelo made it clear that she was the housekeeper and cook, but not a dog handler.

About halfway on our outing I discovered why Tony had taken an old newspaper and a paper bag when we left the house. It was to clean up after the animals. This was something we didn't have to worry about on the farm. Sure, you had to clean up after your dogs, but you got a shovel and collected their little presents. Here you had to collect their little presents with the newspaper and then carry them back home in a brown paper bag.

"Mr. T good morning!" blurted a stranger that just approached us.

"Good morning!" said Tony. "Jimmy this is Dan, he will be staying with us for a few weeks."

"Hey, nice to meet you, Jimmy," I said. Jimmy gave me a strong handshake. He was a few inches smaller than me; I would say he was 5'10", slender built. He wore round eyeglasses and his hair was spiky, somehow the hair seemed out of place.

"Where are you visiting from?" Jimmy asked.

"From Wisconsin."

"Wow, that is far."

"Dan will be staying at our house while we go to Europe," Tony offered.

"Cool, Mr. T. Dan, if you need anything, I live in that blue house," said Jimmy as he motioned with his arm.

"Jimmy, maybe later you can show Dan downtown and go to the beach."

"Sure thing. Today I'm not working at the liquor store. I promised my mom to help her in the garden. She is determined to get the backyard in shape and wants to start having weekly barbecues now that Dad is going to be spending more weekends here and coming back mid-summer. But I think I should be done by lunch time."

"If it doesn't work today, then tomorrow you two kids can explore the town," Tony said.

"OK Dan, I will let you know if I can't, but otherwise I'll stop by about 1:00," Jimmy told me.

"See you later Jimmy," I said as we waved goodbye and crossed the street to the Westfield house.

"Dan, Jimmy is a good kid. He is hard working and has a part-time job in the liquor store that he keeps year-round. Plus, he is the best student in his class."

"He looks like a nice chap."

"Later, I will introduce you to Mrs. Pitchman. She is somebody good to know in case you have a question while we are away. She is old and lives in the green cottage on the corner."

When we arrived at the house, we found Pam standing in the kitchen, wearing a robe with a flower pattern and rollers in her hair. She looked ghostly without make-up.

"Good morning, dear!" Tony greeted her.

"Good morning!"

"Good morning, ma'am," I said.

I just could not address them as Pam and Tony like they had asked me to. I had this sensation as if my parents could watch me and listen to what I say all the way from Wisconsin. I felt that if I didn't address them as Mr. and Mrs. Westfield, I was going to feel a slap on the back of my head, just like my dad did in church when Paul or I were distracted. At least my host and hostess had given up on their request of dropping the Mr. and Mrs. formality.

"Daniel, would you like to go the mall with us today?" Pam asked.

I didn't know what to answer, my first thought was—going to the mall with two fighting teenagers? *No thank you*! But I didn't answer. I observed Tony's expression, trying to get some kind of input on how to respond to my hostess. Going to the mall? I didn't even have money to buy a pair of socks. And the way my future was looking, there were not going to be new clothes for school because I was done with high school and I had not decided to go to college, at least not yet. Plus, I was going downtown and to the beach with Jimmy.

"Dan, you don't mind chaperoning my three ladies?" Tony asked.

He just had given me the signal for which I was waiting. It was clear I needed to go with the Westfield women to the mall. His question was more than a question—it was a gentle order.

"Sir, not at all, I will be happy to go to the mall," I said, which was a lie.

I was imagining the bickering between Megan and Leslie.

What was I going to do with three women going from store to store? Then I thought I may have been invited to try to distract them from their constant arguing. I prepared myself to be questioned endlessly. I had to find a way to turn off listening to their complaints.

"OK, then we are leaving at 11:00," Pam said, "the stores do not open early, but they close by five. It's Consuelo's day off. We'll grab lunch, buy two or three items and come back to prepare dinner."

Listening to my hostess I realized that I could forget about my plan with Jimmy to go around town.

"Sounds like you have a plan dear," Tony said, and Pam left to go to get ready.

"Mr. Westfield, I would like to go and tell Jimmy that most likely I won't be able to go with him to explore downtown."

"Oh, yes, I had forgotten. You can call him, or if you prefer, go and tell him."

"I will go and let him know that I can't go out today."

"OK, Son. Before I forget, let me give you some spending money in case you see something you would like in the mall; you know, a snack or a souvenir," Tony offered.

"Oh no, you don't have to," I said when Tony took out his wallet. My old man's wallet never had been as full as Tony's.

"Dan, just take it. And if my wife wants to buy you clothes, please just let her. Look Dan, we wanted to have a son, and we did but the baby died months after he was born. She always has been shopping for girls, or for me. Today, she may want to buy clothes for you. I hope you don't mind.

"No at all. If that makes Mrs. Pam happy, I will go to the shopping center." I assured him.

"Son thank you. Go and tell Jimmy that the mall got in the way of your plans."

I folded the twenty-dollar bill Tony gave me and went to Jimmy's house. I knocked on the door and a girl that didn't seem older than five opened the door carefully.

"Hi, is Jimmy around?" I asked. She gave me an inquisitive look, up and down.

"Are you a new friend of Jimmy?"

"I hope I will become one," I said.

"Where did you meet Jimmy?" the little tyke responded.

"By that yellow house, we were walking the dogs and…"

"Do you have dogs? My parents only allow us to have cats. Because you don't need to take them walking. But I always have wanted to have some puppies," she continued rapidly, happy to talk.

"You know, puppies grow up and then stop being cute," I said. The girl looked at me like I had told her Santa didn't exist. Then she screamed with a voice that didn't seem to come from a little delicate girl.

"Jimmy! Jimmy! A stranger is looking for you."

"Angie, I told you not to open the door to strangers." I could hear the voice of a woman as she was approaching the door.

"Mom, but he looks harmless. See you stranger!" The girl ran away from the door, but not before she called her brother's name one more time.

"Angie, stop screaming!" the mother blared as she stood in the doorway.

"Hi, my name is Daniel, I am staying with the Westfield family. Is Jimmy available? I need to speak to him," I finally spoke.

"Hello Daniel, I am Mrs. Jones. Just a second, let me see where that kid is. Would you like to come in?"

"No, thank you, I need to get back." Mrs. Jones smiled and went to get Jimmy.

"Hey, Dan what's up?"

"I have been asked to go to the mall with Mrs. Westfield and the girls. I don't know what time I will be back or if I will be able to go with you at all," I explained.

"Are you available tomorrow in the afternoon?" Jimmy asked.

"I think I will be, unless Mr. or Mrs. Westfield have plans for me."

"Then I'll stop by after two. I work the mornings, Monday through Thursday at the grocery store. But I am free after that, except Friday and Saturday when I work the afternoons at the liquor store. Sunday usually I am free all day, but Mom really wants to get the garden done before it starts getting hotter."

"You keep yourself busy."

"It never hurts to have your own pocket money," Jimmy advised.

"No, it doesn't," I said with the twenty-dollar bill in my pocket that Tony had just given me. It felt like I was carrying a fortune.

I liked the concept of your own pocket money. I only had what my father gave me now and then for a soda at the diner or a hamburger. Most of the time I didn't drink a soda with my burger just to save the few coins. That way I could have a treat on another day.

"Then tomorrow I will stop by to give you the Jimmy Jones tour of downtown Manhattan Beach."

"We have a plan, see you tomorrow," I said and walked back to the Westfield house.

The weather was perfect, not too hot nor too cold. There were clouds that morning just like Tony had described the early morning marine layer. I could see myself living there. Doing what? I didn't know. The only thing for sure was that there was no farm to work, and that to me was good.

The rest of the day went fast. We drove to the shopping center through the streets—block after block of houses or businesses. I was used to driving from our farm to the small town nearby on roads surrounded by green fields and trees. I sat in the back with Leslie; she told me on the way to the mall the name of every town we went by. I couldn't tell when we were leaving a town and entering another, because there was no open land between them.

Finally, my youngest hostess told me to pay attention to the color of the street signs or their design, because that was the only clue that you had that you had left Manhattan Beach. We went by Hermosa Beach, then Redondo Beach and then to Torrance. Torrance was big compared to the other towns. We stopped at a fast-food restaurant to grab a burger. Then we proceeded with the day's mission: to find a sweeter for Leslie, or at least I thought it was a one-item shopping trip. I was wrong.

To my surprise the two Westfield girls didn't have any fights about garments, unless I had missed them. In one of the stores as Tony had suggested, Pam told me to go and search for a few shirts, t-shirts, a pair of shorts, and pants plus some swimming trunks. I went around looking for the items and then I tried them on. When I found something that I thought looked good, I just went back to the rack and grabbed another item in a different color. Shopping was simple; why keep looking if you had found something that was a good fit. Pam had a different opinion and sense of style than mine. When I went to meet with the Westfield ladies, they were still looking at the juniors clothing racks trying to find a treasure. Pam studied each one of the garments I had chosen and then took me back to the men's department to discard half of my selection and pick up twice as many as I had. I ended up even with plastic sandals—flip flops. As instructed, I just said "Yes, ma'am" or "No, ma'am", and of course after she had paid for everything, I said "Thank you, ma'am." Megan and Leslie didn't care that their mother was buying me clothes. They were happy getting more clothes than they could possibly need for a two-week trip.

Our ride back to Manhattan Beach was quiet. Everybody got what they wanted, and the sisters were in good spirits. I wasn't sure if my new wardrobe was going to fit in my backpack. In two weeks, I would find out. And just as Pam had anticipated, we got back to the house in time for her to prepare dinner.

CHAPTER 4
JIMMY JONES & THE BEACH

MONDAY, JUNE 21, 1982

THE TWO DOGS were getting used to me, Tony was right. After I had ignored them for almost a day, now they were friendly. During our morning walk, Tony introduced me to a few neighbors. It was interesting to see how the streets were a bit busier on Monday morning with people going to work, as compared to Sunday when it seemed everybody had a late start. As he promised me, Tony introduced me to Mrs. Pitchman. She was old. By the way she moved, slowly and carefully you would think she was almost ninety years old, but her face didn't look older than seventy. She was short and was wearing a big straw hat, a long-sleeved blouse with a floral pattern, and long gardening gloves that went beyond her wrists. She said that she was pulling weeds. I didn't see any weeds, but then maybe she had finished. The two dogs were friendly toward Mrs. Pitchman, which was a surprise because usually they were shy on the street but were barking machines in the house.

Tony left the house shortly after we came back. It was time to get to his business, a funeral home. I went back to my room looked through a stack of *National Geographic* and *Smithsonian* magazines that I borrowed from Tony's studio. Consuelo arrived almost at nine and then by mid-morning the girls finally woke up. By noon I started to get hungry and went to the kitchen to find some food. Consuelo told me there were turkey sandwiches and coleslaw in the refrigerator. I took two sandwiches and a glass of milk and went to the backyard to have my lunch under an umbrella next to the swimming pool. I was done with my first sandwich when Megan appeared with a glass of juice in her hand, she was wearing tight, smooth fitting shorts and a sleeveless top, I could see the knot of her bikini top sticking out in the back. She was ready to head to the beach.

"Good morning, Dan."

"Hey Megan!" I could not say good morning, it was past noon.

"I'm going to beach to meet my friends, would you like to come along?" Megan asked.

"I would, but Jimmy invited me to go to downtown. He is going to give me a tour," I replied.

"Ah, well if you see us at the beach, don't be a stranger and stop by."

"I will."

Megan smiled and left. I thought it was nice she was inviting me to meet her friends, or maybe her parents asked her to invite me. She seemed sincere in her invitation, or maybe she felt that at least she should invite me to the beach to be nice. After all, I was going to be taking care of her dog for over two weeks.

I sat there, looking at the pool wondering why somebody living blocks from the ocean needed a pool. But then I thought if you can have a pool at your house, why not? I got lost in my thoughts; I was thinking what my friends were doing back home. Fred most likely was helping his dad in their hardware store. Matt and Carson for sure were working on their family farms. And there I was sitting under an umbrella staring at the reflection of a lemon tree on the surface of the crystal-clear water. Then I thought about my family, Dad, Mom, and Daisy; for sure my little sister was not happy with me being gone. By then she already had been helping my parents at least for five hours. She wasn't like the Westfield sisters that got up almost at noon and then went to the beach to meet their friends. I had been in California less than three days, and I already could see how different my family's lifestyle was from that of the Westfield's.

"Danny, would you like another sandwich?" Consuelo's voice interrupted my train of thought.

"Oh no, thank you." I instinctively took the plate and glass to take them back to the kitchen, but Consuelo grabbed them from my hands.

"Danny, you need to eat more. You are still growing." Consuelo moved her head sideways and then turned around and went back to the kitchen. I could tell she ran a tight ship, and she was determined to get me to eat more.

The doorbell rang. It was Jimmy arriving just like he said; it was two and he was ready to show me downtown. It had been over forty-eight hours since my arrival and I still hadn't been to the beach, I was ready to see the ocean-blue up close.

"Danny boy, let's get going," Jimmy said as we started walking down the street. He was wearing some red Converse shoes, shorts that were made of an old pair of jeans, a white t-shirt and an unbuttoned Hawaiian shirt. He had sunglasses on top of his glasses. His hair was short but had used gel to make it stand up. I was wearing the swim trunks and t-shirt that Pam had bought me. I thought wearing the sandals was a good idea, but soon I realized that going downhill they were not the best choice, and I didn't like the sensation that at any time they were going to fly off from my feet.

"I guess you already saw the church," Jimmy said as we strolled on.

"Yes, the tower was the first landmark Mr. Tony showed me. As a navigation point."

"Well, then I will show you a place that has been here since the 1920s; that makes it a landmark in this town."

"I guess that is old for this part of the country."

"Yes, it is. You know just twenty years ago there were still farms in El Segundo. My father used to take us to ride horses at a stable nearby."

"Really?"

"Yes, Danny, that is what real estate development can do, turn lands with crops into houses and store fronts. You know where our local shopping center, The Village, is there used to be underground oil storage tanks. The just removed them few years ago."

I couldn't help it, but to me Jimmy talked like one of my old teachers from high school. He was my age but somehow you got the feeling you were talking with an adult, an older adult.

"Well, I hope real estate development doesn't take over all the farms," I said.

"No, no. For that, the population would need to be 20, 30 billion in the world. In addition, new methods of high yield farming would be necessary in order to surrender all the farmland to housing, commerce and manufacturing," Jimmy sagely instructed.

"That will be a lot of people."

Jimmy just nodded in agreement. We reached the bottom of the hill and crossed the railroad tracks. So far, I had not heard any trains go by. Maybe we were too far away up the hill and the sound didn't carry that far, or it was not a daily train route.

"There is landmark number two: Metlox Pottery."

"Wow, I never have seen a pottery factory."

"The train used to come more often to deliver sacks of powdered clay to make pottery. It seems production has slowed down. When I was a kid, I rode the train many a time. With my friends we used to hide in the bushes and wait for the train to go by. It could not have been going more than ten miles per hour because we just needed to run full speed to jump and hold on to a boxcar. Then we jumped off by "hobo bridge," down the tracks because we didn't want to be seen crossing Rosecrans Avenue."

"Did you ever try to go further?"

"No. I knew my father would have grounded me for years. I lost interest in hopping the train after seeing the bone of Ronnie Miller's elbow poking out of his skin. That was not pretty. Lucky for him, Mrs. Thomson saw Ronnie holding his bloody elbow as he emerged from the gully and gave him a ride to the hospital where Ronnie's father worked."

"Did you guys get in trouble?"

"No, Ronnie's dad was too busy working and raising four kids. He didn't have time to go and tell the other parents. If he had told my parents, my father would have ignored the whole incident, and my mother would had given me one of those "be careful" speeches that mothers do. But Dr. Miller was more occupied with other things than to inform the community of his son's mishap."

We kept walking. I could feel the sea breeze, I was able to smell the salt air and see the shimmering ocean just two blocks away. Jimmy said hi to almost everybody we crossed paths with—to the shopkeeper standing behind the counter, the barber waiting for a client, the cobbler. It seemed somehow everybody knew Jimmy. It was a small town, but not that small. The town I was from was smaller and still people didn't know my name; some knew me as Joe's kid, and I had the feeling I was going to be always Joe's boy or the young Smith kid. People knew my brother Paul's name. I always wondered why. Maybe because he was the firstborn and as the first baby, my parents were showing off their first child to the community, or maybe because he did well in sports.

"Here is our third landmark: my favorite diner, the place to go at any hour of the day. It is open all day and all night long. We can have supper," Jimmy advised as the tour continued.

"Not, today. I need to have dinner with The Westfields," I said.

My father had given me a few dollars to at least have a few singles in my pocket. I also had the twenty-dollar bill that Tony gave me when I went to the mall with the Westfield women. When I tried to give him back the money, he told me to keep it in case I wanted to get a soda or a hamburger while they were away. I never had in my pockets so much money.

"Sure, after they leave for their trip, we can come here to have a meal. By the way, when are you leaving?" Jimmy asked.

"Sunday, the eleventh, two days after they come back. I am not looking forward to my first day at the farm, to start waking up at the crack of dawn."

"But at least you still will have a few weeks before classes start."

"No, I didn't apply to any college, and I don't know if I will ever go to college," I said as we got closer to the pier.

"I could have been already in college, but years ago my mother convinced my father that it was better for me if I just kept going to school with kids my age," Jimmy mentioned.

I didn't ask how he could have skipped years of schooling; now and then in magazines or on TV they talk about smart kids graduating from college when others are just finishing high school.

"Where are you going to college?" I asked.

"MIT. Dad thinks it is the best school for me. After graduating from MIT, I can come back and get a master's or PhD from Caltech in Pasadena."

"Wow, you have the next ten years of your life planned."

"Danny, that is more like the next six years of my life."

"Well, good for you. Get it done and then you can start working."

"Danny, that is the scary part. This is my last summer prior to all the serious stuff that starts to happen. I will be leaving behind the Pacific Ocean and the temperate weather, and I will have to adjust to the Atlantic Ocean and dealing with seasons. Who wants seasons? When you can have this year-round!" Jimmy exclaimed and waved his arm expansively as we reached the bottom of the street. We were ready to step onto the pier.

"Jimmy, I must agree. I have been here not even a week, and I don't want to leave. It's easy to get used to this."

It was more than the weather that was making Manhattan Beach appealing, it was being away from my day-to-day responsibilities, being in a house where everything was brand new, and things were not scarce. I was just dreaming like any other eighteen-year-old that doesn't want to rush life, that wants to find a way to prolong the days where the biggest hurdle is to get up in the morning and go to school, see your friends and study just enough to pass and avoid being left behind. Who was I kidding? My reality was so different from Tony's daughters, and that reality was waiting for me as soon as the Westfields were back home and put me on the plane back to Chicago.

"Danny come on! Don't just stand there. Let's go to the end. You just space out big time," Jimmy insisted, and I snapped out of my reverie.

We went to the end of the pier, to the Roundhouse Aquarium; I was surprised to see people fishing. My self-proclaimed tour guide told me that people had been fishing for corvina since before the pier was built. The other inter-esting fact was that there used to be dunes that were 50 to 70 feet high. The sand was sent to Waikiki beach in Hawaii and the beach here became nice and flat. He promised me that he was going to take me to see a park where some dunes still existed. We just stood there; you could feel the waves crashing against the pilings of the pier. I was experiencing for the first time the salty breeze on my skin. You could see jets taking off in the distance and several tankers moored at sea where they were unloading oil for the refinery in El Segundo. I learned that the town of El Segundo next to the airport was named El Segundo, which means "The Second" in Spanish, because it was the second Standard Oil refinery on the West Coast.

Jimmy pointed south to Palos Verdes and told me that maybe during the week we could go driving around the Palos Verdes Peninsula. He then talked about the professional volleyball tournament that took place every summer in Manhattan Beach. We could not have stood there for more than twenty minutes, and I learned more about the area than I was expecting. Jimmy had all kinds of facts on the tip of his tongue. I could tell that when he got on a roll, the information would just keep coming out, which was fine with me. I was not much of a talker, and it isn't every day that you have your own private tour guide.

We started to make our way back to the street. I wanted to get in the water, but Jimmy told me that it was not that warm. I thought that it could not be cooler than the water in the creeks back home when all the snow had melted. He seemed a little uneasy to get to the sand, and I was eager to feel the sand under my feet.

"Let's go and grab a taco, it's my treat. It's part of the tour," Jimmy said.

"Okay, but after the taco I want to go and get in that water."

Jimmy nodded his head in agreement and led the way a block or two up the hill to a small Mexican restaurant.

I was expecting hard shell tacos like the ones I had eaten at a county fair back home. Jimmy got four tacos made with soft tortillas, two carnitas and two carne asada, the first were grilled pork and the second grilled beef. The tacos had onions and cilantro. I didn't know what cilantro was, but I decided that if Jimmy liked it, I was going to eat the little pieces of green leaves. We had one of each of the tacos. Jimmy told me to squeeze some lime and then put some salsa on them. He stressed not to put too much of the dark red salsa, it was spicy. The tacos were ten times better than the hard-shell tacos I had eaten back home. I was planning to go back and try something else from this place after the Westfields left for their trip, even if I didn't have a clue about some of the items listed on the menu. If the rest of the food was this delicious, I needed to try it before my departure.

We finished our snack and headed back down the street to the beach. Finally, I was going to get my feet in the sand. Jimmy seemed to get uneasy as we were getting closer. I could tell because he kept pulling the edge of his Hawaiian shirt like a nervous tic.

"OK here we go. Just ignore those guys over there if they say something."

"Which guys?" I asked.

"The six guys with the surfboards, the blue cooler and the volleyball."

I glanced at the group, and they didn't look like trouble, but I knew I was the new kid in town.

"OK, I will ignore them. Are they trouble?"

"They haven't been for a while," Jimmy said while he kept looking at the group and pulling the edge of his shirt.

"Jimmy, if they are, we can come another day or go to a different spot. You told me this beach is two miles long."

"No, I am not going to cut short today's tour."

Jimmy snapped out of the funk and went down the steps to the beach. We walked at least thirty feet from the group of older guys and just as we thought that they had not noticed us, somebody started yelling *"Jimmy, Jimmy."* Jimmy didn't turn and just kept walking. There was a certain urgency to his step.

"Hey, Jimmy, are you deaf or what?" The guy with the shaggiest hair of the group came running and stood in from of us, blocking our path.

"Todd," Jimmy uttered apprehensively.

"Hey, Jimmy, I thought I had told you to stay away from here," demanded the shaggy one.

"It's a public beach," I spoke.

Jimmy looked upset.

"I was not talking to you, but now that you opened your mouth, tell me what your name is."

"Danger!"

"That's funny boy, because you are looking at danger!"

"Danny, let's go!" Jimmy implored.

"Oh, Danny and Jimmy, that sounds so cute." Todd started laughing, it was a stupid laugh, empty, just an obnoxious laugh. It was almost like he had lost his marbles.

"Hey Todd, look who is here!" One of the other guys yelled and Todd waved to his group.

"You two are lucky my girl is here, and I must go. But do not come back here."

"It is a public beach," I said, and I gently pushed Jimmy's back to get him to move. He had become a statute; he was frozen.

"I'll be watching you two," the loser advised.

We kept walking until we reached the firm sand close to where the waves washed up, then we started walking north until we reached the second lifeguard station from the pier. We walked in silence. Jimmy stopped pulling the edge of his shirt, his hands were in fists, and he was walking in an angry way.

"Let's stay here. We are far away from what those hooligans think is their territory," Jimmy said, "plus, they are not going to come here and create any ruckus. Already the lifeguard has been keeping an eye on them."

"Who are they?" I asked.

"Some guys that always like to create trouble."

"What do they have against you?"

"Todd has destroyed more than one pair of my glasses. He is four years older than me and when I was in second grade, he took my glasses and stomped on them. The second time he did it, he was unaware that one of the nuns was watching the whole thing. That day his father, an airline executive had to stop by to pick Todd up from the principal's office. That was the last day Todd stepped foot in that school. He was expelled from the Catholic school. His father was furious about his kid being kicked out of the place. I remember my mother saying that Todd's parents didn't care too much when Todd did something bad, if it didn't affect their status in the community. My mother called his mother a social climber. After Todd left the school, we learned that it was not the first time he had ended up in the principal's office. He had taken the lunch and lunch money from some first graders. Somehow his twisted mind blames me. In my junior year he destroyed another pair of glasses. I had walked by his group, they were just where they are now, and Todd ran and snatched my glasses right off my face."

"Did you tell your parents? He cannot keep doing that forever," I said.

"No, I didn't. I just try to avoid them."

"You know Jimmy, you aren't seven years old anymore. He will keep doing it and getting away with it if nobody says anything. He may be taller and stronger but that is no reason to be an ass..."

"Well, enough about Todd. Do you want to get in the water?"

"Yes, you bet! I have been waiting to get in the water since Saturday when I saw the ocean while flying in."

"Well, go in then."

"You're not coming?" I said, surprised.

"No, I am more of a land guy."

"Do you know how to swim?"

"Of course," Jimmy replied.

"Then why are you not going in?"

"I'll get in when it is warmer, but I am sure for a boy from Wisconsin like yourself, the temperature is going to be just balmy!"

"Okay, then keep an eye on my sandals and my t-shirt."

"I will. Danny do not go too far out, it's your first time in the ocean, and I don't want to have to tell the lifeguard to go and fetch you," Jimmy said as he sat on the soft sand.

"Do not worry, I am Aquaman."

I turned and ran to the water. Jimmy was right, it was not as warm as I thought, but I didn't care. I could go back home and cross off one item from the list of things I wanted to do in my life.

As Jimmy said, this was my first time in the ocean, and I didn't want to make a fool of myself. I floated around, just letting the waves move me back and forth. Now and then I turned around to see where my new friend was sitting. To my surprise he was surrounded by a group of girls. One of them was Megan. She and one of her friends got close to the water. Megan's friend jumped and stepped back as soon as the first rush of water touched her feet. Megan held on to her hand and started walking out towards the next wave, pulling her. I started to swim to get closer to the shore. I wanted to see the commotion.

"Wendy, come on it's not that cold, it's only going to take you five seconds to adjust. See, Daniel is over there. It's not like you are going to be the only one getting in the water today. Look, there are people already in the water."

"Megan it's cold. You are going to run back as soon as I run in."

"Wendy don't be childish, I wouldn't do that to you, you are my best friend!"

"Hey Megan. The water is perfect, you two should come in," I announced.

"See, Daniel says it is alright."

"Well, Daniel must be from Alaska."

"OK, if you are not getting in, I am." Megan let go of her friend's hand and rushed into the oncoming wave. Surprisingly, her friend followed her; she screamed as soon as the water reached above her waist.

"Come on Wendy, you have done the most difficult part. It's just going to get better."

"Daniel, this is Wendy, Wendy this is Daniel, a friend of the family," Megan introduced us.

"Hi Wendy, how are you doing?" I offered.

"Dan, Daniel, I am okay."

We floated in the water for a while and then I had enough of the Pacific Ocean, and I left the two girls playing there. It was good that Matt and Carson weren't around otherwise they would want to stay chatting with the two girls, even if they started to get overly chilled.

Jimmy came closer with a cluster of girls.

"Ladies, this is Danny, a visitor from the northeast," Jimmy said as an introduction.

"Hi Danny, I'm Mary."

"My name is Susan!" Another exclaimed.

"I am Katie. Tell me Daniel, what do you like to be called: Dan, Danny, or Daniel?" The thin, redheaded one asked.

"I prefer Daniel, but I don't mind Danny."

"I will call you Daniel then," Katie said as she pulled her sunglasses down over her freckly nose.

Her hair was red, a beautiful red. Her skin was white with freckles that seemed to adorn it whimsically. Her voice was velvety, almost like the voice of one of those actresses portraying a femme fatale in the movies my mother liked to watch.

We spent the rest of the afternoon in that spot, talking. Our group grew bigger when two guys arrived and sat there for a while. Then one of the girls left because she needed to help her mom with cooking and had promised to clean her room before the day was over.

We went back to Manhattan Beach Boulevard and went up to a little grocery store with a meat shop, or a meat shop with a grocery store, to get sodas. Then we went back down to the pier and made our way north on the sand. We had lost track of time, and it was almost six.

"Daniel, it's nearly six, we are expected to be back home for dinner," Megan reminded me.

"It's too early; you guys should stay a little longer. Maybe Daniel wants to see the sunset," Katie said, trying to convince Megan.

"No, my father may not be too strict, but if there is something he will not tolerate, it's arriving late for dinner," Megan said and gave me a look conveying that we better get moving, and that if I had any idea to stay and see the sunset with her redheaded friend, it was not going to happen that day.

"I better also go," Jimmy said, and we started walking.

"Me too," said Wendy.

"See you tomorrow, Daniel," Katie said, slowly pronouncing my name.

She kept reminding me of the dames from the gangster movies, the ones in the nightclubs dressed to the nines, with impeccable hair and make-up; always needing somebody to light a cigarette for them while they bat their eyelashes and thank the gentleman with a sexy smile of their voluptuous lips. I was a little mesmerized, when Jimmy pushed me to get going. The rest of the group seemed they were not expected for dinner, or had a different schedule. Megan, Wendy, Jimmy, and I headed up the hill, leaving behind the pier and the beachgoers. As we were leaving, more people were arriving at the pier. The street was getting livelier with people going to the restaurants or to the pier to see the sunset or just to walk on The Strand.

Wendy lived near the church. My first impression of Wendy was that she was quiet, but since we had left the pier she was talking with Jimmy nonstop; she became a chatterbox. Soon we were in front of Wendy's house.

"See you guys tomorrow!" Wendy said as she ran down the side of her house to use the back door to get in. Megan, Jimmy, and I kept walking to our street, mostly in silence.

"Daniel, be careful with Katie; she is my friend. I know her, and you are the new kid on the block which makes you attractive in her eyes. Plus, she likes to collect boyfriends. I know you are just going to be here for a short period of time; don't waste your days inflating Katie's ego," Megan said this as we reached our street.

"Thank you for the advice," I said as my mind was still spinning fast.

I didn't care if she only liked me because I was the new kid on the block. I was going to be there just for a few weeks, it was perfect if she wanted me as a disposable boyfriend. It didn't bother me. Back home I couldn't get any of the girls to go out with me, and here somebody was already giving me some promising signals.

A few more steps and we were back. Megan just waved goodbye to Jimmy, and I said, "See you around."

CHAPTER 5
TO LAX

ON WEDNESDAY NIGHT everybody's luggage was by the door, just as Tony had instructed his family, except Leslie's. She was the last one to bring down her suitcase and only after her father asked her where her green midsize suitcase was.

First impressions are deceiving, I thought Leslie was sweet, just a little moody due to her age, but I was wrong. She was turning out to be a brat. On the other hand, for the few days that I had spent with the sisters, Megan was friendlier and while she seemed a bit arrogant, she was the most down-to-earth of the two. I had seen that the interaction between Megan and Consuelo was smoother than the few words Consuelo exchanged with the youngest of the Westfields. I thought if looks could kill, Leslie would have dropped dead a long time ago.

We had dinner and there was not too much talk during dessert. Everybody went early to bed. During dinner Tony told me that he wanted me to take them to the airport. I had never driven in the city, nor had I driven a car, but Tony assured me that it was an easy drive as soon as you got out of the madness of the airport. I remembered that you just needed to get to Imperial Highway and drive until you got to the water then turn left to take the road to Manhattan Beach.

I had asked Tony during dinner if it was OK for me to go exploring the city with Jimmy. He had offered to take me to Venice, Beverly Hills, and Olvera Street when I had mentioned that I wanted to buy some postcards. He said that I should wait and check out postcards from other parts of Los Angeles before buying only postcards from Manhattan Beach. Tony told me it was OK to go exploring with Jimmy after I had taken care of my chores, looked after the dogs and informed Consuelo that I was going to go out. And of course, he told me not to get home too late, because even if he was not going to be in town, he still was responsible for me.

———

I was getting used to waking up closer to seven. I could hear that everybody was awake. Downstairs Tony and Pam were talking. The dogs were running up and down; once or twice they tried to push the door of my bedroom open, but to no avail. I then heard Megan going downstairs. At a few minutes to seven I decided to go downstairs and make myself helpful and take the dogs for their walk. Tony had said that he wanted to be in the car by eight.

"Good morning!" I said to Pam and Tony. They were in the kitchen and greeted me with their steaming mugs of coffee in their hands. Pam was ready with makeup and hair done. By the door there was Megan trying to fit something else into her suitcase. I was going to offer to sit on it for her to close it, but as I got closer, I could hear the click of the latch, the sound of success. I thought there was a good chance that her suitcase was going to burst open before making it to Europe.

"Hey Daniel!" Megan said when she saw me walking in with an inquisitive look on my face regarding her dilemma.

"Are you ready for your big trip?" I asked.

"Yes, I am. I wish we were already in the airplane flying. Packing and unpacking are my least favorite activities. Well, I better get upstairs and brush my hair before my dad asks us to get in the car."

"Yes, and I better take Bella and Ginger for their morning walk."

"Please take good care of them, I am sure you will."

I just smiled at her comment—the two dogs had become so accustomed to my presence that if they had their way, they would have spent part of the night with me in my room. As soon as I started feeding them, taking them for walks and playing with them in the garden, they started to look to me as another member of the family. The pooches were not dummies, they knew that Consuelo didn't care for them, and they avoided her as much as she avoided them. They were like two magnets repelling each other.

"Daniel, when you come back from the walk, I need you to help me with the luggage," Tony stated.

"Of course," I replied. I didn't understand why he needed my help; one person could take care of the four suitcases. I went and grabbed the dog leashes, shook the box of cereal, and the dogs came running into the kitchen before I even called their names. When I left, Tony was asking Pam to go and check on Leslie who still had not come downstairs. That morning I didn't have to take the full route, the dogs took care of business quickly and I decided to turn around and go back to the house to help Tony with the luggage as he had asked me.

"I can't believe you are still dragging your feet." Were the first words I heard when I opened the door. Tony was telling his younger daughter, who still was wearing her pajamas. I went straight to the kitchen and drank a glass of orange juice.

I didn't want to be a witness to the Westfield morning soap opera. Leslie went running up the stairs to change. Behind her was Pam to make sure her youngest got ready. Megan was sitting in the living room reading a fashion magazine and looked ready to get in the car as soon as Tony gave the order.

I walked to Tony's studio where he was standing by his desk looking at the bills he had told me to mail according to the dates he had written in pencil on the bottom left corner of each of the envelopes.

"Daniel you are back, that was quick. Let's get the luggage in the car."

I followed him and after some doing, all the suitcases fit into the big trunk. The order and placement were complex. Maybe that is why he wanted me to help him to figure out how to fit everything. The carry-on luggage of the three ladies of the house would need to be on their laps on their way to the airport. At 7:55, Leslie came down and was ready, she went and sat on a chair in the dining room, and she looked upset. Then her father told everybody to get in the car because we were going to the airport. I sat in between the two sisters. I was paying attention to every turn. Traffic was light and I was hoping that on my way back it was going to still be light. Leslie didn't talk at all, not even when I dropped them off by the curb. Megan at least said: "have a good time and we'll see you in two weeks."

Pam told me to take care of everything as we had discussed, and Tony told me I knew what I needed to do. The moment had come for the beginning of the anticipated summer vacation of the Westfields. Wearing their finest, and with luggage in hand, they walked inside the terminal while I got back in the car, but this time in the driver's seat. After looking carefully, I pulled out and made my way to Sepulveda Boulevard. I never had driven on city streets, only on the country roads back home, where you encounter a car here and there, and only in town where you couldn't drive more than twenty miles per hour, otherwise the sheriff was going to have a talk with you and later call your dad.

I took a quick right, and I was on Imperial Highway going straight to where the road ends. I could see the blue ocean. I was looking forward to Jimmy's tour of Venice in the afternoon. I turned left and this time I knew that the rancid smell was from the Hyperion plant. Leaving El Segundo behind, soon I was back to Manhattan Beach, parking the car in the garage, where it was going to stay until my host's return. Tony told me he was not going to ask me to pick them up because their flight was going to arrive late, and that you never know how long it would take you to go through immigration and customs. They would return home by taxi.

I went inside the house and the two dogs came out, looked at me, and then ran to the master bedroom. I had this feeling as if I was dreaming. It was surreal to be alone in a big house, a new house in a town near the beach. I was thinking what I was going to do. I didn't need to water the front yard; the dogs were walked and fed, and I didn't have to go to the post office. I decided to wait for Consuelo and left her know I was going to go to the beach. I took a magazine and went to the sit by the pool. The weather was perfect. After turning a few pages, Consuelo arrived.

"Danny, Danny, I am here. Are they gone?"

"Hey Consuelo, yes they are at the airport."

"Was there any trouble with the girls, this morning?" she asked.

"Not really," I said. I decided I was not going to tell her about Leslie not being on time and being moody.

"Was Leslie ok?"

"She was quiet." I didn't see the point telling Consuelo that the younger sister had been brooding in the dining room until the moment that they left. I didn't like to gossip.

"She doesn't like flying. She likes traveling but she doesn't care for airplanes," Consuelo told me.

"Ah, I didn't know."

That explained why she didn't look too happy, but it didn't explain why she still was in her pajamas within thirty minutes of leaving.

"Have you eaten breakfast?" Consuelo asked. She was going to continue her feeding quest.

"No. But I will have something later when I come back from downtown and the beach."

"OK, then lunch it is." Consuelo turned around without saying another word. I appreciated that she was a woman of few words. Since the moment I arrived I had been interrogated by Tony, his family, and the people I had been introduced to. I wanted just to be alone for a while, just to walk around without having a plan. Even if I was going to see Jimmy sometime after 2:00 when we were going to go to Venice. It was different, it was a fun appointment.

———

I had lost track of time looking at the ocean and listening to the waves crash. How long had it been since I came down those narrow streets or alleys, where there is room for only one car and houses are built a few feet from each other, with barely a yard between them, I wasn't sure. Some houses occupied the whole lot without a single square inch of dirt left empty. So different from home. Our closest neighbors were half a mile away, and that was the limit of their land. To get to their house you still had a quarter of a mile to drive. But in Manhattan Beach you could fit a lot of houses in that half mile. Some of the houses I went by were new while others looked old; but all had something in common, the colors used on the exterior: pale blues or greens, beige and white. Most of them were two stories. And then there were the nautical details: an anchor, a piece of net, seashells, a ship's wheel, a statue of a sailor made of wood that had seen better years.

The low brick wall of one of the houses was decorated with sea glass and seashells making it stand out from the other houses on the small block. The other houses seemed boring compared with the exuberance of the blues and greens in the wall.

I looked around me and people had arrived at the almost desolate spot I had chosen to sit and contemplate the blue Pacific Ocean. There were sun worshipers (that is what Jimmy called them), beach goers that lie in the sun and every fifteen or thirty minutes they flip over to obtain an even tan. Then there were a few groups playing volleyball—interesting that until the moment when I saw them playing, I had not noticed the sound of the volleyball being hit. I was lost in my thoughts, and I had forgotten my watch. I didn't know what time it was. But I wasn't the only one lost in his thoughts, there was a guy that had been sitting on his surfboard since I arrived. He was just floating. He only got on his belly to paddle out when the current got him closer to the beach. I was wondering if the guy was going to get out of the water before I got up to get back home. I didn't have to wait too long to get the answer. He turned his board around and soon was getting out of the ocean and walking on the wet sand. He looked at me and changed his direction towards where I was sitting.

"Hey, are you OK?" He asked. He was tall, with short hair, and strongly built. Maybe he was in his late 20s or early 30s.

"Yes. Are *you* ok?" I replied without thinking. He smiled and planted his surfboard in the sand.

"Yes, I am, thank you for asking. I like to come here when I can, and just take in the calmness of the ocean. My name is Jack by the way. I haven't seen you around, are you new in town?"

I gave him a look; he seemed like a nice person, but he was a stranger and was asking me if I was OK and if I was new in town. My parents would not have been proud of me if I was not polite.

"I am here visiting some family friends, and this is the first time I have been by the ocean," I said. I neglected to tell him my name.

"I see," he said. "Well visitor, be careful with Mother Ocean, you never know when the tide can change or how strong the currents are. See you around."

"See you."

I sat there for a few more minutes and then I decided that it was time to start walking back to the Westfield's house before I got ravenous. On my way back, I went by the parking lot of the Community Center and a group of elderly ladies were unloading trays of food and desserts, confirming that it was time for lunch. I was sure at home there was something prepared by Consuelo waiting for me.

The sound of the doorbell woke up the dogs, who came barking from the master bedroom, only to turn around when Consuelo told them to be quiet. It was time for Jimmy to come and get me. I was ready to get out of the house and have Jimmy give me a tour of Venice Beach. I went and opened the door, since Consuelo was going to start vacuuming upstairs.

"Danny boy, are you ready to experience Venice?" Jimmy blasted.

"Hey Jimmy, yes, I am ready to go. Just let me tell Consuelo I'm leaving."

"OK, OK, I will be waiting in the blue Impala."

"Those are some serious wheels you have."

"I only get to drive this car. It's my mother's car. After getting my driver's license, my parents thought to buy me a used car, but that idea lasted two minutes. My father thought that in two years I was going to be gone, and I didn't need a car to go around town. My mother said that I could use her car until the day I go to college."

"Hey, at least you have a car that you can use. At home we only have a beat-up truck and an old, old car that only sees the light of day on Sundays to go to church or when my mother must go into town. Both are running by the grace of God. Let me go and tell Consuelo and then we'll get out of here."

I went upstairs and had to tap her shoulder for her to realize I was there, trying to tell her I was leaving. She was listening again to the little radio, she just said "Do not be late and be a good boy out there." I waved goodbye and ran downstairs, then we left.

Soon we were driving north on Vista del Mar, leaving Manhattan Beach, passing by El Segundo and Los Angeles International Airport. Somewhere while driving in Playa del Rey, Vista del Mar became Culver Boulevard. Playa Del Rey seemed to be smaller than El Segundo, but I didn't ask my tour guide because soon we were driving through some green open space. It was interesting because all of a sudden there were no houses jammed against each other and the road had open space on both sides. This was the most open land that I had seen since my arrival. Jimmy told me it was The Ballona Creek Wetlands and Ballona Creek. He explained how when the tide is high the water comes in and forms canals through the area. Next, we were merging with Highway 1, which in that section of Los Angeles is called Lincoln Boulevard. Jimmy was telling me how his father likes to take them on road trips up Highway 1, sometimes camping, other times staying in bed and breakfasts in small coastal towns. I also learned that Highway 1 is also known as PCH which stands for Pacific Coast Highway and runs 1,675 miles from Fort Bragg, in Mendocino County to Dana Point, in Orange County.

"Dan, now we are in Marina del Rey," Jimmy said.

"I thought we just went by Marina del Rey."

"No, no that was Playa del Rey, The King's Beach. This is the King's Marina."

"That's funny, not too original, but funny," I quipped.

"Danny, California was part of Alta California, and it was part of New Spain. That is why you find a lot of streets and towns with Spanish names, and the words Del Rey are vestige of the Royal Crown of Spain."

"Interesting. I guess we also have that back home but because it is in English, we don't know of any more details. We have a Verona, now I wonder if it is named for the town in Italy. I will ask my dad or my grandpa, he seems to know a lot of history," I said.

"Now, I am curious why Hermosa Beach is not called Playa Hermosa and Redondo Beach Playa Redonda? Why put one word in Spanish and one in English? One day I will find out," Jimmy uttered.

"I'm sure you will Jimmy, you seem to know a lot. Does information just stay in your brain and never leave?"

"Yep, pretty much."

"That must be cool, I have to read and read to memorize something."

"Yes, until there is something you want to forget, and you can't," Jimmy said. "Like Todd breaking my glasses."

My friend was right. It could be a curse and a blessing to have the brains he had. His parents had very high expectations for him. School was a breeze for Jimmy.

"Not being able to forget, I never thought about it that way. Do you speak Spanish?" I asked, trying to change the topic and take the conversation away from Todd.

"Sí. Besides I know a little Italian and some German," said Jimmy in his casual tone of voice. He never tried to impress or brag.

"Jimmy, you are full of surprises."

"Danny, we are in Venice. Let's drive by the canals before we go to the beach."

A few more turns and we were going over the bridges crossing the canals. I could see why they had named the place Venice, because it had canals like the ones in Venice, Italy. Jimmy found a place to park, and we walked around. The canals were not that deep, but they were cool. I took two pictures to show everybody at home. I was being selective with my picture taking; I had two rolls of film, and I didn't want to have to buy more, plus the more pictures I took, the more I needed to spend on developing them.

We got back to the car, and we drove as close as we could to find a parking spot near the beach. We had to go around several times. The place looked different from Manhattan Beach.

"Danny, Venice Beach has its own vibe, it isn't like the rest of the Beach Cities. My father calls it '*Hippie Town.*'"

I already could see what Jimmy was talking about; in the few blocks we had driven trying to find a place to park, I saw two VW buses with flowers and peace and love signs. Just like Manhattan Beach, the houses were back-to-back; not too much space between them. Finally, we found a space big enough for the Impala.

"OK, Danny boy, let's go and explore Venice Beach." We started walking down the street towards the beach, and you could see there were a lot of people coming and going.

"This place is busier than Manhattan Beach."

"More tourists visit this area. There are basketball courts, a jungle gym and the famous 'muscle beach.' Come on let's go this way," Jimmy said and we were right at the bottom of the street. There were people walking and roller-skating.

"Are all of these people really tourists? It's Thursday, are all of them on vacation?"

"Oh no Danny, some are locals, but they may have part-time jobs like me, or work evening schedules and go to work later. The summer is just starting and most schools are on vacation, that is also why there are so many people here on a weekday."

"It must be really busy on the weekends."

"Yes, it is. My father brought us here with our cousins when they came to visit. They wanted to go and see Muscle Beach and it was like a carnival. My cousins and I enjoyed it, but my father promised not to come back. He is kind of serious and doesn't like anything that affects his weekend routine of reading the paper and working on the car."

"Is this Muscle Beach?" I asked.

"You're kidding me; you don't know about Muscle Beach?"

"No."

"On our way back, we will go to *'The Pen'*, that is the place that for some is called Muscle Beach; because the original Muscle Beach was in Santa Monica."

"How do you move a whole place?"

"Nothing was moved, it is more like a title, it was just renaming an area."

"You know Jimmy, you Angelenos like to complicate things," I said.

"Why do you say that?"

"First you have names of street and towns in Spanish, which is nice, but then you have names of cities with a word in Spanish and a word in English, and now you are telling me that just over there was the original Muscle Beach and somehow it ended up in Venice."

"Oh Danny, it's not that complicated."

"I guess it isn't when you have been born and raised here."

"Come on, let's a get a slice a pizza and a drink."

Between a collection of small store fronts selling sunglasses and curios, henna tattoos, and even a massage parlor, there was a small pizza joint. With pizza in one hand

and a soda in the other, we walked across the boardwalk and sat on a grassy area where there were people sunbathing, reading, couples entangled in passionate embraces, and others just like us taking a break and eating something.

"You know Danny, at the start of the 1930s there was black gold bubbling out here in this area. Oil drilling towers stood where some of those buildings are."

"No way, this was an oil field?" I said it was difficult for me to imagine how it would look.

"Yes, I have seen pictures of how Venice Beach looked more like an industrial park than a coastal town. You know there are still operational wells around Los Angeles, and there are four man-made islands, the THUMS Islands off the coast of Long Beach. They look like islands with nice resorts but behind their facades there is only oil drilling equipment," my tour guide mentioned between bites.

Jimmy was right, Venice Beach was so different from Manhattan Beach, and the free spirit vibe was palpable among the eclectic visitors and residents of the area. We finished our snack and then kept walking towards Santa Monica along the bike path. This town appeared less run-down and had finer hotels and restaurants, in addition to a pier. Then it was time to turn around.

We headed back south. More people started to arrive. Standing out among the crowd were girls in bikinis roller-skating past. Their skin tan, sun kissed for weeks, and the strands of their brown or blond hair flying away behind them, making more than one onlooker lose track of what they were doing as the girls glided by like the sea breeze. Jimmy told me that some consider Venice the Roller-Skating Capital of the World.

"Let's stop and listen to this dude," I asked Jimmy as we were getting closer to the sound of an electric guitar being played with intensity, a sound that reminded me of Jimmy

Hendrix. The musician had amazed a good number of spectators, and we were late for the show.

There he was, with a turban on his head, wearing rollerskates and playing an electric guitar with an elaborate paint design, hypnotizing his audience with every scratch of the strings. He rolled about with ease. It was like being at a rock concert, it appeared he was reaching the end of his performance, getting ready to deliver the last note, but then he kept going, two or three times more. Finally, he delivered the last group of notes, and everybody cheered and clapped. The show was over.

An empty tin can of instant coffee was the treasure chest where the audience dropped coins, and some, a bill or two. I took the coins in my pocket and put them in the tin can. I never had listened to live music like that—sure you listen to the radio or watch somebody playing on TV, but being close, it was more intimate even though we were standing on the strand. It was not just listening to the sound, you could feel the vibrations passing by you as they kept spreading and dissipating towards us. That was something else. I was always going to remember that moment from my day at Venice Beach.

On our walk to The Weight Pen (Muscle Beach) Jimmy was telling me that the actor from *Conan the Barbarian* used to train there. Yes, at the time I only knew that Arnold Schwarzenegger was Mr. Olympia and that he was in a movie that I watched on a Saturday night because it was being played with another movie we wanted to see as part of the double feature in our local movie theater.

There were bicycle riders: some just wearing their regular beach attire, others appeared to be going to a Halloween party. There were tourists attired in Dodgers jerseys; Jimmy told me everything about the Fernandomania, and Los Angeles hosting the 1984 Olympic Games. There was a guy wearing a Santa hat with white trim that had become grey, I was sure it had never been washed since the first day he put it on. Then we crossed paths with a group of monks of some religion playing a drum and walking towards the sand. Maybe they were going to have a sunset ceremony of some sort. There were more street performers; people breakdancing, doing acrobatics, some tossing balls and bowling pins. All these people performed as spectators looked on in awe. Then we got to the gym at the beach.

"Here we are! Muscle Beach at Venice Beach, or the Weight Pen," said Jimmy.

"Jimmy, I was thinking this place should be renamed."

"Why?" Jimmy gave me an inquisitive look.

"Well, if Mr. Olympia trained here, then maybe it should be called Venice Mount Olympus."

"That's funny, that's a good one," Jimmy laughed at my corny comment.

"You know, next time when I talk about Muscle Beach, I am going to incorporate your comment."

"I am OK with that, just make sure you give me credit."

"I will," Jimmy promised.

We looked around, they were getting ready to close the place, some serious body builders were still lifting a lot of iron. Consuelo came to my mind; she would have been so happy just feeding those guys the amount of food they needed to build and maintain the level of muscle they had. That would have been her dream come true—cook, and feed somebody a lot. She wanted to give me seconds during lunch, and she was already preparing dinner to leave for me. I thought she should be working in a restaurant instead of being the housekeeper for the Westfields, but of course I was not going to tell her that. Pam would have killed me.

On our way to the car, we meet a girl with a thick snake over her shoulders, she was on her way to the beach. I guessed my mouth dropped open because she smiled and asked me if I wanted to pet it. I shook my head side to side.

There was no way I was going to be touching it. I don't have snake phobia, but I prefer reptiles with legs.

"What is that smell?" I asked Jimmy.

"That's incense. Some burn it because they find it calming, others because it is some kind of spiritual thing and others just to get the stench of weed and beer from their over-crowded apartments. Really, you never have smelled incense?"

"Nope, it must be a city folks' thing. There are smells on the farm, but you just deal with them. We do not have incense burning to cover the stink of 'money from the pigs.' If I did that, I may just end up burning the barn down and then there would be a lot of smell of hay burning. Plus, my ass may end up burning after a good lashing from my dad."

"What do you mean with the aroma of money from the pigs? And does your father still spank you?" Jimmy was giving me a perplexed look and smiling a bit.

"One of our neighbors has a lot of pigs. It doesn't matter how much he cleans their pens. You can smell the animals and the stench of their poop far away before you reach his farm. To anybody that dares to tell him that he has the most stinking farm, he replies that at least his farm smells like money. He has been able to make a good living by raising pigs. You know, everybody wants bacon or sausages with their breakfast, ham in their sandwich, and a nice big greasy pork chop for dinner. No, my father doesn't spank me, but if I were to do something so stupid such as burning the barn down, he may just have a heart attack. Things have been a little difficult on the farm."

"Is the stench from the pig farm worse than the smell from the Hyperion plant in El Segundo?" Jimmy inquired.

"No, the Hyperion plant smell is worse, that smell is plain nasty."

"And we are just going to be driving by for the six o'clock

batch, which is especially rotten," Jimmy said as we were getting in the car.

"Are you serious?"

"I will let you be the judge of that. We will be driving by soon."

On that note, we started our trip back to Manhattan. Between laughs we made it to Manhattan Beach. I don't recall the stench of the Hyperion plant that day, I remember the vibe in Venice was something else, and so very different from any of the towns I had gone to. I couldn't wait to tell the guys back home about Venice.

CHAPTER 6
THE PALOS VERDES MERMAID

SUNDAY, JUNE 27, 1982

SINCE THE WESTFIELDS LEFT, I spent my time taking care of the chores that they assigned me the first thing in the morning, and then I went out walking in different directions until it was time for lunch. Consuelo prepared hearty lunches, maybe because the upkeep of the house was lessened with the family gone. I was fortunate that while I like sandwiches, I was enjoying eating dishes I never had heard about before. She prepared something called *chilaquiles verdes.* There were tortilla chips and shredded chicken breast drenched in green salsa and garnished with onions and cilantro. On top of this she placed a sunny side-up fried egg, just because she said I needed additional nutrition.

It was the first day that I was going to be completely alone in the house; Consuelo had Sundays off, and yes, she had left me rice, beans, and a saucepan of *chili colorado* (pork in red sauce). Even with the family gone she managed to keep herself busy. The day when I returned from my Venice Beach tour, I found that the dirty clothes I had been piling up in one corner of the bathroom had been washed, and were neatly folded on the bed. I wasn't expecting her to do my laundry, but she beat me to it. When I thanked her and told her I could do my own laundry, she told me that it was her job to do the laundry, and if I didn't mind, she was going to take care of mine just like she did for Tony and his family. I at once understood the washing and drying machines were in her domain, and it was important for her to keep it that way. Therefore, I was not going to try to convince her I could take care of my own dirty clothes. I still had over a week to go, and Tony and Pam made it clear they liked to keep Consuelo happy, otherwise I would never have been asked to take care of the two dogs.

I was going to the beach by myself. Jimmy was out of town—his father arrived from his business trip on Friday and was taking the family to Santa Barbara for the day. But he promised to give me a tour of Beverly Hills and Hollywood Boulevard on Wednesday. I had no plans and I decided to watch TV in the morning. I soon got tired of watching music videos and surfing the different channels trying to find something decent to watch. I thought if I was in Manhattan Beach I should be at the beach and hang out there instead of being confined by four walls.

I had seen Katie one day on my way to the beach when she was on her way home. We talked a little and I almost asked her for her phone number but she left before I got up the nerve. She was acting a little different than the first day I meet her. Not too *femme fatale*, maybe because there was no entourage around her.

I took a towel, a banana and a book, and headed to the beach even if it was close to lunch. I had decided that I was going to have a taco in the small Mexican place when I got hungry. I was feeling positively rich with the twenty dollars that Tony had given me for the mall. The money was constantly making me aware of its presence. It was time to spend some of the bills. Plus, I already had scheduled some yard work for Mrs. Pitchman. She had decided to change the flowers in her planters and flower beds, and I was expecting to get few dollars for the gardening work. I decided I could have a couple tacos and maybe even splurge and get a soda.

The beach was busy. I went and sat near to one of the lifeguard stations, the closest to the pier. I took off my shirt and sat there reading my book. Between pages I looked around, checking out the rest of the beachgoers. I scanned the area looking for Megan's friends, but I couldn't find them. The time passed and I was getting hot and decided to take a splash in the water. I knew my stuff was going to be safe there. The water felt good, I just floated around, letting the waves take me back to the beach then draw me back out, when a group of girls caught my eye. It was difficult not to focus on them. Their bikinis clung tightly and were orange, yellow and green neon—colors that were magnets. They were arriving at the beach, laughing and being playful; behind them there was a guy carrying a cooler. The girls had beach bags and a volleyball. They set up camp near one of the volleyball nets closer to the water.

My stomach started to growl and a trip to the little Mexican restaurant on Manhattan Avenue was in order. On my way to lunch I walked by the encampment of new beachcombers; they were drinking from plastic cups as colorful as their outfits. I must confess that I was staring, plain rubbernecking so that I didn't notice the beautiful brunette coming to join the group and wearing a metallic powder-blue bikini that was very tight. She had her hair in a ponytail, was wearing a big beach hat and a white unbuttoned camisole. She was giggling when I found myself standing in front of her, within inches of colliding. She said "Hi" as she went around me, I replied "Hello" and followed her with my eyes for a second, then turned around and increased the tempo of my steps, but I couldn't walk as fast as I wanted to in the soft sand.

It was a hot day, and more people were arriving at the beach. I went by a small pizza place and the smell of pepperoni almost made me change my mind to buy a slice of pizza and drop my goal of trying something from the Mexican eatery, but I carried on and made my way up the street. I got to the little restaurant and was looking at the menu trying to decide what to get when I saw a guy with beach blond hair walking by with a plate, holding a flour tortilla with something inside.

"Hi, what is that?" I asked.

"Dude, this is a carne asada burrito. It's a bomb. It has beans, rice, cheese, and grilled steak."

"Sounds good, thanks."

"It *is* good!" he said and went to sit in a booth facing the street.

I decided not to look at the menu and just order the highly recommended carne asada burrito. When I got it, I understood why it was good. Besides being tasty, it was a good pound of food wrapped inside the tortilla. As I ate my burrito, I was looking at the people coming and going in the place, mostly beach goers needing a bite, some barefoot.

With my belly full, it was time to head back to the beach and spend a few more hours reading and enjoying the sun. I was hoping to see Megan's friends and hang out with them. I decided to head back to the same spot where I had been sitting, even if that meant I was going to have to walk by the group of neon-clad girls. I was going to try to look the other way. I didn't want to get caught really staring; once had been too many times. When I reached the bottom of the street, I scanned the beach, and I saw they were playing volleyball. I thought it was perfect; nobody was going to notice me walking by. But then just when I thought I had not been seen, I heard a sweet voice.

"Hey Billabong, would you like to play?" And the volleyball landed right in front of me. I turned around and the brunette with the powder-blue bikini was coming to fetch the ball and she said, "Do you want to join us? We are short one."

"Sure, but I never have played."

"There is nothing to it, just hit the ball when it comes your way and try to send it over the net to the other side." First, she looked at me inquisitively and then she explained what I needed to know about playing volleyball.

"Val come on, there is more to it than that," the only guy in the group said from the other side of the net.

"We want Billabong to join us, not to scare him away," Val responded.

"Billabong?" I said, not understanding why they were calling me that.

"Your t-shirt. Come on, you will be playing with us." Val didn't wait for my answer, she started walking and I decided to give it a try and followed her.

"OK, I will join you," I said.

"Hey, I am Oscar, and this is Lori and Eve," he said as he gestured towards each of the girls.

"My name is Daniel."

"I am Valerie, but I prefer be called Val, and this is Samantha."

There was something about Valerie, she had a beautiful big smile, and she was unpretentious.

"Come on, let's play. You two now don't have any excuse, we are even," Oscar said, and Val went to serve.

"Oscar, you will need to go and get drinks if you guys lose," Valerie said.

"Sure, that is *if* we lose. But I doubt you will win with Billabong on your team," boasted Oscar.

"Hey, I think he's a natural," Samantha said.

Between laughs and tips from Val and Samantha, I was able to hit the ball. Quickly I understood that I just needed to keep the ball in the air at all costs to keep the play going. Oscar stopped talking trash as the minutes went by. I was a lucky volleyball rookie, I managed to save some balls to the delight of my teammates that were into giving you high-fives after a winning a point. Also, they were screamers, they screamed if we got a point, they screamed if we lost a point—just screaming *ah!!!, oh!!!, mine!!!!*

Soon we had the lead and were close to winning. I didn't know how we got there but I was happy that we were not losing. Val was serving and Oscar returned the ball to me. I just sent it back to him and we did that a few times, it was like we were playing ping pong, and then I barely touched the ball leaving it on the net, just going over to the other side. Lori tried to reach for the ball which was falling straight down like a rock. Eve ran to assist her, but Lori sent the ball into the net, and it bounced away from them. Samantha and Val started to celebrate our victory.

"Let's play one more," Oscar said, hoping to even things up.

"Sure, after we drink a cold soda," Val replied.

"OK, I will be back. Hey Billabong, keep an eye on them and don't let them get into trouble," Oscar advised.

"Trouble?" said Eve.

"Hey, wait, I'll go with you," Lori said and followed Oscar.

"Well tell us, you aren't an Aussie so where are you from?" Samantha asked.

"I'm from Wisconsin. Why is it that you thought I was from Australia?"

"Because of your t-shirt, Billabong is an Aussie brand," Samantha replied.

"Ah, I didn't know. Somebody gave it to me."

"Then are you on vacation here, or just moved? Tell us, what is your story?" Val asked.

It was difficult to concentrate as my heart was beating and my mind trying to turn. She then smiled, waiting for me to tell them my life story.

"I am here until July ninth. I am staying with a friend of my father."

"What else?" Samantha insisted almost impatiently.

"It is my first time in California," I replied, somewhat breathless.

The girls were surrounding me, staring at me and waiting for more. It was somewhat surreal.

"Daniel, tell us more. Where do you go to college? Do you have a girlfriend? Do you have siblings?" Eve pressed.

They were determined to learn more about me. I was realizing that everybody I met asked me about college, or college was part of their conversations. And that was the topic I wanted to avoid because I didn't apply to college, and I didn't have any idea when I was going to apply and if I was going to apply.

"I'm not in college, I just graduated high school and I'm going to wait two years before I apply. I have a younger sister and an older brother."

My interrogators just exclaimed "Ah" when I said that I wasn't going to college.

"Girlfriend?" Val asked, she was persistent and beautiful.

"No, I do not have a girlfriend." All the girls smiled but Val had the biggest grin.

"Val doesn't have a boyfriend," Eve offered, and Val reacted by kicking sand on Eve's legs.

"It's time you tell me about yourselves," I proposed.

I couldn't believe it, how they started talking nonstop until Lori and Oscar came back with the drinks. It was like they had been keeping a vow of silence for years and then they were free to say everything they couldn't say in a long time. In those short minutes I learned they were from Palos Verdes and referred to Palos Verdes as PV. They pointed where PV was—the big hill in the distance, when they realized I didn't know where it was. Only Eve lived in Manhattan Beach, and she was Val's cousin. They liked to come to the beach in Manhattan because there was not really a decent beach where they lived. They told me if they had brothers and sisters, what college they were going to attend, and more —information my brain didn't have time to record. I was getting dizzy listening to them when Oscar and Lori came back.

We spent the rest of the afternoon playing a few more sets, listening to music from a small boombox. The girls kept changing the tapes and then replaying one or two songs. The ones that suck in my mind were "Don't you Want Me" and "I Can't Go for That." I learned that Val was the best swimmer in her high school, and she was known as "PV's Mermaid." She had won a lot of swim meets, which looked good on her college applications, and she had been offered several scholarships to private and public universities. She decided to attend Stanford, the school her mother went to. Val was humble; she didn't like to talk about her swimming accomplishments, but her friends loved to. She sat there and smiled.

It was almost six o'clock when the girls started to collect their things to get back to Palos Verdes, and at that moment Katie and some friends came by. Katie's *femme fatale* attitude was back. She stopped by our group to say that she had been looking for me, all the while not acknowledging my new acquaintances and hanging herself on my arm like I was one of her belongings. I smiled at Katie and gently freed my arm from her grasp. I told her I had been there for hours, and I tried to introduce her to the Palos Verdes group, but Katie was dismissive, and pulling her glasses an inch down her nose to look over the frame, she said "I have seen some of them. Daniel, I hope to see you later to watch the sunset together." Katie and her entourage left, as Oscar and the girls were chuckling.

"Oh, Daniel let's watch the sunset!" Oscar imitated Katie.

"Wow, she is a little too Sunset Boulevard," Eve said.

"Sunset Boulevard?"

"Daniel, don't tell me you have never watched *Sunset Boulevard*?" Samantha exclaimed.

"No, I haven't. I think one day my parents were watching it, but I went to my room."

"Daniel, you need to watch it. Your friend is as dramatic as the main character of the movie," Eve said.

"She is not really my friend," I clarified for Val's benefit.

"Eve's parents have a vast collection of tapes. Her father works in the film industry and is obsessed with film noir movies," offered Oscar.

"Oscar, I don't like how obsessed sounds, I would say my father is a big fan of black and white films. He believes one day there will be channels just showing old films. And I think it will be awesome," Eve explained.

"As you can see, like father like daughter," Oscar added.

"Maybe before you leave, we can have a movie evening in my house and watch "Sunset Boulevard" with Daniel."

"Eve, that's a great idea, let's do it," Val chimed in.

I had recuperated somewhat by this time and gathered my thoughts a bit. I agreed to the movie idea, coolly suppressing my enthusiasm.

"Dan, you are alone on this one. I am not going to spend an evening watching old movies," Oscar insisted.

Shortly we were leaving the beach. I headed back to the Westfield's house, and they went to the parking lot to get Oscar's car and drive back to Palos Verdes. We agreed to meet on the beach on Wednesday and play a few sets. I had a fleeting thought of going to find Katie, but it was getting windy and I didn't want to deal with her Sunset Boulevard attitude. Plus, I was ready to eat the *chili colorado* that Consuelo had prepared. I liked Katie, but I found Val to be more my type of girl, Katie was like the bad girl and Val was sweet. I was looking forward to seeing her again.

CHAPTER 7

FOURTH OF JULY WEEKEND

FIREWORKS? OR THE STARS?

AFTER HAVING SPENT Sunday on the beach playing volleyball with the crowd from Palos Verdes, it was time to start the week. First thing on Monday I helped Mrs. Pitchman with her garden. I thought I was going to spend two hours max helping her change the flower beds. The project turned into a whole day affair. I had to forego my trip to the beach. She asked me to be at her house as early as I could because she wanted me to go with her to the nursery and help her buy all kinds of flowers, pots, and bags of soil. We returned with a load that would have been the envy of any professional gardener. After I off-loaded all the goods, Mrs. Pitchman looked at the sun and her watch. Then she told me our action plan, based on the amount of shade in the areas she wanted to work on. You see, Mrs. Pitchman's skin was really pale. She already had several painful visits to the skin doctor, and he wasn't too happy with her gardening. But gardening was her hobby. She told her dermatologist she wasn't going to spend the rest of her life indoors because that would kill her quicker than skin cancer. I respected that she knew what she wanted, and she was going to make it work.

The whole day I felt like a jack rabbit jumping from the backyard to the front yard following the shade. I told her I could do everything based on her instructions. Still she was determined to be by my side, watching my every move, waiting for me to have ready the area for her to put the plants in the holes. I wondered if she didn't trust my green thumb to be as good as hers. I thought it was a team effort though I could have finished in half the time if she had left me alone. It took longer to be back and forth trying to find the shadiest place to work in. It was fine with me because she paid me by the hour, and I didn't have anything else to do besides wanting to go to the beach. The few extra dollars in my pocket were welcome, and I still had more days to hit the beach.

Arriving at the Westfield's, I knew Consuelo was not going to be happy if she found soil from my dirty shoes on the carpet. For that reason, I went to the back yard and took off my shoes and socks; I made sure my jeans didn't have dirt ready to fall. When I was convinced that I was clean enough, I went inside the house and faced the inquisitive eyes of Consuelo. She could see I didn't want to get in trouble with her. She was happy and impressed that I didn't leave a trail of dirt to the guest room. Later after having eaten three slices of the meatloaf that Consuelo had prepared, I went to bed early, I was tired.

Tuesday morning I spent in the house. I didn't want to go to the beach because I woke up to find the street engulfed in thick fog; the air felt damp and cold. The fog didn't change my early morning routine though. I had to go out for a least five minutes to take the pooches for their walk. As soon as I was back from the morning chore, I went back to my room to write postcards and read magazines. When I started to get hungry, I went downstairs to eat some cereal and found

Consuelo vacuuming. As soon as she saw me, she asked me if I wanted a hamburger. I was going to settle for some sugary puffed rice from a colorful cardboard box, but a hamburger was an offer difficult to turn down. Consuelo was happy, she was going to cook something for me.

In the afternoon Jimmy took me to Hollywood Boulevard to show me the Chinese Theater. The street performers were walking up and down the block. A Marilyn Monroe impersonator blew us a kiss when we went by. After parking on a side street, we took a brisk walk to see some of the stars on the Hollywood Walk of Fame. I must say that I was a little disappointed. The sidewalk looked grimy. A good hose-down was in order, or a torrential downpour to clean the dirt and whatever else was stuck to the sidewalk. I took a picture of Frank Sinatra's star for my mom. We walked around and went in some of the shops. I bought more postcards as souvenirs. We went back to the car and drove to Pink's Hot Dogs stand because in Jimmy's words "It was a must do when you are in the area, it is a landmark you can taste." It was not time for lunch or dinner, but it was time for a good hot dog.

After cleaning the ketchup from our fingers, we drove back to Sunset Boulevard, which was the route we were going to take on our way back. Jimmy pointed at the Chateau Marmont where John Belushi died. I got confused with Sunset Boulevard and the Sunset Strip. Jimmy explained that the area of Sunset Boulevard where some of the historic night-clubs and bars are, like The Roxy and Whisky a Go Go, is called The Sunset Strip. Soon I could see that it was the happening place, the epicenter for nightlife – marquees announcing the latest acts, bar names in neon lights, restaurants, billboards. It was a visual display of what the place had to offer after dark. Jimmy rattled off a list of artists that had played in the places as we drove by. Some of them sounded familiar and for others it was the first time I heard of them.

The Doors I knew because my brother liked their tunes. My father disliked their music, but my mother thought Morrison was cute. Maybe it was his leather pants that she liked. I never asked her, not that she would have answered the question. Jimmy said he would have liked to go to one of those events, but his parents wouldn't let him. I didn't understand why not, Jimmy seemed to be the most trusting and quiet kid I had ever meet. I couldn't imagine him getting wild on the Sunset Strip or any other place.

We turned left to leave behind Sunset Boulevard and head south. We drove by a place called The Troubadour on Santa Monica Boulevard, Jimmy told me it was famous because John Lennon, Elton John, Bob Dylan and many more had played there.

With few more pictures in my camera and a handful of postcards, we headed back to Manhattan Beach through neighborhoods. Jimmy didn't want to take the freeway, he found it too impersonal. He said it was going to take us longer, but it was worth it.

We had been driving for a while in silence, listening to a rock station when Jimmy spoke: "I am trying to convince my mom to let me go to see the landing of the Space Shuttle *Columbia* at Edwards Air Force Base."

"Really, you can just go and see it land?" I asked.

"Yes, you just need to get there the night before to park, and then just wait and pray that the weather will be ideal for the landing," Jimmy replied. "My mom will let me go only under two conditions: the first condition is that my father has to say "yes," and the second condition is that I do not go alone," Jimmy explained.

"That sounds easy enough."

"Well, my dad is not going to get home until Friday and then I will be facing a round of parents' 'ping-pong' approval."

"What do you mean by ping-pong?" I asked.

"You know when your mother sends you to ask your father for permission, and then your father says, 'ask your mother.' Then you go back and forth two or three times like that until you either tell one of them he or she said OK, or one of them is forced to give you their approval to whatever you were asking, just so you stop."

I knew it too well. His parents were just like mine in that regard. Father always said, "Go and ask your mother," only for my mother to say, "If your father is OK with it, then it is fine with me." Then I had to turn around and convey to my father what Mom said word for word, and then either he got up from his chair and talked to my mom or he just said "OK, OK, go." I liked how Jimmy called it the parents' ping-pong.

But he was not only trying to convince his mom, he also was trying to convince me to go with him, to the high desert.

"Would you like to go with me?"

"What? I can't. I need to take care of the dogs."

"Bring the dogs. Or my little sister can take care of them," Jimmy said as we had to stop for a red light. He turned and smiled, then the smile disappeared, and he continued: "better bring the dogs because if my little sister takes care of them my mother may end up telling the Westfields in passing."

"Yeah, that wouldn't be good if they knew," I concurred.

"Danny boy, the only option I see is we take the dogs with us."

I couldn't believe he was recommending I take the dogs and maybe get in trouble with Tony. I just thought what would happen if I lost a dog in the middle of the desert. Tony would be angry, and my father would be furious.

"Jimmy! I don't know if I will go, I need to think about it. If I go and something happens to those two dogs, then I will be in big trouble with the whole Westfield clan and my father will ground me for a long, long time."

"Take your time, think about it," Jimmy soothed, "on

Friday, I will need a decision. I know my parents will say yes."

Soon we were back in Manhattan Beach, the streetlights were on and Consuelo was gone for the day. I was alone, and after having dinner and a glass of milk, I went to bed. I didn't have any interest in watching TV or reading. I wanted it already to be Wednesday; I was looking forward to spending time with Val.

I woke up to a beautiful morning; the fog was gone by ten. I waited until noon to leave the house and go to the beach to see if the PV group was back. With a towel over my shoulder and a five-dollar bill in my pocket, I marched down the street. I was walking without looking when I heard my name. It was Katie who was going to the grocery store with her mother.

"Hey Daniel, look at you, a regular beach bum. Am I going to see you later?" Katie said as she waved her mother away—her way to let her know that she was going to stop to talk with me. Her mother just told her to not take too long.

"I don't know. I'm meeting some friends."

"Wow, you just have been here less than two weeks and you already have friends."

I didn't like her tone.

"Well, yeah," I replied. I didn't see the point of her question. I thought somehow she got it in her head that because she was one of the first girls that I met, I was not going to meet other people or that I had to spend time with her every day I was going to be in town.

"Oh, let me guess. Are you friends the Palos Verdes kids, the ones I saw you playing volleyball with?"

"Yes," was my answer to the inquisition.

"Be careful with them, they are spoiled kids from the peninsula. See you later Daniel," she cautioned in all seriousness.

You would have thought that Val and the rest were dangerous criminals. I didn't bother to reply to her comment, and I was not planning to see her later. Katie turned around to see if I was looking at her as she strode off. I remained expressionless as she quickened her steps and went into the store.

As if seeing Katie was not enough for the morning, in my way down to the pier I saw Todd.

"Hey Dan, where is your sidekick, Jimmy? Is he afraid to come to the beach? He shouldn't be, he just needs to be away from us," Todd said as he stood there giving me an arrogant look.

He had fake tough-guy written all over him, even if he thought otherwise. He believed he still was in fifth grade and was terrorizing kindergarteners, just like he did to Jimmy. It was clear that Todd would crumble the day he met somebody who could see beyond his façade and was willing to give him a lesson. But I was not that guy. I was going to be there only for a few more days, and Jimmy was going to go to college soon. There was no point in creating trouble—not for me, not for Jimmy.

"You know, he works in the mornings, not like other people I know whose only work is to take air from others," I said as I passed him by. I was not going to give him any more time than he deserved, and that was already zero.

"You turned out to be quite the philosopher. But I must tell you something, you aren't welcome at the beach. Tell Jimmy I am happy he isn't coming to the beach anymore," Todd pronounced.

"Todd, you don't understand, you aren't the reason why he isn't here. Stop believing that you have any power whatsoever."

I didn't wait for his reply, I kept walking and left him standing there. I knew that since he was alone, he wasn't going to do anything, plus there were people everywhere and he wasn't going to keep going on with his antics.

Down the incline, I reached the beach and to my joy the

group of girls clad in neon-colored bikinis was in the same spot. But there was another guy with the group besides Oscar. A guy older than the rest. He had the looks of a movie star; he looked like he could have been the younger brother of Robert Redford.

As soon as I got closer to the group, Samantha said, "here comes Danny Billabong."

"Hey, how is the PV crowd?" I asked.

I got a reply in unison that they were doing well.

"Phil, this is Daniel, he is visiting from Wisconsin," Val introduced me.

"Hi Daniel, my little cousin can't stop talking about you."

"Phillip, stop it," begged Val.

"Hey Daniel, they told me you are a natural at playing beach volleyball."

"It was just beginners' luck," I claimed.

"Val, I will come to get you in two or three hours."

"Okay, Phil."

"See you later and nice meeting you, Daniel." Phil took his shoes and started jogging effortlessly over the sand towards the pier and up Manhattan Beach Boulevard.

"OK, let's play. But this time I get Val and Samantha," Oscar said.

"No, we want Daniel on our team," said Val.

"Oscar, do you really want to change teams? Come on, let's play together and avenge our loss," Lori pleaded. It was obvious she liked Oscar and wanted to be with him.

"OK, you guys are going to have to get the sodas, this time," Oscar replied and went to the other side of the net to join Lori and Eve.

"Only if we lose," Val responded.

We started to play. Soon we were losing by several points and as much as we tried to catch up, we couldn't. We'd score one point just to lose the next. We were a point from having to get the sodas, but they missed the serve. Then Samantha managed to serve an ace. After a few plays we were tied. Every time we touched the ball Samantha and Val were screaming as if their screams were going to keep the ball in the air. Eve sent the ball to the area that Val was covering; she tried hard to reach it, she dove for it, and she got her hand under the ball but couldn't hit hard enough to get it over the net. We lost the point and the set. Our opponents jumped up and down celebrating like they had won the Olympics. I high-fived Samantha, and realized that Val was on the sand screaming.

"Ouch, my finger. It hurts!" Oscar's team stopped celebrating their victory and ran around the net to join Samantha and I that were helping Val to get up.

"What happened Val?" Lori asked.

"The ball landed on my right thumb and jammed it against my hand." Val was holding her hand and grimacing with pain. We went to the towels and sat there, wondering if her thumb was injured seriously as she kept looking at her hand.

"Samantha and Daniel, get some ice when you get the drinks. We didn't bring a cooler today," Oscar said.

"Come on Daniel let's head to the store."

"Hey, I am getting hungry. Oscar let's go to get some nachos. You guys can pay for the drinks at the restaurant," Lori said.

I thought of how much the nachos and sodas were going to take from my five-dollar bill. I knew the sodas were cheaper in the store.

"No, let's go to the little Italian place and get a pizza while Daniel and Samantha get the sodas," Lori added.

"I vote for pizza and because I am injured my vote counts more," Val offered.

"I guess we have our marching orders. You guys go for lunch while I stay with Val," Eve said and the four of us started walking. I would have preferred to stay with Val but instead I was on soda detail. As soon as we were far away from Eve and Val, the others started talking about Val's injury.

"Val's parents are not going to be happy," Oscar said.

"I know. After last year's scare with the ankle, they were clear they didn't want her playing volleyball," Samantha recounted.

"Why not?" I said, without wondering why her parents were so concerned, or if she had some ailment preventing her from playing. It seemed that I said something odd because everybody stopped walking, and they looked at me like I should have known.

"Daniel, Valerie is the best swimmer in Palos Verdes and the South Bay, she is one of the best swimmers in the state. She got a scholarship to go to Stanford. If she gets injured during the summer, that could jeopardize her scholarship in the long run. Her parents have not been doing too well to afford to pay full tuition at a private school," Lori clarified the situation.

"Oh, I get it."

"Yes, there is a lot at stake if the 'PV Mermaid' gets injured," Oscar emphasized the point.

"She was on a partial scholarship at high school," said Lori.

"She needs the athletic scholarship because while her grades are good, they are not that good for an academic one," Samantha added; she knew a lot about Val's schooling.

"Wow, that must be a lot of pressure," I said.

"You bet, Billabong," Oscar replied.

I had given up that he was going to call me by my name, I guess my summer nickname was going to be "Billabong." Maybe I would get the guys at home to start calling me Bill-abong, and with luck the rest of the town. I wanted once and for all not to be called Joe's youngest boy, or Paul Smith's little brother. Yeah, I liked the idea "Billabong Smith."

We got the sodas, pizza, and ice and when we got back to our spot on the beach, Jack the older guy that I had seen earlier sitting on his surfboard, was talking with Val and Eve. Everybody seemed to know him.

"Hey Jack, what are you doing here. Did my brother send you to spy on me?" Lori asked.

"Lori, no I am not spying on you. I just came to walk on the sand."

"Daniel this is Jack, my brother's best friend and he is a spy."

"Hi Daniel. We met the other day. And Lori, stop saying that I'm a spy. I am not."

"Well, you are so mysterious, you work for the government, nobody knows what you do, and you travel around the world," divulged Lori.

"You girls, always making up stories. My job is not that glamorous, and I just prefer not to talk about it. I better get going."

"Dude, are you not staying to have a slice with us?" Oscar asked Jack as he opened the box with the pizza.

"No, I can't," Jack answered and reassured Val, "little mermaid, you are going to be fine. The thumb doesn't seem broken. Ice it and in a few days the swelling will have disappeared, the bruising may take longer."

"Thank you, Jack. I hope so because otherwise my parents are going to ground me for the rest of the summer."

Jack walked away and as soon he was far enough away to where he couldn't hear us, the girls started talking.

"For a man like that I'd forget about college and just stay at home and make babies with him," Samantha gushed.

"You're not the only one. I want to be next to his pillow every morning when he wakes up. He is so mysterious and handsome," Eve added.

"You two are delusional, I think he goes for older women, like older than him, like in their late thirties," Lori claimed.

"You ladies can keep talking about Jack while Billabong and I eat the pizza," Oscar opened the box and offered me a slice. That quickly ended the fantasizing about Jack.

I sat next to Val and asked, "are you okay?" She shook her head, saying yes.

She wasn't wearing her sunglasses and I could see her eyes were red like she had been crying. During the twenty minutes that we were away, her thumb had swollen and it started to take on a purplish tone.

Just when we had finished eating the pizza, Jimmy showed up and five minutes later Phillip stopped by to pick up Val. He was not too concerned when he saw his cousin's oversized thumb. Phillip was a water polo player and had seen his share of finger injuries. He agreed with Jack that her thumb was going to be OK, but told her to forget about her volleyball days, if she didn't want to be grounded.

After Val left, we stayed around just for half an hour. Jimmy, and I went back to the Westfields. We spent the rest of the afternoon watching music videos and talking about Val and Katie. Soon it was time for him to go home to have dinner.

———

Everybody had been talking about the fourth of July. People were asking me if I was going to see the fireworks, or if I was going to go to a party. The idea of going with Jimmy to see the Space Shuttle *Columbia* land couldn't leave my mind. It was a once in a lifetime experience, something I knew I wouldn't get to do back home. I was tired of reading about stuff like that in the magazines that Fred let me borrow. I still had film in the camera. What better opportunity than to use some of it. If I took the two dogs with me then I would know that they were okay, and nobody would know that they had left the house. The only thing was if Tony called to check on things, I was not going to be there to answer, but then I could say that I was sleeping or outside by the pool.

Friday arrived, and Jimmy came knocking at the door in the afternoon. His parents told him he could take his dad's car to go to the see the shuttle land, but only if he went with a friend. The pressure was on. He had not invited anybody else, and he needed to convince me, not that I needed too much convincing.

"Danny, come on. You can bring the dogs so as to avoid them barking all night long because they are alone in the house. You know the neighbors will call the police, and then Tony will know," Jimmy said.

"Jimmy, I don't know if the dogs will be okay traveling all those hours. And what if Consuelo discovers we are gone?"

"She won't know you are gone. We'll leave after she goes home. There is no point in arriving before lunch to Edwards. If we get there a little later than dinner time it will fine. We can find a spot to park the car, look around, eat some sandwiches, and then sleep. In the morning we will be ready for the landing. It's going to be a big event; it is the fourth of July, and President Ronald Reagan is going to be there."

"I am not too convinced. What if the neighbors see us leaving with the dogs?" I was already convinced, but I wanted to see how Jimmy was going to handle it.

"We will be leaving around dinner time. Everybody will be busy eating. Danny boy, they are only two small dogs. Bring their stuff and they'll be fine."

"OK, but you are going to help me with them," I insisted.

"Sure. Just make sure to bring their food, their bowls, water, and their beds."

"As soon as Consuelo leaves, I will get ready the dogs' kit."

"I'll bring some snacks for the road and for the morning," Jimmy assured me.

"I'm going to ask Consuelo to prepare us some sand-wiches. If she asks, I will tell her that they are for the beach."

"Excellent."

The TV had been on; it had been only background noise until the news began and the anchor started talking about an unbelievable story. The prime-time story was about a guy that tied a bunch of helium balloons to a lawn chair, took off from San Pedro, and for many minutes had been flying over Los Angeles. Even pilots of airplanes approaching Los Angeles airport got to see him.

"Danny, I bet you don't have this type of story where you are from," Jimmy noted.

"No, we do not."

The next day Consuelo left the house not knowing that I was going to leave minutes after she had walked out the door. As expected, she has happy because I asked her to prepare sand-wiches for Sunday. She even prepared coleslaw and potato salad to celebrate properly the Fourth of July. She said, "You can't have a proper Independence Day lunch at the beach without two American summer dishes: coleslaw and potato salad."

I was sitting in the living room waiting for her to leave. As soon as I heard the door close, I went around the house searching for a bag to put the dogs' stuff in. I couldn't find one, then I just went to the garage, took an empty box, and put their food, bowls, water, and toys in it. I had to venture into the master bedroom to find what they slept on and take it with us. I felt I was being a snoop; after all the days alone in the house I never thought about looking into the girls' rooms or the master bedroom. I kept myself to the common areas. I marched into the master bedroom to find the two pooches sleeping on a thick padded cushion. Next to it there was a blanket full of dog hairs. I assumed the blanket was also theirs. I didn't want to disturb the sleeping balls of fur until Jimmy came to pick me up.

Jimmy arrived within five minutes of Consuelo's departure. I had taken the food that Consuelo had prepared and packed it in a cooler.

We loaded the dogs, their stuff, and our provisions into the car. And without any witnesses we drove away. Jimmy handed me a piece of paper with the route, a big *Thomas Guide* map book and two folding maps. I was going to be an active copilot. I had to follow the route on the map as we passed major intersections and check the list of directions written on the yellow piece of paper. Jimmy also wanted me to write down the time when we passed the main points in his route. He said he wanted to have it as reference for future trips.

The dogs were not too happy at the beginning of the trip until they settled in on their blanket and cushion. They fell asleep quickly, or at least that's what I thought.

I had seen from the air the size of the city, but driving through it was something else. There was no traffic, and we were going at least sixty miles per hour. We just kept going and going through different neighborhoods; the freeway exit signs passed by one after the next endlessly. I was wondering if there was a landmark to see or just blocks of houses as far as you could see. Jimmy didn't talk too much; he was paying attention to the road. He told me his eyesight was not that good at night—it was not bad, but things were not as clear as during the day. Besides, dusk is the worst time to drive during the day for everybody, for people with or without glasses. At least that twas what Jimmy said he had read somewhere.

We started to go up a hill leaving behind the lights of the city. I thought we were finally out of town. To my surprise, in few minutes, a tapestry of glowing lights as far as I could see appeared in front of my eyes.

"Danny boy, welcome to the San Fernando Valley or 'Porn Valley' like some people call it."

"What?" Did I just hear Jimmy say "porn"?

"This is where most pornographic movies are shot. San Fernando Valley is the porn movie mecca," Jimmy advised.

"How do *you* know so much about it?" I asked.

"Come on Danny, it's common knowledge. And some adult magazines have passed by my hands. I didn't buy them. A classmate found them when he was helping an elderly couple clean their garage. He shared his bounty with his friends."

"Wow, that is a nice friend. Where is he now?" I asked this because I thought Jimmy didn't have any friends. He had mentioned names from when he was younger so far; he greeted a lot of people, but he didn't mention any current friends, nor had he introduced me to any of his close friends.

"He is in Palo Alto. His father is a top surgeon and a college professor. Two years ago, he was offered a job in the Bay Area. It was a no brainer," Jimmy said.

We kept driving through the San Fernando Valley. There were no visible signs of the porn industry that Jimmy had talked about; it looked the same as the rest of Los Angeles. Jimmy had told me to remind him to get gas when we were getting close to the intersection with Highway 5. He wanted to make sure we filled up the thank before getting out of the city. His father recommended to keep the tank full because with all the people attending the landing, the gas stations close to Edwards Air Force Base may run out of petrol.

At last, we were leaving the city behind, the endless blocks of asphalt jungle. Driving through a sparsely inhabited area, we started to gain altitude. The highway cut through rolling hills. The city traffic was gone. Cars were driving at steady speed. For miles the only lights were from the oncoming traffic. Now, the closer we were getting to the air base area, the busier the roads were becoming.

"Do you know how many people are expected for the landing?" I asked.

"A few hundred thousand at least," Jimmy said.

"You said hundreds of thousands?"

"Yeah, in 1981 when it landed there were almost 400,000 people. With this being the holiday weekend and the president making an appearance, maybe more people will show up."

There were signs, flashing lights and highway patrol cars directing traffic to the parking area, a spot called East Shore. It was the designated viewing site on Rogers Dry Lake at Edwards Air Force Base. The whole thing reminded me of a drive-in theater: lines and lines of cars and RVs waiting for the spectacle to start. Now, I could see why we needed to arrive the night before the event. Parking took time. We were slowly moving; we could see the line of red lights in front of us like a bright red snake moving in the darkness. There was an RV in front of us and a pickup behind. Finally, we reached our spot, turned off the car and got out. It felt like a carnival – laughs coming from different directions, kids running around, the smell of hamburgers and the rare, subdued smell of marijuana. There we were in the middle of nowhere, surrounded by more people than the population of the county I was from.

The people in the RV next to us were a couple in their 60s. They came out of their large vehicle and introduced themselves. He was a retired engineer who had worked for some of the aerospace companies in Southern California. She was a retired accountant that also had worked in the aerospace industry. Both were excited to be there. They felt they were part of history and not just because of their presence at the landing, but because of the projects that they had worked on during their careers. Projects that made a contribution to the building of the shuttle. They graciously offered us the use of the WC in their rig. Until they offered, I hadn't really thought about those details. Why should I? I was an eighteen-year-old kid from a town where nothing happened, and now I was going to be witness to an extraordinary event.

The dogs were restless with all the commotion around them, but after a while they calmed down. I never thought that I was going to end up sleeping with the two furballs curled up next to me. They hadn't seen their masters for days, and I was the only familiar face around them. Yes, they had their bowls and blanket, but they were not in the comfort of the Westfield's master bedroom. They had been taken away from what they had known all their lives, and I was the only link to it. Now they were sharing the interior of a station wagon parked in a dusty lakebed in the California high desert.

The next day at sunrise when we got out of the car, we could see the full size of the event. There were cars as far as we could see in every direction. The smell of coffee filled the area. Ron, our RV neighbor offered us a fresh cup of coffee; I wasn't a coffee drinker back then but at that moment a cup of the steamy liquid was what I needed. People were walking around, there was nothing to see, but everybody needed to stretch their legs. Our neighbors in the blue pickup were two guys from Cambria. I didn't know where Cambria was, and I had to pull out the folding map for them to show me the small town on the coast. They traveled further than us to get there and they recommended that next time I was in California I should explore the Central Coast. It took me a good decade to do it, and I wasn't disappointed when I saw that their description of the area where they were from lived up to its billing.

I took the dogs out to take care of their business. Somehow, they were still on a schedule of walking around at 7:00. It became obvious quickly that their fur was going to get dirty, something I hadn't contemplated and now it was too late.

The shuttle was expected to land in the morning, sometime after 8:00 am. While we waited, we wandered around the sea of cars and RVs. Jimmy was carrying one dog, and I was carrying the other. There were tents with first aid personnel. As breakfast we had the sandwiches prepared by Consuelo. Soon the word was that the shuttle was landing as planned. Our neighbors kept listening to the local radio station reporting the progress. We decided not to go to the fence where a lot of people were pressing to see the shuttle land. Ron said we could get on top of his RV and view it from there, plus we had the dogs to deal with. Ron's wife, Tess, took a liking to the two animals. She offered to keep them in the RV out of the heat. I didn't think twice and agreed. Then I saw Bella running free—she had escaped when Tess opened the door to give us a cold drink. I ran as fast as I could, and I found her being petted by a girl with a big floppy hat.

"Is this your dog?" she asked.

"Yes," I replied while trying to catch my breath.

"Hey Son be careful; this is not a place for an animal like that. It could get lost in no time and maybe get squashed when all the cars start to move," the father of the girl advised. His words conjured up a stream of images from having to report to Tony what happened, to my father waiting at my return and giving me the sermon of my life.

"I will be careful sir!" I picked up the dog that was quite happy to have found somebody to pet her and to have run free for a short time. I could see Tess waiting for our return, relieved that I was able to catch up with the animal.

"Oh, Danny, I don't know how it happened. I opened the door, and she went out like a flash of light," Tess explained.

"No worries, she's back. I will put on the leash. Let me bring their blanket, they may just lie down and forget about the outdoors," I said, trying to console Tess.

"That's a good idea."

With the dogs secured and comfortable, I went back to the

top of the RV waiting for the moment. Soon a jet took off, it was the plane that was going to escort the *Columbia* shuttle as it approached. We couldn't see a thing yet; Jimmy had taken his parents' binoculars, and he let me use his. We were scanning the sky and then a dot appeared, every millisecond getting a little bit bigger and bigger. It was something else, like a black wedge. It looked more like a dark triangle than a flying machine. Ron informed us that the shuttle was more like a glider than an airplane. It didn't seem like it belonged in the air—it was very strange. I was awestruck when a sound that I never heard in my life echoed through the skies–a sonic boom. People were reacting to the sound, the anticipation was building, the space shuttle became visible to the naked eye. It leveled off and we could see more than the blank underside of the shuttle. The space shuttle had one shot only—it couldn't turn around. It seemed it was moving slowly but it wasn't, it looked at the same time gracious and clumsy. Finally, it was getting close to landing and in an instant, everything was over. It went past by our eyes and touched the dry lake runway with a puff of dust.

Everybody started to cheer, there were American flags flying. Jimmy and I were jumping up and down so much that we felt the RV moving.

The show was over or at least we thought so, but later there was a fly-by of a Boeing 747 Shuttle Carrier Aircraft carrying another shuttle, *Challenger*—one huge craft carrying another. It was a sight to be seen! We roared in celebration of the technological achievement and the pure spectacle.

After that it was time to leave. Slowly everybody started to get ready. We got down from the RV, thanked Ron and Tess for their hospitality, and took the dogs back to the car. They had made themselves at home in the vehicle, but it was time to start our journey back to Manhattan Beach.

On the film in my camera there were only three pictures – one of the sunrise, one of the thousands of cars, and one of

Jimmy and I on top of the RV taken by Ron. I didn't bother to take pictures of the landing. Ron recommended to just enjoy the moment because it was a moment of a lifetime. He said, "It is going to last a second, you want to register it in your memory, not on the film. You need to be present." He was right, my picture would not have been able to fully capture the moment. I still remember the minutes when we saw the Columbia approaching, the cheers of the thousands of people when it landed, and the other-worldly nature of a black triangular wedge that appeared suddenly and looked out of place in the sky.

Monday morning when I went down to have breakfast, I found Consuelo standing in the middle of the kitchen. She gave me an inquisitive look and smiled. I was expecting her to pepper me with questions.

"Did you have fun yesterday?" she asked innocently enough.

"Yes, it was a lot of fun. Consuelo, thank you for the sandwiches, the coleslaw, and the potato salad. Jimmy liked it. We ate it all," I said this trying to avoid more questions. I was hoping that the mention of the food would distract her.

"Danny, you took the dogs somewhere, they are all dirty," she said, almost stern.

"Yes, I took them out a little."

"I don't need to know what happened yesterday. But you need to wash those dirty dogs and wash their bowls. I will take care of the cushion and the blanket."

"Wash the dogs?" I mumbled.

"Yes, wash the dogs. Mr. Tony and Mrs. Pam will expect to find the dogs how they left them—clean. It is better they don't know that the dogs were running wild getting dirty."

If Consuelo knew that one of them ran wild in the middle of a parking lot on a dry lake, I wondered what she would have told me, but I was not about to share that. I assumed she didn't want to know where I took them, in that way she was not my accomplice.

"Follow me," Consuelo said.

I walked behind her to the laundry room where she showed me a cabinet with miscellaneous cleaning products and rags. In one of the sections there was a pile of towels, and bottles of dog products. One of them was a shampoo.

"Wash them in the bathtub of the master bedroom, I was going to clean the room tomorrow for Pam and Tony's arrival, but I will clean it today after you finish washing the dogs. Just make sure those two don't run wet all over the house. Close the door of the bathroom and stay there until they are dry, use the hair dryer if need be."

Consuelo was serious but not angry. She had more seniority in the Westfield household, and I was just a temporary nanny for the dogs.

I was given a mission: to get the dogs clean without making a mess. If I wanted to stay on Consuelo's good side and no mess was going to be made. I wanted to avoid any questions from Pam and Tony regarding what happened to their beloved hounds. They were going to be clean. Soon I found out they liked to be bathed. I dried them as much I could, then I grabbed one at a time to take them to the back-yard. We stayed there until they were completely dry. Consuelo was happy. The dogs were clean. I was tired and somewhat sad. My days in Manhattan Beach were coming to an end.

CHAPTER 8

MOVING OUT, MOVING IN

TUESDAY, JULY 6, 1982

IT WAS my last day alone at the Westfield's house. They were arriving on Wednesday sometime after six in the evening. I had taken care of all the things they had asked me to do. The dogs were now spending most of the night in my room and that was even without their blanket or cushion; they had grown on me and I on them. Consuelo had washed all my clothes, and I had packed what I was not going to use in the few days I had left. My flight was taking off on Friday. I went to the beach that Monday, hoping to see the PV crowd but I didn't see anybody I knew. I just walked around and sat on the sand and listened to the waves for a few hours.

Jimmy invited me to eat at the local diner in downtown Manhattan just in case I didn't have time on Wednesday or Thursday with the Westfields back in town. Consuelo had left for the day after having dusted every corner, making sure everything was spotless. I was just sitting in the living room waiting for Jimmy to ring the doorbell and march down the street to go to have my first and last supper in a restaurant in Manhattan Beach. I had been eating Mexican food from the place on Manhattan Avenue or a slice of pizza from the little Italian place on Manhattan Beach Boulevard up from the pier. Jimmy rang the doorbell and the dogs came running from the master bedroom barking like they were really going to defend the household; I knew they were more show than substance.

"Hey Danny boy! Are you ready?" Jimmy inquired.

"Ready and hungry. Let's go to eat at this Manhattan Beach institution that you keep talking about," I said.

"This is for you." Jimmy handed me something wrapped in newspaper. I thought the packing job was cool.

"Wow Jimmy, thank you. I don't have anything for you," I said, as I started ripping the newspaper. Under it there was a lunch bag, and inside was a white t-shirt with the Body Glove logo that I had become so familiar with by observing at the bikinis of Val and her friends.

"You don't need to give me anything," Jimmy said. "It was fun to show you around town. You're cool. There aren't too many people that like to listen to my endless list of facts. You know, I just can't help it; information just sticks to my brain."

It was the first time that Jimmy had given me a clue why he didn't have too many friends. He was a cool kid, a little bit nerdy, but cool. I wished I had the brains he had, and had received multiple offers to go to college, to study what I didn't yet know.

"Hey, *you* are the cool guy. You know, if you find out that you don't like what you are going to study, you always can be a tour guide, you have all the facts ready," I said.

"Yeah, I can see buying a van, painting on the sides 'Jimmy James Tours,' driving people all over the city to take them to the different landmarks. Anyway, I thought you needed a Body Glove t-shirt in your closet. You already have a Billabong. You were missing the SoCal brand, the local brand."

"A local brand?" I asked.

"Yes, the founders of the company are from Manhattan Beach."

"Really?"

"Yeah, they are super cool. They were one of the pioneers of the modern wetsuit, that is why the company is called Body Glove," Jimmy explained.

"Wow, thank you Jimmy. I like it a lot, and now I can tell my friends I got I real Body Glove t-shirt."

We headed to diner; it had been two weeks since my arrival. Now the streets, the Metlox pottery factory, the train tracks, everything looked so familiar, and I had gotten used to living in Manhattan Beach fairly quickly. I wished I could stay longer, but the reality was that by Friday night I was going to be back at home. I was going to take a plane that was going to deliver me back to reality, to my family and to the farm.

Dinner at local diner was perfect for a hungry teenager. I had their meatloaf special, and Jimmy had a pastrami sandwich. We recounted the highlights of my stay in Manhattan Beach. Jimmy also told me of other tours he would give me if one day I came back during the summer when he would be on vacation from MIT. I invited him to visit me, and we also talked about Val and Katie. I wanted to hang out more with Val, but we were from two different worlds. She was the girl from the hill, and I was the kid from a county in Wisconsin, hundreds, and hundreds of miles away.

After dinner we went down to the pier just to walk out to the end and turn around. The breeze was strong. Looking north I could see the flashing lights of planes taking off from the airport. The sight reminded me of my impending departure. We went back up Manhattan Beach Boulevard, past the Metlox factory where most of the lights were off, then headed back to the street. Jimmy said he was going to stop by on Thursday to say good-bye. I entered the house and went right to the guest room, with the two dogs following me up the stairs.

————

Wednesday evening had arrived. I was watching TV after having eaten some of the chicken dish with vegetables which Consuelo had prepared in case the Westfields arrived hungry and in time for dinner. It was around 8:00 when I heard a commotion in the street and then Bella and Ginger came running down the stairs, excited because their humans were back. I got up and opened the door. Leslie was the first to come into the house, with a sweater tied around her waist, a bandage around her right hand and a big straw tote over her shoulder. Nothing had changed with the youngest of the Westfield girls. She just said "Hi" then she passed me by. She didn't acknowledge Bella which was exuberantly showing its excitement for the return of her young master. Leslie went straight up the stairs and closed the door to her room for everybody to hear. Megan came in next, dragging her luggage. I stepped up to help her, and she was more gracious than her younger sister.

"Hi, Dan, thank you! Did this little monster give you any trouble?" she said as she picked up Ginger who was bursting with happiness in her arms.

"No, she was really well behaved," I replied.

Of course I omitted the episode of Ginger running out of an RV in the middle of a sea of 500,000 people. Megan went in and went directly to the kitchen. After putting Megan's bag by the door, I ran to help Pam and Tony with the rest of the luggage. Tony was on the sidewalk counting the bills to pay the taxi driver.

"Did you have a nice trip, Mrs. Westfield?" I inquired.

"Hi, Daniel. Yes, we did, but I am glad to be back home. Today was a long day, and our flights kept getting delayed. I don't know what time it is and if I should be awake or asleep."

"Happy to hear you had a nice trip, and welcome back," I said and followed her to the house with her suitcase.

"Daniel, tomorrow you need to tell me everything that happened."

"Yes Ma'am."

She went and joined Megan in the kitchen, and I went out to greet Mr. Westfield.

"Hey sport!" Tony said with enthusiasm.

"Welcome back Mr. Westfield!"

"Oh, I am glad to be back home. You don't know what it was to be two weeks every day with teenage daughters having meltdowns about anything. I missed the days when they were little girls." I just smiled and followed Tony to the house. "Daniel let's talk tomorrow in the morning. Right now, I need to eat something and go to bed. I'm tired and I haven't been feeling that well."

"Consuelo left a chicken casserole with vegetables," I said.

"Oh great."

"Good night, I will see you tomorrow sir."

"Good night, Daniel."

Everybody looked tired after traveling for hours, it had been a long day to get back to Manhattan. I felt my presence was not needed and went upstairs to the guest room. I could hear them talking in the kitchen and within a few minutes Megan was closing the door of her room and there was silence downstairs. I was falling asleep when I heard Bella scratching my door, she had been left out of Leslie's room. I thought about not opening the door because I didn't want Leslie to have a tantrum since the dog now was sleeping with me, but I gave in to the cries of the animal and let her in.

I woke up and I pulled opened the wood blinds to see what type of day was waiting for me outside. It was a gloomy day; the street was engulfed in thick fog. Bella was alert waiting for me to get ready. As soon as I opened the door, she ran down the stairs. She didn't bother to go to Leslie's room to try to get in. Bella must have given up on her young master. Ginger passed me by and also shot down the stairs.

A quick trip around the block and the dogs and I were back at the house. As soon as I entered the place, I could smell the fresh brewed coffee, telling me one of the older Westfields was awake.

"Hey Dan, I need to talk with you when you are done with the dogs," Tony said from the threshold of his studio.

"Yes, sir, I will be there shortly."

I went quickly to the kitchen to feed the dogs and put their leashes away. I had a glass of juice, and I was wondering if somebody had told Tony about my escapade to see the shuttle *Columbia* land, or he had gotten a message from a neighbor complaining about something. Or somehow I had forgotten to mail one of the letters he had left, but I knew I had taken care of everything they asked me to. The dogs were clean and happy, the grass and plants were as green as when they left, and everything was in place. But I still felt uneasy, there was a sense of urgency in Tony's voice.

I marched to his studio, there was only one way to find out. I stepped in and he pointed to the chair across from his desk. He had dark circles under his eyes and was wearing a flannel robe over his pajamas. His hair looked half combed.

"Daniel, how was everything in our absence?"

"It was quiet, no problem with the dogs and I stayed out of the way of Consuelo. I also helped Mrs. Pitchman with her garden. Jimmy was kind and gave me a tour of Venice Beach and Hollywood Boulevard and Sunset Boulevard. I went to the beach. I mailed all your letters, and I didn't have to take any messages," I reported to Tony.

"Great. I was going to call you to see how things were going, but with the time difference and always running around I never got to. There is something I want to talk to you about. While I didn't call the house to see how you and

Consuelo were doing, I called the office to check how things were going there, and I found out that…"

As I listened to Tony's words, I couldn't help but to feel the bottom of my stomach becoming uneasy.

Did somebody from his business see me taking the dogs away? I stayed quiet and composed as much as an eighteen-year-old could whose parents had engrained in him over the years not to lie and be sneaky. I knew what I did was not bad, but I had refrained from disclosing my escape with the dogs. I still was not going to say anything until listening to what he had to say. Just when I thought he was going to confront me with the escapade with the dogs, he continued, "I'm losing an employee earlier than anticipated."

"Oh, that's unfortunate." I was surprised he was sharing with me.

"My oldest employee wants to retire, which is okay. We have been preparing for it and he has been slowing down. We hired last year somebody to start picking up his work. But what I hadn't expected was that he was going to move to Oregon with his son, who also works for me on an as-needed basis and is going with him. I do not blame them. The life of the city can get to you, and being in the middle of trees is more alluring than living surrounded by thousands of houses in every direction. I was wondering if you wanted to stay longer in Los Angeles and help in the mortuary, just for a few months. Just until you figure out what you want to do, and I decide what I am doing with the business in the long term," Tony explained and finally got it out of his system.

I was speechless—my chance to stay in Manhattan Beach was knocking at the door.

"I don't know, I need to check with my father, he needs me back at the farm and you must have other people that you can hire," I said. The words just came out of my mouth. A true eighteen-year-old closing the door on an offer by mentioning that there must be someone else to help. If Tony's jet lag condition made him think it was a wonderful idea for me to stay longer and help in his business, why did I need to plant a different idea?

"Of course, you will need to talk with Joe, and I will also talk with your father. Look Daniel, you did everything we asked you to do. The dogs seem happy, the front yard looks great, and everything is in place. You are a known quantity. The help I need is not for a full-time position. Also, it doesn't have regular hours, it could be six hours one day, two hours another, or working the weekend nights. I thought it would be a good summer job for you," Tony offered in a soothing tone.

"Yes, I think it is a great opportunity," I said eagerly, now that I knew I was going to have time to be at the beach, and on top of that, I would have a few more dollars in my pocket.

"I just need to figure out where you are going to live." Tony's words took me by surprise. Somehow I thought that I was going to keep living with the Westfields. I am sure my face showed my shock because Tony followed up right away, as the good salesman he was.

"Daniel, at your age you want to have your independence, your own little space. I believe I can find you a room in a decent place. I have an acquaintance that owns several apartment buildings, and two on-a-lot properties. I am sure she must have something available."

I considered how thoughtful Tony was, trying to get me a place of my own, but later I realized that it was one thing to be there alone taking care of the dogs but something different for me to be living there for weeks or months with them. Maybe Tony was OK with it, but later that day I overhead Pam asking him to make sure that I was gone by Friday as originally planned. On Friday, either I was going to be taking a plane to Wisconsin or moving out to whatever dwelling Tony could find for me.

We agreed that I should talk with my father, and then

Tony could talk to him. He wanted to get everything settled by the end of the day, Thursday, because my original flight was on Friday. I called my father, but he was in the fields. I talked to my mom, and she was not happy about the new plans. But then to my surprise she agreed.

"Daniel, you are eighteen, and as much as we want to keep you in the house, you can decide what to do. I wish you were here to help your father, but that would not be fair to you. Paul left the house, and he never looked back. I cannot expect you to do something different. Call in one hour, your father will be back. Daisy, your father, and I will figure out how to manage. I know if you come back, you still may end up leaving the farm. At least out there Tony will be keeping an eye on you."

My mother had surprised me. I just needed to talk with Father. Before Tony left for work, we agreed that I was going to call my father in an hour, and that Tony would call him after I had informed him I already had talked to my dad.

I was in the guest room pacing around waiting to make the call. The house was quiet, the ladies of the house were sleeping. Tony told me most likely they were going to be sleeping all day because with the time difference their sleeping schedule was out of sync. Consuelo arrived and I told her what I thought was great news, that there was a chance I was going to be staying longer in Manhattan working for Tony.

"Oh, dear boy, no, no! Danny you are a good boy." It was strange that she said that.

"But I am going to be working and nothing will change." I found myself explaining my future to Consuelo who was grimacing as if I was committing the biggest mistake of my life.

"Yes, you will be working, but there are so many temptations in this city. The city is not good for good boys like you. Oh, dear Lord! I hope you don't become lost!" She put her hands to her face and then turned around and went to the kitchen. To this day I can't understand her over-the-top reaction.

The call with my father was quick. He sounded disappointed that I had accepted Tony's offer, but then he had similar words like the ones from my mother. He liked that I was going to be under the supervision of Tony. It was interesting that at the end of the call he said that he did not blame me and that at my age he was training to fight in World War II. Me staying in Manhattan Beach for a few more months until I figured things out was nothing compared to going to the Europe during the war. After hanging up the phone, I called Tony right away.

I was staying. I needed to go and finish packing my things; I was going to stay, but I wasn't going to be sleeping at the Westfield's on Friday.

I didn't see the rest of the Westfield family until dinner time. After lunch, I went to Jimmy's house to tell him the news that I was staying longer. Then I went to the beach to walk in the sand and think. I didn't want to spend time at the home. I had overhead Pam telling Consuelo that finally I was going to leave, and the house was going to be back to normal. Consuelo didn't respond to her employer's comment. There had been more drama in the house. Around lunchtime Leslie was complaining that Bella was missing. The dog wasn't missing. She just didn't connect the dots. If she closed the door after not having seen the dog for two weeks, the dog was going to find the person that had been taking care of it for so many days. Sitting on the sand, I thought the trip to Europe had made Pam and Leslie more irrational. I didn't think the jet lag could be blamed for that.

When Tony got home, he looked exhausted. He didn't have the luxury that the ladies of the house had, to sleep off the jet lag. He had to run the family business. After he poured whisky over ice, he called me to talk to him out on the patio.

"Daniel, I spoke to your dad, and I promised him and your mother that you will be okay and that I would keep an eye on you. I found you a place to live. It's not much and needs a lot of work. Miss Benson, Allison, said she will let you live there for free for two weeks and also pay you a good rate, if you help her fix it up. She also mentioned that you could help her with some of the miscellaneous repairs on her apartments. This may work well for you—some hours in the mortuary and some hours helping Allison. I was thinking of taking you to talk with her today, but I had to catch up with things at the office."

"Thank you, Mr. Westfield."

"Oh, it's the least I can do for you helping us. Tomorrow, after breakfast I will take you to Mrs. Benson. Let me go and see how Pam and the girls are doing."

I stayed sitting in the backyard for a few minutes and then I went to my room to wait for dinner. Consuelo had left a bowl of salad, beef stew and cooked noodles. I went down for dinner within a minute to 7:00. Even if I didn't want to see the rest of the clan and I didn't want to hear their complaints of how tired they were, I had to have dinner with them. I hoped Leslie wasn't going to bring up at the table anything about missing her dog. I helped set the table because as usual, the Westfield ladies were no place to be found until their father went to fetch them for dinner.

To my surprise Megan came down with a little paper bag and handed it to me. There was a leather bookmark that said "Made in Italy" and a postcard from Venice. The postcard had written on the back: "Thank you for taking care of Ginger!"

Dinner was quiet. Everybody seemed as if they were having a hard time adjusting back to LA time. Tony broke the news: I was staying, and he had found me a place to stay. Pam looked happy, Megan said "Cool," and Leslie was indifferent. When Pam asked Tony where I was going to be staying, her expression changed when she heard Miss Benson's name. She quickly changed the conversation.

The next day, I took the dogs out for the last time, and as soon as I got back and had some cereal, we were off to see Miss Benson.

We drove a few blocks away from the beach and headed south. The streets were new to me. In my two tours with Jimmy, we always went north. Soon we were parking in front of a Bungalow-style home, with a white picket fence. There were roses against the porch and pots hanging from the porch beam with red geraniums. Tony headed to the door and rang the doorbell. Miss Benson opened the door with a big smile. She looked to be in her early forties, wavy brown hair, tall, and with impeccable red fingernails.

"Oh, dear Tony, you were serious about coming this early. I haven't even had time to change into something nicer." She was wearing a flowery cotton dress that could pass for a pajama, a summer dress, or a house robe. Later I realized that most of her outfits looked the same—cotton dresses, loose, some with sleeves others without. She stepped out of the house and kissed Tony on both cheeks. I thought that maybe Pam didn't appreciate how Miss Benson greeted her husband.

"Allison, you look lovely as always."

"Tony, Tony, you are always the charmer. And you must be Daniel."

"Yes ma'am. Daniel Smith," I extended my hand as I introduced myself.

"Oh please, don't call me ma'am. I feel like you are addressing my mother. I am Allison Benson, and you can call me Miss Ally. Oh, Tony, you didn't tell me how polite this kid is. Okay, let me show the room that is going to be all yours if you want it."

She reached inside the house to grab a big floppy pink hat, a stylish pair of shades with thick white rims and a key ring that would have made any janitor or security guard envious.

She stepped down the porch and we followed her to the driveway taking us to the backyard and the garage. She was wearing strappy sandals that at every step took looked like they were going to fly off her feet. Her toenails were painted in the same red color as her fingernails. A color that my mother would never have considered. Mother used to say that red toenails were not for a lady. I thought Miss Ally's toenails looked fine and she seemed to be a lady. Up we went on a wood staircase with cream colored paint peeling off. I noticed that Tony was looking intensely at Miss Ally's legs and behind as she went up the stairs. Tony let Miss Ally go up until her legs were at his eye level, then he followed her. She opened the door, and we went in.

"As I said to Tony, it doesn't look like much, but it has potential."

"Oh, this will be perfect for Daniel, and he can help you to get it ready in no time. What do you think Daniel? Your own pad."

"Sure, I can help Miss Ally to clean it and get it ready," I replied.

"Well son, I will leave you with Allison to discuss the details. How about you start working in the mortuary on Monday. This way you will have three days to get your new digs ready. On Monday I will pick you up; it is your first day and I will give you a ride, the office is just a few blocks up the street."

Tony almost ran out of there after thanking my new land-lady and getting more kisses from her. I was looking around, the place was a mess, there were spider webs everywhere, a mattress was rolled over in a corner. Stacks of framed paint-ings half covered with a dusty sheet were against a wall, another painting was in the other corner. An easel was leaning against another wall and the curtains had seen better years.

"Tell me Daniel, what do you really think, now that Tony

has left? I thought you guys were coming to look at the place and not just leave you here. I have the feeling it isn't what you were expecting. I appreciate sincerity above all," Miss Ally said with hat and glasses in hand.

"I was expecting something cleaner, a place with some furniture. Not a storage room that needs a lot of work." She gave me a look and moved her hand signaling me to keep going. I continued, "I wasn't expecting to move out of the Westfield's guest room into this. Tony said that he had found a place for me to stay, and I imagined it a little differently."

I felt mixed emotions looking at the place that was going to be my room. It was a dump; a messy storage room on top of a garage. The thought crossed my mind that I could have been on a plane on my way back to my family, to my room on the farm, to my bed with clean sheets. But instead, I was standing in the middle of a cluttered, dusty, and dilapidated room.

"That was not nice of Tony, leaving you here before we got the place ready. I thought you guys were going to come and see it, and if you were OK, we could clean it before you moved in. I see Pam's ways have been rubbing off on him. Look, he came and asked me if I had something available in one of my properties. I have a unit available in one of my apartment buildings, but it is out of what Tony said was your price range. He expressed it was urgent to find you a place because you couldn't stay in the house longer. But I never thought longer meant no more than twenty-four hours. I suggested this room and he didn't see it. I was clear with him that it needed a lot of work, and he said you were good at that. Are you good with tools?"

I was not liking what Miss Ally was telling me, I felt that Tony was only helping me because he was in a pickle and needed help in his business and that he saw my eagerness as something he could use. He showed me a carrot and I had gone for it. I hadn't talked with Tony about how much I was going to be making. I didn't know what housing went for, or if I was going to have enough money for meals. What was I thinking? After a brief silence I replied, "Yes, I help my father back on the farm with a lot of things. Plus, I always enjoyed the auto shop classes at high school."

"Good. This is the deal: you get to stay for free in this room for two weeks with the condition that you clean it, paint it, and repair anything that is broken. After that we go month by month. Tony said this is temporary, and I don't know if I would like to have you living here in the long run. I had been thinking to use this place as my art studio, but I never manage to find the energy to clean up this mess. What do you think?"

"Tony said you need help with your properties. Can I get the room for free if I help you with your properties?" I didn't answer her question.

One of my buddies back home always used to ask for things, even if sometimes it didn't make sense. He said if you didn't ask, you never knew. Like the time he asked Mr. Johannes if he needed help getting rid of the pieces of wood after fixing his barn and fence. My buddy sorted the wood, sold some of it to Mrs. Smith as kindling, and some to Mr. Parker as wood for small project. The rest we used for a bonfire. Now I knew that most likely Miss Ally would say no, but I didn't have anything to lose. I was in a city hundreds of miles away from home, with a questionable income from a part time job that had not started, standing in a messy place where I was supposed to sleep that night.

"No, you can't have it for free. Still, I like you Daniel, you are direct. It could be a good deal for you and me, but it can get messy. I can't guarantee you an exact number of hours per week. There are weeks that nothing happens and then there are days where it seems everything is breaking. Months can go by without vacancies, then I have two or three units giving their notice in the same month, and I need to get them ready to rent again. I will pay you by the hour. What do you think?"

"What will I be doing?" Again, I didn't answer her question. I wanted to know more before agreeing. I knew in the end I was going to have to sleep there.

"Small jobs that handymen, plumbers or gardeners do not want to show up for because it takes them longer to drive to the property than to do the work. Professionals like the big jobs and most of the time what I have are small jobs. My properties are not big enough to have a live-in manager, otherwise the manager could take care of these things. Also, when somebody leaves, sometimes they leave stuff in the garage or in the unit, and I need to take the junk out. Do you think this is something you can help me with?"

"It sounds good to me. Plus, it looks like I don't have another choice. But I don't know yet how much Mr. Westfield is going to pay me," I responded.

"I am pretty sure he will be paying you at least minimum wage. You *do* have other choices," she offered.

"Really?"

"Yes, you fix the place and have two free weeks here in this room. You work with Tony for a week, and you may decide that you do not like it. If so, you go back home to your family, or you decide to find a job in your second week here. Actually, you have three choices: working for Tony, going back, or staying doing something else," Miss Ally explained.

"I see. OK, I will help you with your properties. I will see if I like working in the funeral home, and next week I will decide if I stay here for the long term."

While it seemed my first week outside the Westfield's home was shaping up, I still was feeling uneasy about my adventure. It was taking a 180 degree turn into the unknown.

"Well, it looks like we have a deal."

Miss Ally extended her right hand to shake on it. I

extended mine, and I hoped I wasn't shaking on my second mistake in the last forty-eight hours.

"Well, let's get to work. We need to make a list of what we need to buy from the hardware store. I will be back with pen and paper, I am sure there must be some here but who knows where." Miss Ally turned to leave, but she stopped in the doorway and said, "Daniel never say you do not have a choice. There is always a choice, always options. You just need to stop and think of the different possibilities." Then she left.

As soon as Miss Ally left the storage room, I looked around. I realized there was a small bathroom behind one of the two doors on the opposite side to room, the side that was against the alley. It was a three-quarter bathroom with a small shower, one of those showers that is prebuilt. It was just big enough for a regular size person to stand in. There was no shower curtain—the first item for the hardware store list. I went to check what was behind the other door. It was a closet, stuffed with more junk. I was afraid to start moving things out of it, I thought if I remove one item it would create an avalanche. I didn't need more things crowding the room.

Miss Ally came back. She had changed. She was wearing a pair of tight jeans, red canvas tennis shoes and a white cotton top with mother-of-pearl buttons. You could tell she took care of herself. With paper pad in hand, she went around the small room. She told me what to toss out and what she wanted to keep in the garage. Of the items she didn't want was all the artwork under the sheets that had been collecting dust for several years. She said they were the "masterpieces" of her last lover. She wanted them in the trash. The paintings were not bad. I was neither an art dealer nor a connoisseur, but they looked better than the paintings Mr. Rosenbaum sold back home. There were at least forty of them. I asked her if I could keep them and sell them. I thought I could get few bucks for this artwork. After a little bit of hesitation, she said it was a great idea. She only asked that I sell them away from Manhattan Beach because she didn't want people telling her ex-lover that they had seen somebody selling his paintings. She told me most of the contents of the closet could go to the trash, they were mostly items left behind by her ex. I didn't ask her about what happened to her ex.

Before leaving for the hardware store, she showed me the garage. To my surprise it was well organized. There were shelves, most of them empty, a big toolbox, a nice workbench and a washer and dryer, which she told me I could use. She pointed to pieces of wood in a corner, it was a bed frame that I could use. She saw that I was smiling, thinking that I was going to sleep on a bed that night. She said she had a chair and a small table that she wanted to get rid of, and what better place than to put them in my room.

We went to the hardware store, and she bought everything we needed. On our way back, to my surprise we stopped at a mattress store and Miss Ally bought me a futon and a pillow. I never had heard about futons until that day. She swore they were better than mattresses. I was just happy that I was going to sleep on something new instead of the old spotty mattress. Across the street from the mattress store there was a sandwich shop; we went in, and she bought me a sandwich, a side order of potato salad and a soda, even if was not lunch time.

My second surprise of the day was when Miss Ally came up to the room. I heard her footsteps on the squeaky wood staircase. I thought she was coming to check how things were going, but she was not alone. She was bringing me a visitor—it was Jimmy James.

"Daniel, somebody is looking for you. I can't believe you haven't been here a day, and you already have visitors. He seems like a good kid, so he can visit you. By the way, I forgot to mention I have two rules, maybe more, but these are the two most important: rule number one, I don't want you bringing girls here, and rule number two is I don't want you drinking or smoking with your friends. Like I said, Jimmy looks like a good kid and I may know his mother, so he is welcome."

"Thank you, Miss Ally!" Jimmy James blustered.

"Do not thank me yet because Daniel may put you to work. You are an extra pair of hands, and it's just what he needs to be able to get this place ready before bedtime."

"Sure, I will help him."

"Good!" Miss Ally noted with her head and turned around. Then she went down the stairs. Jimmy walked around and then stood by the window, waiting to see her go into the house.

"Wow, Danny-boy, it looks like you got a rotten deal. You lived two weeks in the Westfield's house alone, with Consuelo cooking meals, and now this is the best that Mr. T can find for you? I don't like it; this is a little rotten, not just a little, this *is* rotten."

"It's good that you didn't see the place two hours ago," I said.

"Danny are you sure you want to stay here and work for Westfield?"

That was the first time Jimmy had called Tony Westfield just Westfield. He never again addressed him as Mr. T nor as Mr. Westfield. Years later he told me that on that day he lost his respect for Tony for moving me into that dump. Instead of letting me stay in his house for few more days until the room was ready to move into.

But I was warming up to the little apartment and kind of liked it—my first place.

"Yes, Jimmy I want to stay and work for a while until I figure things out. I may change my mind next week. I have this room for free for two weeks," I said trying to convince myself I had made a good decision and that it was going to be temporary. Interestingly, the day before, I was thinking that I was going to be in SoCal for the long run. I was going to start working for Tony and then maybe find a better job and call sunny California my home.

"OK, if you say so. I have three hours before I must get back home for dinner. What would you like me to do?" Jimmy said.

I only had known Jimmy for less than three weeks and he was proving to be a good friend, just like my friends back home. I knew if they had been there, they would have helped me clean the place in no time.

With Jimmy's help I finished moving all the paintings to the garage. It was a two-car garage and Miss Ally kept her truck most of the time on the street. Jimmy said he had a plan to sell the paintings but first he needed to talk with his great aunt. He didn't want to reveal his idea, but when he went through the contents of the closet, he put some things in a box and labeled "ACME Plan." I was too busy putting paper on the floor and painting the walls. But I stopped when Jimmy exclaimed "WOW!" I turned around and it was an old bicycle.

"Danny-boy, these could be your wheels."

"Do you think it works?"

"Of course! The tires need air, the chain needs grease, it needs a mirror, maybe replace the seat, but dude, this is the best beach cruiser. You can ride to the pier, to the mortuary instead of walking. You just need to be careful because there are more cars than bikes on the streets."

"I don't know, it looks a little beat-up, look all those scratches and the paint is peeling off."

"Danny come on, see the potential. Imagine how it's going to look after cleaning it, installing a new seat, a mirror, and painting it."

"This is the second time today that somebody tells me that something has potential; first Miss Ally about this room and then you and that old bicycle."

"Danny, sometimes you just need to have a little imagination. Things may not look like much, but think about it, if Miss Allison lets you keep the bicycle, you are saving yourself some shoe leather and coins in bus fare. You just need to spend no more than a few bucks to get this back operational. I know that most of my classmates would love to have a bike like this."

"You're right, it's just that I can't see when I'm going to finish with this room."

"After we finish painting it, it will look great. It already looks better than when I arrived. Go and ask Miss Ally if you can keep the bicycle."

Jimmy was more excited than I was. I needed a break; I went to ask my landlady about the bicycle. She right away said, "Sure."

Jimmy was right. The room looked way better when we finished painting it. Without all the junk that was there also it looked bigger; it was the same size as the two-car garage. Jimmy left and he said he was going to be back on Sunday to help me get my bicycle in working order. After he left, I felt alone, tired, and hungry. But I still needed to clean the floor and the bathroom. This was when Miss Ally came to check on my progress.

"Look at this! It looks bigger and brighter. Can you believe this was the same place you saw in the morning? You have transformed the dump that Walter left into a living loft." She walked around and checked the handle of the closet door that a few hours earlier was loose and ready to fall off, "Daniel, be proud of the work you have done; you could easily outdo some of the handymen I hire to help with my properties."

"I never thought I was much of a handyman," I muttered.

"Daniel, you never know how good you are until you get to compete or compare your work to others. Never sell yourself short. Anyway, you must be ravenous. I'm ordering some Chinese food, my treat. I figure it is the least I can do after everything you have done today. What would you like?"

"I don't know; I never have had Chinese food."

"Never? That is unbelievable. Tell me, do you like rice? Beef? Pork? Chicken?"

"Yes, I like rice and everything you mentioned."

"Good, then I will order a variety of dishes, and we will find out which ones are your favorites."

"Thank you!" I said. I was truly thankful that my landlady was thoughtful and at least my dinner was resolved. I had so much to do, that where I was going to get dinner had not crossed my mind.

"I will call you when the food is here."

Forty minutes later I was sitting at the kitchen table of Allison Benson. In front of me there was a display of small white boxes decorated with red dragons on the sides. My hostess told me there was white rice, fried rice, spring rolls, sweet and sour chicken, beef in spicy sauce with broccoli, orange chicken, and noodles with pork. It was a cornucopia of Chinese food. And of course, there were fortune cookies. My face must have lit up when I saw all that food. I had managed to clean the bathroom and take a shower and had changed before the meal arrived. I felt better in clean clothes, and with a room that was looking more like living quarters. I only needed food to be completely happy.

Miss Ally handed me over two paper plates. She said that they were the cheap kind, and you always need two to support the food. Her instructions were: "Dig in, try everything."

I ate everything, but my favorite dish was the sweet and sour chicken. We ate in silence, my hostess understood there was no point in trying to talk to a hungry teenager when food was in front of him.

Soon we were opening the fortune cookies. My first message was: "Do not panic" and the second was: "A goal is a dream with a deadline." I took a third cookie, and it was empty. I decided I didn't want any more messages.

There wasn't anything to do after eating, and no dishes to wash. Miss Allison put all the leftovers in the refrigerator and told me if I wanted some for lunch, I just needed to ask. Then she brought to the kitchen a bag with sheets and towels. It would have been nice to have them when I took the shower. I had to use one of my clean t-shirts to dry off. Next, she pointed to a box that I hadn't noticed before. It contained a saucepan, a plate, a bowl, a cup, a glass, and some silverware. I took the items to my new room, and she asked me to come back to the kitchen because she had something else for me: a hot plate to heat up food.

That night I slept with the futon on the floor. I was tired, and I didn't want to deal with putting the bed together. A new futon and clean sheets were everything I needed to sleep.

The next day, when I opened my eyes half asleep, I didn't know where I was. Everything looked so different from the floor level. The sun was shining into the room unobstructed, there were no curtains to stop the rays from hitting my face. Around me there were all my worldly possessions: my opened suitcase, my backpack, the box with the household goods Miss Ally had lent me, and the hot plate. I pulled the sheet over my head knowing that I was not in a dream. I could have been back home, waking up to a wonderful breakfast prepared by my mother. You could always count on her Saturday special of hash browns, crispy bacon, homemade muffins, and scrambled eggs. I was getting hungry just thinking of what I was missing, but still I thought that it was a good thing to be in an empty room not knowing what I was going to do in the mortuary and how much I was going to get paid. At least I had the weekend to finish making the room livable and fix the beach cruiser. I needed something to eat, and I wanted something other than Chinese leftovers for breakfast. I was not expecting Miss Ally to buy breakfast for me or invite me to have an omelet. I needed to fend for myself, and I didn't know if there was a store or a diner nearby, I didn't remember seeing one when I drove with Tony.

When I was ready to go explore the area, I saw that Miss Ally was working in the yard.

"Good morning, Daniel. Were you able to sleep?"

"Good morning. Yes, I slept well. I was tired."

"Wait, I have something for you." She took off her gardening gloves and ran to the house. She came back with a piece of paper.

"Here, I made a map of the neighborhood showing where you can find food." The map looked like something a kid had drawn in kindergarten. But it gave me a good idea where I was, where the local store was, and where I could find a bite.

"Oh, thank you. This was what I was planning to do, go and see what I can find," I said.

"If you want a simple and affordable breakfast, then got to the Star Café, they are just three blocks away. There are some shops and diners around it, on the same street. On your way back you can go a block closer to the water and stop by the local store. It isn't a big supermarket, but they have vegetables, fruit, fish, and meat. In addition, their deli is well stocked."

"Thank you, I may just do that. I'll be back soon."

"When you come back, we can move the chair and the table upstairs. Also, don't let me forget to give you an extra sheet. I don't have curtains, but I thought you could use a sheet as a curtain."

"Sure. Thank you."

I decided to go straight to The Star Café that Miss Ally recommended. Tony had paid me to take care of the dogs, so I had money for a hearty breakfast. After breakfast I looked around the street. There was a Chinese restaurant that had a sign with a red dragon hanging above the door. I knew this was where dinner was from on the day before. There was a hamburger place which opened at eleven and that had a help wanted sign on the door. I thought this could be a job opportunity. At the end of the street there was a fine dining restaurant—at least that was what it said on one of their windows. I was sure I was never going to eat there.

Then I started walking toward the local grocery store. I went in and I didn't bother to see the butcher section. There was no point in looking at beef and fish since there was no way I was going to be preparing a full meal on the hot plate. I went directly to the canned goods section and picked up two cans of spaghetti and meatballs, a can of split pea soup and a can of clam chowder. I didn't have a refrigerator so I couldn't buy anything perishable like milk for cereal. Looking around I saw evaporated milk and I grabbed a can. I was going to buy a box of cereal, but the oatmeal was cheaper. My eyes went to the box of mashed potatoes and I grabbed it, I only needed to add water. Picking up two apples and two bananas, I was ready to pay. It was the first time I was buying groceries for myself. Sure, I had gone with my mother to the store or to run and buy something we needed at home, but I never had been in a store figuring out what to buy to eat later that day, and with my own money.

On my return, I took my bag upstairs and then went to tell Miss Ally I was back, and we could move the chair and the table. She gave me the sheet that was going to serve as a curtain and some clothespins to hang it, plus the chair. Then she helped me bring the small table up to the room. When she looked at the sheet hanging, she went to get scissors to make two panels out of the old sheet which had a flowery pattern. She came back with two red ribbons to tie the panels and let light in during the day. Things were improving.

The next step for me was to put together the bed. When I was done, the place looked way better than the day before. It was spartan living, but it was clean, plus I had my own bathroom and something to cook on. It was my first place away from home.

CHAPTER 9

THE BAR FIGHTER

WEEK OF JULY 12, 1982

I WOKE up several times during the night, worried I was going to be late for my first day at work. I didn't know what I was doing. Tony told me I was going to be helping mostly at night and as needed during the day. I knew the position was part time and it never crossed my mind to ask for the details. I assumed somehow because the position was part time that at least I was going to work twenty hours per week. Every time I woke up, I wondered if I was going to help with the bodies or just answer calls, not that I had a great deal of knowledge of what went on in a funeral home. I didn't know anything about any other business besides what I knew of farming. I could explain the whole lifecycle of crops and how to take care of farm animals, but that was the extent of my knowledge.

Tony always wore a suit to the mortuary, but he was the owner. I decided to wear my new pair of khakis and a button-down shirt, two items from the wardrobe that Pam had bought for me. The same Pam that later wanted me out of the house in a hurry.

As promised, Tony pulled over in his gleaming black Cadillac in front of Miss Ally's house at 8:00 a.m. to pick me up. He waved to Miss Ally who was drinking her coffee sitting on the hanging bench on the porch.

"Good morning Mr. Westfield," I said eagerly as I was looking forward to my first day at work. By Monday morning I was not feeling too unhappy with my new dwelling, or the way Pam and Tony rushed me out of their house. Jimmy still thought it was a rotten deal.

"Good morning, Daniel. Are you all settled in?" Tony inquired.

"Yes sir."

"That's good Son, everybody is looking forward to meeting you. They are a good group of people, you will see. I thought it would be a good idea for you to spend the first three days working all day. You will get to meet the team and become familiar with what needs to be done. Next week you will work as needed." Tony said.

I thought cool, I was working twenty-four hours on my first week, it was promising.

We drove two or three blocks to the main road and then two blocks south when he pulled into the funeral home. It was bigger than the one we had back home. We parked behind the building. There was hearse, a limousine, and a van. The hearse and the limo had the golden signage "Westfield Mortuaries." I didn't know he had more than one mortuary. Tony took a small briefcase from the back seat, and we went ahead to the back door.

"Come on Daniel, let me show you around. Frank should be here shortly; you will go with him to the LA morgue to pick up a body. Upstairs is an apartment. That is where Esther lives, she is the live-in manager of the place. We are required by law to have somebody living on the premises. Through that door is the prep room, where we get the bodies ready for the funerals. I will let Frank show it to you, it's his domain."

"Good morning, Tony, and you must be Dan." A petite lady, with highly stylized gray hair and red lipstick, came out from the lunchroom. She was holding a cup of coffee that was ready to spill over.

"Yes ma'am, I am Daniel."

"Oh, Daniel don't call me ma'am. Please call me Esther. I am the accountant, receptionist, and live-in manager for this place. I will be processing your check on Friday."

"Check?" I said surprised. I thought Tony was going to pay me in cash just like he did for taking care of the dogs. Esther looked at Tony inquisitively seeking guidance.

"Dan, do you have a savings account?" Tony asked.

"No sir, I do not."

"OK, then you need to open one. It's easier to cash a check when you have a bank account." Tony turned to see Esther and said, "Esther, please pay Daniel with cash this week. Next week with a check."

"Will do. Daniel, after lunch please stop by because I will need you to complete a few forms for me, for the payroll," Esther asked.

"Yes ma'am. Oh, sorry about that."

"Don't be sorry, kid." She tapped my shoulder with her free hand as she balanced the cup of coffee with the other. I learned in the coming days that her cup of coffee was always filled to the brim. She was skilled walking to her desk with it, as skilled as an acrobat walking on a cable.

Tony continued showing me the place. He showed me the chapel where the services and viewings were held. He explained that I was going to be in charge of making sure the room was ready for the services: to clean it, set up the lights and the crucifix, if needed, plus arrange any flowers that were delivered. Esther was going to discuss with me how to answer the phone and what information I needed to collect when people called and she wasn't available, or during her days off, which were Saturday and Sunday. It sounded like I needed to say goodbye to my weekends. Then we went to the casket display room and spent a lot of time there. Tony was explaining to me the different features of the models, the materials they were made of and the costs. I thought all caskets were the same. While he was talking enthusiastically about the price ranges and the quality of the material, I was thinking, what difference does it make to be buried in the basic model or the top-of-the line? If you were dead, you couldn't feel if the bottom of the casket was plush or not. I didn't ask if Tony had other locations, or if the embalmer worked in different places as needed. I didn't have an idea of what the supply or demand for caskets and services was. I didn't have any idea of the business at all.

Tony asked me to wait in the little waiting area or the lunchroom for Frank to arrive. He needed to review some documents and make a few calls before he went to check on the other locations. I still didn't ask how many locations he had, and I thought I could ask Esther or Frank; maybe they were willing to divulge more about Tony's business. My mother always told me not to be asking people about their businesses, not to be nosey even if I wanted to be. I decided to follow my mother's advice. I sat there looking at the place; it looked somber. I don't think it was my imagination, but the wallpaper, the dark carpet and the heavy drapes gave the place a solemn look. The sconces and lamps had crystals matching the chandeliers. The furniture was heavy, made of dark wood.

Soon Frank arrived. Frank Roberts was a character, and he was the embalmer. Frank was thin as a rail, tall, with a bald spot on the back of his head, and grey hair—whatever he had left. His eyebrows were thick and wild. It was as if the hair he was missing on his head had migrated to his eyebrows, they were bushy. I must confess that a few times when the hallway was dark, and he came out of the prep room, he gave me a fright.

"Are you the new kid from out of town that is going to be helping us out? Where is the boss?"

"Yes, I am. My name is Daniel. Tony is in his office."

"Nice meeting you, Daniel, I'm Frank and I am the embalmer. You know, I take care of the bodies, get them ready for their last event. I need to get some paperwork done and then we'll leave for our excursion to the morgue." I never thought I would hear the words excursion and morgue in the same sentence. I always thought about an excursion as a fun event. I sat and waited.

"OK Sport, let's go," Frank came back holding a manila folder.

We went out of the building and Frank walked towards the van. "I guess this is your first time riding in one of these," Frank said when I stood there looking at the converted van which had nothing in the back but a gurney. You couldn't tell it was a mortuary vehicle except for the curlicue emblem affixed to each side of the van, up high towards the rear.

"Don't worry, they're just like any other car. It doesn't matter if you don't have to ride in the back. That is when it does matter because then you are dead. C'mon get in."

I opened the door. I knew that there was no body in the back, but I knew there was going to be a body there after stopping by the county morgue.

We started driving through streets that I never had seen before and then we got on the Harbor Freeway.

"Tell me Dan, how did you land this job?" Frank asked as he was holding the steering with all he had. We were in a section of the freeway where cars were merging, trucks were passing us by and people just driving way faster than us. I told him the story of how Tony called my father to take care of the dogs, and the rest.

"I see. Well, I am happy you will be helping, because I am getting too old to be doing more than my embalmer duties. I am still here because every time I have tried to leave, Tony convinces me to stay one more month."

"Yes, I will be helping part time." I offered.

"Yeah, even when we have a lot of work, it is difficult to have a full-time person taking care of the miscellaneous stuff. Esther, Tony, and I used to manage this location well. But now that Tony spends more time being a salesman, things are different. We need help during the busy days."

"What do you mean being a salesman?"

"When Tony started in this business, he was an embalmer. Then came the opportunity to take over the location that you just saw. Old man Cain didn't have a family to leave it to, and he was tired of owning the business. This is when he sold it to Tony and the place became the first of the Westfield Mortuaries. Old Cain moved to Florida to enjoy the warm weather; he said he wanted to die suntanned, surrounded by warm bodies, and if it was during a hurricane, even better. Then just like Cain, Tony's business was almost a one man show. He did everything around the mortuary, the flowers, the set-up, everything. Then an opportunity for a second location happened. That was when I started working for him. But those were the early years in the business. The success of his first location got him the second location, then everything changed, and he became a salesman. Which has paid off, because now he has three locations. I don't think he will stop expanding, he is good at what he does and has the energy to do it."

"A salesman? But people die and they need to be buried."

"Yes, people die, but there is more than one mortuary around here. He spends a lot of time building relationships with the local hospitals, the nursing homes, the church. You know, making people aware that Westfield Mortuaries are ready to take care of all the details when you need to say goodbye to a loved one. Also, you need to be skilled at selling the extras to people in grief."

"Oh, I see."

"Yes, and Pam and the girls are high maintenance. The cash must keep flowing for those three to be happy. OK enough of that," he said abruptly.

"When do we need to get bodies from the morgue?" I asked Frank, trying to make conversation and show some interest.

"When the person dies due to a crime, in mysterious circumstances or they were not under the care of a doctor, or their family asks for an autopsy."

"Who are we picking up today?"

"We are getting 'The Bar Fighter'."

"'The Bar Fighter'?" I replied. I was curious how Frank knew the nickname of the individual. Then I realized he sometimes assigned names to the people that passed through his brief care.

"We are picking up a guy that died in a bar fight, hence 'The Bar Fighter.' It is going to be a simple service at the graveside. We are going to pick him up today, tomorrow the family will stop by, and the day after tomorrow he is going to rest."

I didn't ask anything else on our way to the morgue. The traffic was heavier the closer we got, and I could tell Frank was concentrating on driving.

"Hey, Valley Boy, I am here for a pick-up," Frank addressed the security officer tending the entrance. He was a bit younger than Frank.

"Frankie, Frankie, long time no see. You had forgotten us."

"We haven't had business coming from this fine establishment."

"Oh, now you are just getting folks that die peacefully in their sleep."

"Something like that."

"Well, you know the drill. The boys are going to be really happy; yes, they are going to be ecstatic to see you. And not because it is you, but because we are overflowing. I was hoping you were taking more than one." Frank and the security guard laughed. I just smiled.

When Frank asked me if I wanted to stay in the van or accompany him, I thought I should go and see the whole process. My mother used to say, just like most mothers do, to be careful what you wish for. The building where the morgue was had seen better days. It was a sturdy building with thick cement walls that looked like it had been built in the 30s. After taking care of the paperwork, we went to get the body. I was not prepared to see a room full of corpses, a few in plastic bags and few of them only with a sheet or blanket for cover. All had a tag tied to their big toe. It was an apocalyptic scene.

"Hi JT, I see you got extra customers."

"Hi, Frank, how many are you taking?"

"Just one."

"Just one? You don't show up for weeks and you come to pick up just one. Wow, wow, now you even have a sidekick?"

"Daniel, this is James Thomas, known as JT. It's Daniel's first day at Westfields."

"Daniel, because you are with Frank, you can also call me JT. On your first day, they are giving you the whole tour. OK, let's go for your dude."

We walked into the crowded room which was lined with occupied gurneys. There was a smell that I never had known in my life. It was thick—somewhat musty, somewhat sweet. I could feel it traveling into my nostrils, then down my throat all the way to my lungs. The smell of the dead, dead bodies that have been stored in the crowded room for who knows how long.

"Lucky you, the body is here and not there." JT pointed at a gurney with a heavy short man and motioned to the corner where there were bodies on shelves all the way almost touching the ceiling.

"Yeah, JT it's our lucky day. Let me see what you guys did," Frank said. "Oh, come on! Now you just cut them open, you didn't even close them," Frank exclaimed as he came close to the corpse.

I didn't want to analyze the man in the bag.

"Hey man, I just take care of the storage, I don't dissect them. You can close him up, you are one of the best," JT responded.

"Daniel let's go before JT starts throwing rose petals at us with his compliments. Just because they did a mediocre job."

"Frank, we are busy. I'm going to tell the guys you said that." JT seemed truly hurt.

"I thought you guys were too busy to have time to gossip," Frank said as we rolled "The Bar Fighter" to the van. Frank had put the pall—a rug-like green fabric with the name of the mortuary woven into it—over the body to cover it.

"Let's see, let's see." Frank looked at the time on his watch when we got inside the van. "Are you hungry Daniel? Because I know the best sandwich place and it's just a mile away."

"But we have a body in the back."

"Yes, we do. What is going to happen? He isn't going to run away is he, or be late for lunch?"

"No, I guess not. OK, let's go to the sandwich place you are talking about," I said even if I didn't like the idea of having a body in the van while we ate sandwiches. I assumed Frank knew what he was doing. I just was hoping that we weren't going to have to eat sitting in the van. Also, I needed to wash my hands, the plastic bag with the body felt kind of sticky.

———

Frank recommended the torpedo sandwich that had all kinds of cold cuts. I went for it, and he treated me because it was my first day. I was happy I was able to wash my hands before eating and there were picnic tables to sit at.

Soon we were back at the mortuary, rolling in our customer.

"Do you have something to do? Would you like to see what I need to do?" Frank asked.

"Esther told me to stop by to see her after lunch because I needed to fill out some paperwork," I said.

"If you want, I can wait while you ask her if you can do the paperwork later, after I finish getting 'the Bar Fighter' ready."

"OK," I said, and I went to talk with Esther who told me the forms could wait.

I went back to the prep room to find that Frank had removed the body from the plastic bag. There on the prep table, lay the lifeless bar fighter, there were bruises on his face and two stab wounds. There was still dry blood on his skin. He had died in the alley behind the neighborhood watering hole where he spent hours after work. Frank had read the brief chronicle of events in the local newspaper. I stood there while Frank stitched the torso back up in order to close the main cavity of the body. Inside went the breast plate which had been snipped away from the ribs, plus a bag of organs similar to a bag of the giblets you find in a turkey. It was not as easy as the stitches I saw my mother make when mending something by hand. Frank had to fight his way into the skin with a needle that was large and broad. It was sturdy and had a curve to it for ease of use. He tugged at the heavy waxed brown thread and Frank stitched back shut the large opening that the autopsy created—a long incision down the center of the torso with incisions at the top of the cut like a "Y". This same incision, inverted in the groin area was also stitched up. When that was done, he cleaned the body.

Then he started working on the head. He cleaned it and gave the man a shave. No shaving cream was needed as there would be no nicks, no bleeding. Frank used a disposable razor and went about it somewhat roughly unlike shaving a live person. He combed the man's hair and then he went to a cupboard and took out a little jar; it was makeup foundation, and he applied it as thickly as needed to cover the bruises. Then he took another jar and applied it all over the face. He was like a painter, blending the lines between the different tones. Frank told me that while the skin tone was going to be different than when the man was alive, at least it was going to be uniform, and his family wouldn't have to see the bruises on his face, which would just make the moment more painful for the grieving family.

In order to be sure that the mouth of the body would not somehow pop open, or even open just a bit, Frank pushed back the upper lip and shot in a small metal screw or plug with a fine wire attached to it. He did this with a handheld tool that was much like a small rivet gun. He pulled back the lower lip and shot in the lower wire just below the gum line, then he joined the wires together from the two screws and twisted them tight. Next, the lips of the face had to be joined together so they would not part during the viewing. This was done with the same somewhat broad, curved needle using the same brown thread. It took quite a bit of skill to sew into the interior of the lips, but the curvature of the needle and its design aided in this. Frank told me that glue could also be used, but he preferred the stitching method.

After tucking the last bit of the thread into The Bar Fighter's mouth, Frank moved on to the eye caps. These were small cup-like pieces of plastic with small perforations and extrusions that prevented slippage of the eyelids. They were placed over the bare eyeballs after lifting up and pulling back the eyelids, so the face of the deceased wouldn't get a sunken look.

I was then asked to help dress the body. The family had dropped off a white shirt and a blue suit. We put the underwear and the suit pants on him. Next, we cut the white shirt and suit coat right down the middle, starting at the center of the collar, with a pair of scissors. We then got each half onto the body. We put the body into a casket the family had selected. Frank stitched together the collars right behind the neck, using the brown waxed thread. When we were done, Frank went around the casket studying the dressed body.

"Daniel, we are done. Mr. Bar Fighter is no more. He is now the dead brother, or son, to be missed and friend that will be remembered. Mr. Smith is ready for his family; he is ready for his last farewell," Frank said in a solemn tone.

Listening to Frank's words, I understood the importance of what Frank did. He had given back dignity to Mr. Bar Fighter. He was giving him the opportunity to be remembered as Mr. Smith, and not the man found dead from a bar fight who died in a dark filthy alley.

CHAPTER 10
MALIBU

THE CON ARTIST WEEKEND, JULY 17, 1982

ON FRIDAY, Jimmy finally revealed his plan about how to sell the paintings. He had asked his great aunt if we could use her station wagon for the weekend. The plan consisted of loading as many paintings as we could in the car, the easel, and the box of items that still Jimmy had not divulged the contents of. We were going to go beyond Santa Monica to Malibu and maybe to Santa Barbara to sell them. It was a weekend trip. It was perfect, I didn't have to work in the mortuary that weekend and Miss Ally didn't have anything for me to do.

I thought that was the whole plan. But Jimmy didn't reveal to me the most important part—how we were going to convince people to buy the paintings. That he kept a secret until we were far from Manhattan Beach.

Early Saturday morning, Jimmy showed up at my place. He had the old station wagon of his great aunt ready and filled-up with gas, plus a cooler with provisions. After we loaded everything, we took off on our art selling road trip. This time Jimmy took the 405 Freeway and then the 10

Freeway all the way to the end where it becomes Pacific Coast Highway or Highway 1, by the sand in Santa Monica. Before leaving Santa Monica behind, Jimmy pulled over in a beach parking lot telling me he had to stretch his legs. I thought it was strange he wanted to stop; it was just an excuse to reveal the rest of his plan.

"Danny boy, is this wonderful or what?" he said as he opened his arms as to show the vastness of the Pacific Ocean in front of us.

"Yes, it is. What's going on Jimmy?" I asked. I noticed that he had the nervous tick he got when he was uncomfortable.

"Nothing is going on."

"Oh, really? Come on, tell me. Wait a minute, don't tell me you stole the station wagon."

"No, I didn't. Aunt Lizzy let us use it for the weekend, her only condition was to return it clean and with a full tank of gas. Well, there *is* something else."

"I knew it!"

"I need to tell you the last part of the plan about selling the paintings."

"It can't be that bad."

"No, it's actually a great idea but you will need to execute it," he said, and I didn't say a word, I just shrugged my shoulders signaling Jimmy to spill the beans.

"Danny, I thought people would buy the paintings if you give them a reason to buy them besides the fact that they are good paintings. I thought, if we say that you paint and sell paintings to get money for college, they will be more inclined to buy them."

"But I don't paint and I'm not even going to college." This idea blew me away, I believe my jaw dropped open.

"OK, you are not a painter. And you are not going to college, not yet. You said that you didn't know. *They* don't need to know. If they ask, you can say that you are saving money, and if you save enough, you will apply next year. Which you may still do."

"OK, I see where this is going. But I think you will be far more convincing than me," I said attempting to get out of it.

"Oh no, I was the mastermind of this and got the vehicle. Plus, Miss Ally gave the paintings to you, they are yours."

"Okay. You're right."

"There is one more thing," he said as he took the cardboard box labeled "PROJECT ACME" out of the car. "It will help if you wear this, and you paint on site."

"What!"

"Look, it's just a painter's smock and an artist's beret."

"Jimmy, you lost your mind. I thought we were just going to sell the paintings. I didn't think I had to act."

"I'm telling you, this will help us sell the paintings."

"I will fake that I am painting, but I am not going to wear that smock. I may wear the beret for a while and see if people stop by."

"OK, that works. Now let's go."

Jimmy was happy that we reached a compromise. The way I saw it, we were already over an hour away from Manhattan Beach and we had all the paintings in the car. We were committed, and I could use a few more dollars in my wallet.

We pulled over into a gas station that had a big mechanic's garage next to it. We talked with the owner, at least we thought he was the owner. He agreed we could setup on one side of the gas station. We parked the station wagon, and Jimmy took out the easel. I was avoiding it. Then we took out of the station wagon the bigger paintings. There were about ten. We wanted the bigger paintings out; we thought that they would command a higher price. Then it was time for me to act like I was an artist. Jimmy had found one painting that was half done but that looked decent and that I could do some brush strokes on and wouldn't like a total amateur.

The first hour only two people stopped to get gas. They looked at us, but they didn't bother to get closer and check out the paintings. It was around nine. Jimmy was confident that traffic was going to increase as day went by. And it did. Just before lunch, a car with two elderly ladies stopped for gas and to put air in one of their tires. Jimmy ran to help them and shared my story of poor student raising money for college. Jimmy piqued their curiosity and soon they wanted to see all the paintings we had, even the smaller ones. They bought three of the small ones and went on their merry way. Then more people started to stop. It was a busy intersection and just as Jimmy predicted, the gas station got more traffic just after lunch.

When we had no potential customers, we ate the sandwiches and fruit that Jimmy had brought in the cooler from his house. We also discussed our options for where we were going to sleep. I didn't know anything about the area, but I was happy that Jimmy let me decide where to stop next. We needed to find a spot in one of the campgrounds of the several state parks on or close to Pacific Coast Highway. Our last option was to find a spot in the closest camp—Sycamore Canyon. After securing the spot, we planned to go into Oxnard to have a hot meal. Jimmy's original thought was to drive to Carpinteria and try to make it before sunset when all the state parks closed; but if for some reason we got delayed on the way, or the park didn't have campsites, we would have ended up with no place to camp out. Sycamore Canyon State Park was the best option.

By five o'clock we had sold seven paintings, and we knew our next destination. We thanked the owner of the place by filling up the tank and we headed north.

What a drive, the Coast Highway hugging the mountains; we had the windows down and the sea air was coming in. You could hear the waves crashing onto the boulders protecting the edge of the road from erosion. The light of the afternoon sun seemed to give a golden glow to the scenery. Still to this day, every time I see a car commercial filmed on that section of road, I remember that warm afternoon.

Soon we were entering the park, and it was our lucky day because there was a spot. We were going to spend the night there, so we left a few camping items at the site to mark our place. We quickly went to Oxnard and found a market. To our surprise the market had a section where they served food, there were chairs and tables to eat inside. They also had a big bakery section; the baker was just putting fresh sweet Mexican pastries on the shelves. Jimmy and I walked around, deciding what to buy. We approached the counter in the food section and asked for two burritos to go. The area was impregnated with the aroma of a dish I didn't recognize. We asked the lady preparing the burritos what smelled so good. She answered it was the "menudo." Jimmy and I didn't know what menudo was. She could tell and explained to us that was the stomach and feet of the cow boiled with chiles and spices, a traditional Mexican dish for Sunday mornings. She raved how it was the best cure for hangovers. We thanked her for the information, and we took the burritos. Then we went to fetch some fruit and pastries and headed back to the campsite.

The next day we woke up as soon as the sun was up. I told Jimmy I wanted to go across the highway and walk on the sand for a while before we headed to Santa Barbara. I ran across the highway, took off my shoes, and ran towards the waves. Then I found a big tree trunk that must have washed up during a storm and sat on it. There I was—on a little strip of sand, the vast Pacific Ocean in front of me, the mountains behind with the sound of the waves and the seagulls. Life was good. I was where I wanted to be, and I didn't worry about what was going to happen next. At least for the summer, I was set.

Jimmy came searching for me to tell me it was time to stop my contemplation—it was time to hit the road.

We got to Santa Barbara, and it was more difficult to find a place to setup our mobile art gallery. Jimmy liked to refer to it as our art show on wheels. We tried two gas stations, and they said no to our request. Then we stopped in a small supermarket and the manager told us "There is no way you are going to sell stuff in my lot, get out!" He could have been a little polite. He almost followed us to the car to make sure we left.

We were giving up when we found a big gas station with ample room, also with a big mechanic's garage and a carwash. The owner told us we could be there, but if one of his clients complained, we were going to have to pack our stuff and go. Everything was going OK, we had sold three painting by lunch, even with the late start, but then a police car stopped by. We thought the officer wanted to buy a painting, but he didn't.

"Where did you kids get these paintings?" the officer asked.

I looked at Jimmy and Jimmy looked at me. Jimmy's mouth looked like it had become hermetically sealed, he remained silent. I thought it was up to me to handle the situation. After all, the paintings were mine and Jimmy was just the mastermind. The officer was taking a close look at the signatures on the paintings.

"My landlady gave them to me after helping her clean a storage room. They belonged to her ex-boyfriend, and he left them behind when he moved out," I said. There was no point in lying.

"Yes sir, and Daniel is selling them to get money for college," Jimmy piped up.

"Where are you kids from?"

"I am from Manhattan Beach," Jimmy eagerly answered.

"Sir, I am from Wisconsin, but I am living in Manhattan."

"OK kids, you look like decent chaps. But if you are going to pay for college by selling paintings you are going to need to sell a lot of them. Don't get in any trouble!" The officer turned around and went into the minimart to get a cup of coffee and then left. We stood there in silence until the police car left the gas station.

"Danny, close call, just imagine if the officer didn't believe us and he would have called my parents."

"What's the big deal if he had?" I asked.

"I told my mother that we were going to go camping in Malibu, not that we were going to come to Santa Barbara to sell paintings."

"What's the difference? You haven't done anything wrong" I said.

"Except I lied to my mom. My dad doesn't tolerate lying. He would have grounded me for the rest of the summer."

"Jimmy, Jimmy. Nothing happened."

"Hi!" A tall blond with freckles and hair to her shoulders interrupted our discussion.

"Hey!" I answered while Jimmy only waved his hand.

"Are these your paintings?"

"They are mine, but I didn't paint them. My landlady gave them to me." Somehow, I didn't want to lie to her.

"Well, I know somebody that may take them off your hands," she said with a big smile.

"You are not joking, are you?" Jimmy asked.

"No, I am not. Why should I? Here is the address of my aunt's gallery. She owns a gallery, and she is an interior designer. I am sure she can use some of the paintings you have here.

"What should we tell her?" I asked.

"Tell her that Bethany sent you. Don't take too long to decide, she is closing today at 4:00."

"Okay, thank you Bethany," I said, and Jimmy again waved.

She turned around and ran to her lime green convertible by the first pump. We were talking with the police officer when she had arrived to get gas.

"Danny what do you think? Should we stay here, or go to Bethany's aunt's gallery?"

"Let's go. If we stay here, we may not sell any more. If she buys them all then we still have time to look around before we go back to Manhattan."

"Yes, I told Mom that I was going to be back no later than nine."

We packed the paintings in the station wagon, thanked the owner of the place and went in search of Bethany's aunt. The gallery was in old town Santa Barbara. We parked in one of the six spots behind the gallery. We decided to take four of the paintings with us and entered the gallery trying to look sure of ourselves. I even wore the artist beret. Behind a chrome desk with a glass top, there was a woman. Her hair was grey and highly stylized, her lips were a light pastel pink, and she was wearing the type of glasses that are attached to a chain; her chain was golden with small pearls. She was flipping through the pages of a thick art book or catalog; it was a mighty book. When she heard us coming, she closed the book, removed the glasses, and let them hang from the chain. She stood up. She was as tall as Bethany and she was wearing tight black pants that stretched perfectly, a white silk blouse and a red blazer over her shoulders.

"May I help you?" she asked in a refined tone of voice.

"Yes, we are looking for Bethany's aunt. I am Daniel and this is Jimmy," I informed her.

"Oh, what happened with that dear child of mine?"

"She sent us because we are selling some paintings. We met her in a gas station," Jimmy said.

"I see. I am Charlotte Auclair, but everybody calls me Charlie. Tell me, who is the painter?"

She looked at us inquisitively for a second, then her attention was fixed on one of the paintings Jimmy was holding. A painting of geometrical shapes in all kinds of blue hues. Most of the paintings the ex of Miss Ally left behind were of flowers and landscapes, but there were a few paintings that I found weird, they were of geometrical shapes with splashes of colors.

We didn't lie, we told her the story how I got the paintings and that we were selling them from Malibu to Santa Barbara. She listened while she took the blue painting and put it on the desk. I stood by her desk while Jimmy walked around the gallery.

"Daniel, I will need to call your landlady to confirm your story and then we will talk about what I can offer you for this. Do you have more in this style?"

Jimmy and I looked at each other. She was interested. I recited Miss Ally's phone number while Charlie dialed it using a pencil, sticking it in the rotator ring of the phone, I guess she didn't want to damage her perfect manicure, the polish on her nails was an intense fuchsia. It was our lucky day Miss Ally was at home to take the call. Miss Ally told her about the ex and how she ended up with the paintings. Charlie listened patiently for a good three minutes just nodding her head and saying here and there, "Oh that was awful," or "I see," or made a sound agreeing with whatever Miss Ally was saying.

"OK, young businessmen. Let's see what else you have. Can you bring in the paintings that are in the same style as this?" Charlie said smiling when she hung up.

"Yes, of course."

We ran out of the gallery and started going through the paintings we had left. The ones she wanted were on the bottom.

"Danny, can I negotiate the deal?" Jimmy asked with a serious look on his face.

"Sure man. I don't know anything about this."

"Neither do I. But I looked at the prices of some of the painting she has, so let's ask for the stars. Plus, the convertible that Bethany was driving is expensive."

"Jimmy, I trust you."

"Okay, then don't say anything about the price, just agree with me if we need to walk away from her offer. I think she really wants the blue painting and who knows, maybe one of these."

I agreed and we went back into the gallery.

"These are the other three paintings in that same style," I informed her. Her eyes went directly to a painting in purple and dark blues. She took the frame from my hand and walked to the front door then went to the sidewalk to see the painting under the natural light. She was transfixed.

"Remember Danny, do not say a word," Jimmy said in a voice as low as he could and almost without moving his lips. You would have thought that he was a ventriloquist.

Charlie came back with a big smile on her face. "Let's make a deal. How much do you want?" she asked.

"Charlie, we would like you to make the first offer. Which one would you like to keep?" Jimmy replied.

"For a good price, I will keep these four."

"Great, how much do you offer? Jimmy said. It was interesting that he couldn't deal with Todd while walking on the beach, but he was calm negotiating with a professional art dealer.

"I will give you $200 for the four paintings."

When I heard the number that came out of Charlie's mouth, I was ready to jump up and down. But I remembered what Jimmy said, and I just stood there, emotionless.

"Charlie, $200 just for the purple one. And we will negotiate the rest," countered Jimmy.

"You are talking about $200 for just one painting?"

"Most of the paintings hanging in this gallery are over $1,000 dollars. You only have a painting that comes close to this style, and it's thrice as expensive of what you just offered us for the four paintings. I believe $200 for the purple one is a deal."

I couldn't believe Jimmy's coolness. I thought that she was going to kick us out. For a split second she showed her amazement at Jimmy's comment, then her expression became cold.

"I want to hear what you have to say. You are the owner of the paintings, not your friend," Charlie asked me. She was serious.

"Charlie, they are my paintings, but Jimmy is the one that negotiates," I said with a straight face.

"Unbelievable. Did Bethany put you up to this?"

"No, she just told us to come and talk to you because you were always in the search for art," I said.

"I am sure she told you that. Unbelievable. OK, $175, for the purple one. $125 for the other three," Charlie said with exasperation. She was holding the purple painting tightly and kept looking at the blue painting.

"How about $175 for the blue and the purple each, $250 for the other two, and $40 dollars for each one of the ten paintings we have in the car. To make it an even $1,000 dollars," Jimmy persisted.

"I only want these four, and I haven't even seen the other ones to pay you $40 dollar for each of them."

"Come and see them. We would like it if you kept them all. With you, they will find the right home and be properly showcased," Jimmy plugged away.

"Fine, let me close the door and I will see what you have."

Jimmy and I took the four paintings she wanted. Jimmy thought this would signal we were ready to walk away if she didn't accept our terms. After a minute she joined us in the back, behind the gallery.

"Let's see," I said as I opened the back of the station wagon. The first painting was of a house near the ocean with white walls and red tile roof. There was a sunset and somehow when you looked at it you could feel the breeze of the ocean and the warmth of a summer evening.

She put her hands together and brought them to her face like she was going to start praying.

"Bring all the paintings inside, I need to inspect them before I decide."

She took the purple and blue paintings from us, and she went inside. Jimmy and I brought the rest in, and discovered we had an extra painting. We brought everything in–maybe she would like the extra one.

"Daniel and Jimmy, I hope you are not in a hurry because this may take a while. Just take a seat while I inspect them." She pointed at the two modern chairs in front of her desk, and just like her desk, they had a chrome finish; the seat and the backs of the chairs were in brown upholstery. My father would never have sat on those chairs. They were the type that don't have four legs, but more like the seat sits on top of two letter C's. My old man didn't go for anything funky looking. Once he couldn't believe it when my mother liked a dresser that was painted in a rich dark red. He liked furniture to be only stained and varnished.

Charlie started her inspection of the paintings that she was not interested in, or at least so she claimed. She looked at the front and the back of the canvas, then she studied the frame. She looked at the signature of the artist closely, and then she moved to the next painting. When she reached the four she wanted, she didn't inspect them too much.

"I will give you $900 for the ten paintings. Some of the frames will need to be replaced," Charlie said.

"Charlie, you know that most of those frames will be

changed anyway if they don't fit your client's décor. $1,000," Jimmy stated calmly.

"Daniel, too bad you aren't a painter because if you were, you would have a tough sales agent. One thousand for ten paintings. I see you brought an extra one and I am not going to keep it."

"Okay Charlie, we have a deal. You decide which one you do not want." Jimmy extended his hand to shake on the deal. I followed suit.

"I am going to write you a check, and if you have any issues cashing it, here is my business card and have the bank call me."

Charlie walked in front of the paintings, took one of a simple beach sunset, and handed it to me. She didn't want it. She excused herself and went into a little office in the back that we hadn't noticed until then. She came back with a checkbook, one of those big business checkbooks. She asked for my information to make out the check. I was watching her write the three zeroes after the one and I couldn't believe it. Charlie took the check and gave it to Jimmy.

"Jimmy, as Daniel's agent here you go."

"Thank you, Charlie!"

The door of the back was open and there was Bethany.

"Hi guys! Hi Auntie, did you buy something?"

"Bethany, yes I did, and it cost me a pretty penny."

"Oh, auntie, I am sure you can sell those painting to your clients for a small fortune."

"Dear child, I don't understand why you don't want to be involved in the art business. You have the best eye for art, you can spot it miles away."

"I don't love art as I love physics," Bethany said as she studied the paintings, walking on her tippy toes. Saying she loved physics was like saying she loved cupcakes.

"Are you studying physics?" Jimmy asked, eager to have found somebody else who liked difficult subjects to learn.

"Yes, I will start this year."

"MIT?" Jimmy inquired, hoping he would have a friend at MIT before even getting there.

"No, I am going to Stanford. I can't take the cold weather."

"I'm going to MIT," Jimmy said with a touch of pride.

"Oh no! What is wrong with you two kids. You, Jimmy should go into sales, marketing, and you, Bethany Auclair, into fine arts. Come on Daniel give me a hand with these, need to take them upstairs, while these two talk about Physics," Charlie uttered shaking her head.

I followed her upstairs; there was a room that served as frame shop and then an area with more art for sale.

"Auntie, can Jimmy and Daniel come to my birthday party?" Bethany inquired.

"Sure, it's your birthday party. Just please don't tell anybody how you two sold me ten paintings in less than an hour. My reputation will suffer," Charlie said with a smile.

It was the first time she smiled. The tough art dealer persona was gone. She was just Bethany's aunt for the rest of the day.

Bethany gave us detailed instructions to her house in case we might lose her. But she was good and didn't step on the gas when we got to the freeway. We headed south to Montecito, and we followed her up the hill. The houses were big, and they were not jammed in like in Manhattan Beach. We stopped at a single level house, it was wide and sprawling. It was easy to park because her party didn't start until five thirtyish and it was not even five. She opened the door of the house, and we came into this enormous living room facing west with an unobstructed view of the ocean. That was the reason the house was so wide. Every room in the structure had that view. She introduced us to her uncle and then ran to get ready, bounding away with a bit of excitement.

We learned that Bethany's parents had died in a car accident when she was seven and she had been adopted by Charlie and her husband. We met most of Bethany's friends, and Jimmy talked with almost everybody in the party. We ate hamburgers and hot dogs and at seven o'clock we had to leave the party if we wanted to be back to Manhattan on time. We couldn't stay for the birthday cake.

We got to Santa Monica and the traffic was not looking good. Jimmy got off the Santa Monica Freeway or the "10" as most locals referred to it, and we stopped at a gas station to call his mom and inform her that we were running late due to traffic, and that he was going to take me home.

"Is she OK with it?" I asked Jimmy as he was getting in the car.

"Yes, she is. She was happy I called instead of having her guessing where we were."

We took the surface streets back to Manhattan and soon we were back to Miss Ally's place after having had an amazing weekend.

"Here Daniel, here's your check," Jimmy said as he handed it over to me.

With Bethany's arrival to the gallery, and going to her party, I had forgotten that Jimmy had the check.

"Jimmy, thank you, I would not have gotten this without you."

"Hey, it was a fun weekend, and Bethany said she may come to LA next week. I may get to see her," there was clearly anticipation on his face.

We said goodnight. With the watercolor of a sunset over the beach in my hand and a check for one thousand dollars in my wallet, I went back to the room on top of the garage, ready to sleep. The next day was Monday, and I was expected to be at the funeral home by ten.

CHAPTER 11
ENTANGLED

WEEK OF JULY 19, 1982

I WAS happy that Jimmy had convinced me to fix the beach cruiser. He was right, it was going to save the soles of my shoes. I could go to work, to the bank and to the store way quicker than if I had to walk. I had a late start at the mortuary, which worked for me not having to get up so early. I learned to appreciate the minutes of morning sunlight while still lying in bed. The streets' morning busyness was gone by the time I was riding my bicycle. I arrived at the Westfield's mortuary and in the parking lot there was an extra van parked in the back next to the rest of the mortuary vehicles. I didn't remember having seen it during my first week.

I opened the door, and standing in the hallway there was a tall, nerdy looking guy with big square eyeglasses, his hair combed to the left. He looked like he had just got out of the shower. Later, I realized that his hair always looked that way. It only changed when he had a haircut and the barber decided to comb it differently, which was short-lived. He was wearing brown slacks, a shirt with short sleeves in a greenish color that I thought was peculiar. Complementing his ensemble was a tie with dark brown, green, and beige diagonal stripes. He had a cup of hot coffee in his left hand.

"You must be Daniel. I am Terry," he said.

"Yes, I am Daniel. Nice to meet you, Terry."

"You are going to be my sidekick today," said Terry with a big smile. I didn't smile, and he right away added, "you will be helping me with a pickup from a hospital in Long Beach."

"Good morning, Daniel! Tony wants to talk with you two," Esther said on her way to the break room to refresh her cup of coffee.

"Let's see what the big man has to say," Terry sounded eager. He quickened his step and got in front of me. It seemed he wanted to ensure he was the first to walk into the boss' office.

"Hey boss," Terry said and went to sit on the only empty chair in Tony's office. Tony usually had two chairs in his office, but they were moved around if they needed to be used in one of the services or for a meeting with family members discussing arrangements.

"Good morning Mr. Westfield," I said as I entered the office and stood in front of Tony's desk.

"Well, I see you guys met. Terry is the embalmer for the Santa Monica mortuary. He needs to go to the main hospital in Compton to make a pickup. I also asked him to help you find a suit, since we have a service on Saturday morning, and I want you to help with it."

"Yes sir," I dutifully responded.

"Terry, I need you to change your plans. We just got a call, and you need to pick up a body from the hospital in Torrance. I was told an elderly lady didn't make it out of the operating room alive. It was a risky surgery, but she and her family decided to go for it."

"The one by the mall?"

"Yes," Tony replied as he pulled a folder from a tall grey metal filing cabinet in the corner of his office.

"That works boss, we get the body and then we go to the mall for his suit," Terry exclaimed.

I was horrified at the thought of going to the mall with a body in the van. His comment made me believe it was their standard practice—to go and pick up bodies and then run errands or have lunch. All while the corpse was waiting inside the van.

"Terry, you know better," Tony grunted as he gave him a stern look. He was not in the mood for any small talk or jokes.

"I know Tony, first we go to the mall and then we go to the hospital. I was joking for Daniel's benefit."

"Please don't joke," Tony chastised Terry. Then he opened the manila folder and started reading the piece of paper in it; like we were already gone.

"Understood. Come on Daniel, we've got our marching orders."

We took the van from the Santa Monica mortuary and just as we were merging into traffic Terry asked, "Have you ridden in one of these?"

"Yes, last week with Frank when we went to the morgue."

"What! In your first week you got to go to the morgue?" he blurted as if it was the biggest, most wonderful adventure of a lifetime.

"On my first day," I added.

"You're kidding me. On your first day you went to the morgue? I didn't go to the morgue until after a month."

"No, I'm not. Before lunch on my first day, I went to the morgue."

I felt like adding the extra information, I was enjoying how Terry was holding the steering wheel a bit tighter just thinking of *my good fortune*.

"You know, working at the morgue is my dream job," Terry confessed.

"Why?" I inquired with surprise. For me, it didn't seem like the place I wanted to spend forty hours a week.

"Why? Because you get to see the most interesting cases going through a morgue in a city the size of Los Angeles. Crime victims, accident victims, suicides, mysterious deaths. You name it and you get to see it there. It's not fun just to embalm people and try to make them look better than in life. And all for what—for their relatives to have a nice memory from when they saw them last, even if they hardly wanted to see them at all when they were alive. A funeral is more for the living than for the dead. They are dead cold, and they are gone," Terry explained this to me.

"I see. I wouldn't like to work in the morgue even if it was one of the last jobs in town," I reiterated my position.

"Then mortuary work is your thing," he probed.

"I don't know yet. I was asked if I wanted a job for the summer and I accepted. I don't know if working in this business is my thing," I replied. I was not going to go into details telling Terry my life story. He didn't seem as cranky as Frank, but I trusted Frank more than Terry. There was something about Terry that I didn't like.

Listening to Terry, I gathered that there were at least two types of morticians, one type that loves making somebody presentable for their last event, like Frank, who wants the deceased to have their dignity until their last minute. The other type were morticians that did it because it was a steady job while they waited for their dream job, whatever that could be, and liked working in the morgue.

Terry liked to talk; he was happier talking than listening. It was okay for me to be listening. On our way to the mall, he explained to me the different services a funeral home provided: getting the body from a hospital, from a house, from a nursing home. Embalming the body if the funeral needed to wait a few days, shipping bodies to other parts of the country or transporting bodies to other parts of the state, and the list went on and on. I thought he would have been able to keep talking if we hadn't gotten to the parking lot at Del Almo shopping center.

"Let's get you a suit," Terry said he knew exactly where to go; it was a different shopping experience than the one I had with the Westfield ladies. Their mission was to hit as many stores as possible and inspect every rack. Terry's mission was to go in, buy a suit and get out.

"What is your jacket size?" Terry inquired.

"I don't know."

"Well, try this and this," Terry said. He handed me two suits from a thirty percent off rack; a black suit and a charcoal one. "Wait, take this one." He gave me a dark navy blue.

I went into the dressing room and tried the charcoal suit. I liked the color, I thought if I ever needed a suit for something else, I could use it. The slacks looked like they were missing three inches at the bottom. It was a no-go. Then I tried the black one. The shoulders were tight, and I felt as if I had lost the mobility in my shoulders. I inspected the dark navy-blue suit. It could pass for black in the right light. To my surprise it was a perfect fit and looked like it had been tailor-made for me. I went outside to show it to Terry to see if it was acceptable.

"Terry, I think this is the one."

"Yes, that is the one," he said and went to the cashier to wait for me. He paid, took the receipt, folded it carefully and put it in his wallet.

In the van he told me to make sure the suit was always presentable, and that Esther would reimburse me for any dry cleaning. He noted that I could expect to get a second suit in two or three years. When I heard him say years, I just thought that was really far away in my world. There was no way I was going to think that far off. It was just my second week; I didn't know if I was going to be there that long.

We got to the hospital, and we parked behind the building where the delivery area was. Soon I learned it was also the loading area. We went in by a back door and there was a guard checking the comings and goings. Terry talked with the guard and signed for the two of us.

"Daniel, remember never ever enter or leave the hospital by the main entrance, that is reserved for the living. We always use the back door."

"Right!" I replied. It was logical, it would not be good for business if people perished and made their exit where there were hopefuls seeking health. It would be the last thing somebody would like to see while waiting in a hospital.

It was a big place, but we walked down a short hallway, and took an elevator reserved for authorized personnel only. We got out of the elevator and the morgue was the second door to our right. Terry walked in front of me and entered first. I followed pulling the gurney behind me. We greeted the attendant who was eating gelatin from one of those cups that they give you in the hospital. I wondered if the hospital provided meals to its employees, or he just had been given some of the leftovers, or maybe he simply liked hospital food.

After pleasantries and paperwork, we went into the refrigerated room. There were no visible bodies like in the downtown morgue. The room looked clean. Clean enough that the guy eating his gelatin came in with us to show us where the body was, with the cup of green gelatin and spoon still in his hand.

The bodies were stored in a big floor to ceiling cabinet, with chambers and drawers made of stainless-steel. He pointed to the first column and the bottom row drawer with his spoon.

"This one," Terry inquired before pulling the handle. The attendant nodded his head in agreement. Terry pulled the drawer out to its full length. Then he maneuvered the body of the elderly lady. I just stood looking at Terry move her to the gurney, and we left the attendant to finish his gelatin.

We headed back to the mortuary to drop off the lady. Frank was waiting and he was going to get her ready. She needed to be embalmed and sent to a funeral home in Utah for her final funeral and burial.

We turned around and went to the public hospital in Compton. Terry reiterated that if I went to pick up a body, I had to park in the back. I repeated that I got it. This hospital had a different protocol from the one in Torrance. There was phone by a door next to one of the loading docks. You had to call to have the door opened, then check in with security to go to the morgue.

The guy in charge of the morgue was smiling when he saw us arrive. While Terry took care of the paperwork, I just stood close by.

"Your drawer is the third from the left and second from the bottom," the friendly attendant informed us.

"What do you mean 'Our drawer'? We are picking up *three*," Terry insisted while he stood with his arms crossed, signaling he was not going to move until he got an answer.

"Yeah, you are. The three bodies are in there!" the attendant grunted.

"Guys, guys, why you do this?"

"Hey, the hospital had a busy week, and they fit nicely in one unit," the hospital worker claimed.

Terry gave a look to the attendant and then pulled open the drawer. There were two girls bruised and looked like they were in the first years of elementary school, plus a disfigured toddler that was wedged between them.

"Come on Daniel, you need to help me with this. They are entangled."

"What?" I uttered. I wasn't expecting to be handling bodies. I wasn't prepared to see children that had their lives cut short due to the high amounts of alcohol in their father's blood. At least that was what Terry shared with me before arriving to the hospital.

"Come on Daniel, you are going to help me untangle these kids. We aren't going to be taking all of them at once. We are going to have to use a little more care."

"If you had been here last week, you would have consolidated the bodies just the same," Mr. Smiles carried on as he observed our efforts.

Terry didn't bother to acknowledge the comment of the attendant.

We made two trips. First, we took the smallest of the girls and the toddler. Just in the exact moment when we were going down the ramp, a gust of wind came from nowhere and lifted the pall off the gurney, exposing the small bodies. Terry screamed at me "Hold down the pall. There may be people in the windows."

I pulled the green Westfield mortuary cover over the heads of the children and then looked up. In a window on one of the top floors there was an old woman with her hand over her mouth in horror, and in a window on a lower floor, a guy readying his paper shook his head and turned away from the window.

"Daniel, if you ever come by yourself to get a body you need to make sure you secure the pall," Terry reprimanded me.

His tone of voice reminded me of my literature teacher in high school when giving an emotional speech about one of his favorite authors. Also, his attitude was as if he had already told me, and I had failed to secure the cover. I wondered how many times that had happened to him, when he was alone and nobody saw his blunder.

I assured him, "I got it. I need to strap down the pall, and I should always enter and leave the hospital using the back door."

He asked me to stay by the van while he went for the third

body. On the way back to the mortuary he explained the three children had died in the hospital, their internal injuries were too much to survive. I noticed that the oldest of the girls' face was severely bruised. Terry mentioned that she was going to need extra make up if the family wanted an open casket service. The mother was in coma and the father had died in the auto wreck.

Terry dropped me off at the mortuary and for the rest of the day I couldn't stop thinking about the dead children. You know that most people will die after decades of living. It was a shock to see the three lifeless kids. It took me several days to shake the images from my head.

———

The week went fast. Monday, I had spent most of my day with Terry. Tuesday I was asked only to help for a few hours to get the place clean for the viewing of the elderly lady that we picked up from the hospital. Her closest family wanted to have a family ceremony before she was sent to Utah for her more elaborate funeral.

I went down to the prep room to see what was going on. Frank had a body on the "cooling table," as it was known by some in the business. This table was maybe seven feet long and shoulder width. Its edges were about two inches high, so this lip would contain any liquids. It could be adjusted for height by cranking a wheel beneath it and was white with a porcelain finish like a bathtub. The table sloped downward a bit toward the foot, and this angle could also be adjusted. The bed of the table itself had these slight indentations, pointing downward to the bottom. There were many of them, like fish bones on a spine, little channels to aid in the flow of fluids downward toward the drain.

Frank was starting into the embalming process. I wanted

to see what it was all about, and I thought I'd give it a try just to try something different.

Frank handed me a scalpel and pointed to a spot below the collar bone on the body. I tentatively started slicing in, hoping the spot was correct. The skin was tough, and I wasn't making much headway. My thinking was that the skin would easily part with the application of the blade—but this was not so, and I applied more pressure, finally getting down deeper to the desired depth. Either the scalpel was exceptionally dull, or this fellow had an unusually tough hide.

Frank now took over; my curiosity having been satisfied. He took a handheld instrument of polished chrome that had a little loop on the end—a smooth hook about five eights of an inch in diameter. He inserted this tool into the incision I had made and pulled out the carotid artery, which was tough and rubbery, yellow in color.

Next, Frank cut the artery and jammed one end of it onto another instrument, making sure it was thoroughly affixed. The other end of this instrument had a rubber, surgical type hose that led to a machine sitting on a platform near the sink. This pumping device had a glass tank atop of it which we had filled with embalming fluid earlier.

Frank probed into the incision I had made and severed a vein that was paired nearby the carotid artery. He switched the pumping machine on, and it began to hum and throb.

We watched the level of embalming fluid dropping lower. As this fluid pushed through and displaced the blood in the man's body, it flowed out of the cut we had made and made its way down the cooling table into the drain.

———

Wednesday, I was told I was not needed, and I thought I was going to be able to go to the beach, but Miss Ally needed my help. One of her tenants had to move before the month was over and she wanted to clean the place and get it ready to show. I said goodbye to the beach and hello to the toolbox, the paint brush, and the cleaning supplies.

The apartment was a studio in a building with eight units. It was located two blocks from the water in Hermosa Beach. The place wasn't a total dump but needed to be painted and the bathroom and kitchen required a good scrubbing. Because Miss Ally wanted the place ready as soon as possible, I spent all Wednesday and Thursday getting it ready. Those two days she provided me with meals. I didn't have to find something to eat, and it was a relief not to have to eat canned food. She dropped me at the unit and then around lunch time came to check my progress and see if I needed anything else from the store. Around seven she stopped to pick me up, already with a bag of fast food for me to devour when I arrived at my little room on top of her garage.

Tony had been okay with me helping my landlady instead of going to the mortuary on Thursday. Then I had to get up early on Friday to go the mortuary and take care of everything that he wanted me to do and go through the details of a Saturday service.

At noon I was done with my day, I had Friday afternoon for myself. I went to the bank to deposit the check from the sale of the paintings in Santa Barbara. The bank manager called Charlie to verify she had given me the check; I took $200 dollars cash with me. I was going to see Jimmy on Sunday and was going to give him the money as his commission for negotiating the sale. My intention was to forget I had $800 in the bank. I realized that it had been a lucky break having sold those paintings. It had been a once in a lifetime event. After having been paid by Tony and Miss Ally, I realized that I had to work most of the week to not eat canned food every day for the rest of my life.

Saturday, I helped with my first service. It was a viewing in the mortuary and then a graveside service at the cemetery.

Tony told me to stay near him and pay attention to what he did. I was tired by the end of the graveside service. Not because of how much I had to do, but due to standing alert and attentive in the hot sun wearing a dark suit. I was looking forward to Sunday.

CHAPTER 12

SOCIAL LIFE

LAST WEEK OF JULY 1982

THE FIRST WEEK when I started working, I had this idea in my head that I was going to have time to go to the beach and hang out with the Palos Verdes kids, get to see Val, and spend time with Jimmy. What I found out soon was that my schedule was erratic. I had days in which I spent half my time helping Miss Ally just to run to the mortuary or vice versa. Then I had time off when Jimmy was working. The few days that I was able to go to the beach, I didn't get to see the Palos Verdes kids. The only one that I got to see was Katie, but that didn't last.

It was a Wednesday. I had the whole day off and decided to go to the beach, take my bicycle and have lunch in the little Mexican place. Just when I was arriving at the pier, Katie was coming down the hill with a folding chair on her back. I waited for her, and we went to sit on the soft sand by the first lifeguard station. We talked for a good half hour. Everything seemed to be going OK until Katie said something that brought back to my mind what Megan told me about her.

"Daniel, then you are not leaving anytime soon," she inquired without looking at me.

"I don't think so, I want to stay at least until the end of the year," I shared with her.

I kept changing my mind. The truth was I didn't know what I wanted. One day I thought I was staying for few more weeks and other days I saw myself staying for months. When she asked me, I thought it was a great idea to end the year in California. I had considered staying until the snow in Wisconsin melted away. After all, I wanted to experience a winter in sunny California.

"But I thought you said you needed to get back to where you are from," she challenged my new plan.

"Well, I convinced my father to let me stay and help Mr. Westfield in the mortuary."

"Ugh, then now you want to be a mortician?" she scoffed.

"Not really. It's a job for a while. I don't aspire to becoming a mortician. I'm just helping with what they need me to help with. I also help my landlady with her rental properties."

"What do you mean?"

"You know, handyman work—gardening, cleaning, getting places ready to rent."

"Then you are cleaning toilets?" She looked at me and then at my hands as if I was holding a plunger.

"Yes, I do clean the toilets. They need to be cleaned before a place is shown to potential renters."

"And you are not planning to go to school?" She persisted. It was almost an accusation.

"Not yet," I replied, annoyed. I was getting a tired of her questioning. I didn't see where the conversation was headed.

"You know Daniel, I am not feeling that well. I better go home. Plus, tomorrow I have an important date with Richard, he is kind of my boyfriend," she said as she got up and folded her chair.

"Let me help you with your chair and walk you home," I offered. After all, she wasn't feeling well, I could make sure she made it home.

"No, that's not necessary. Stay and enjoy the day before you go back to clean toilets or handle dead people. Goodbye Daniel," she snickered and walked away.

"Bye Katie, feel better," I replied even if I didn't like her comment. I wanted to give her the benefit of the doubt since she was not feeling well.

She left, or at least that is what she wanted me to believe. I decided to leave just after lunch and go to check out the other beaches south of Manhattan.

Just as I was getting on the bike path, on the other side of the pier, there was Katie sitting next a group of guys playing volleyball. I was sure it was her. I hadn't seen anybody else with that red hair of hers which you could see for miles. She never left to go home, she just had lost interest in me, just as Megan had said. I stopped being the new kid on the block. In her eyes I was a guy cleaning toilets and handling dead people. There was nothing wrong with the jobs I had; I was earning money in an honest way. Her comment and attitude bothered me a little and as I rode my bicycle south. I realized her opinion was meaningless, as was she. As far as I knew she didn't even have a summer job.

———

It was the last Thursday of July and Mr. Westfield asked me to his office. He wanted to know how I was feeling so far, helping in the mortuary. I expressed that I was happy helping out. He asked if I was happy in Manhattan Beach, or if I was considering going back home soon. I told him I liked Manhattan, and I wasn't thinking of returning home soon.

"Dan, that sounds good, I would like you to help us for a little while longer. Of course, you need to clear it with your parents even if you are already eighteen years old. If you want to call your folks to tell them you are considering staying longer, call them from one of the telephones here in the office. Just tell Esther, that way she is not surprised when she reviews the bill."

"Tony, thank you. I will try calling my parents in a few days."

"Sure, when you are ready to call them. Hey Dan, I want to ask you a favor," Tony pointed at the chair in his office for me to take a seat.

"Megan was going to take Leslie to a party on Saturday, but she is not feeling well, and she doesn't think she will be able to make it. Would you mind going with Leslie to the party?" Tony asked me, changing the conversation from my future to serving as chaperone for his youngest.

"Do you just need me to drive her to the party?" I was trying to probe because I didn't understand why Pam or Tony couldn't drive their youngest to the party.

"More than that, I would like you to go with her to the party. Megan was going to go with her. Daniel, the party is in Hermosa Beach and there will be kids much older than Leslie. We thought you may like to go and meet more people your age, all while escorting Leslie," Tony articulated this in his astute salesman style—selling me the idea of expanding my limited social circle by serving as chaperone for his spoiled child.

"OK, I will go with her. Is she okay with me going with her?"

"She needs to be, otherwise she isn't going. She understands that she isn't old enough to attend the party alone."

I had my doubts accepting the invitation, but I didn't have anything to do on Saturday night and Jimmy was going to be working. I thought, how bad it could be?

Saturday arrived and I had been asked to be at the Westfield house by six to take Leslie to the party. I was going to be driving Pam's car; it was the oldest of their cars. Tony drove an American sedan that was new. When I arrived, Pam opened the door. This was the first time I had seen her since she vehemently wanted me out of the house after their return from Europe. After the pleasantries, she told me Tony was in the backyard with Leslie waiting for me.

"Hello," I said to the pair sitting under the garden umbrella.

"Hi Daniel, come and sit with us. I want to talk with you kids before you leave."

I nodded my head and went to sit. Leslie was smiling; she was wearing a blue skirt and a pink oversized blouse. Her hair was pulled up in a ponytail and she was wearing lip gloss.

"Daniel, you will be driving, therefore you can't drink, plus you are only eighteen years old. You guys are expected to be home no later than ten. I can't think the party will go later than nine, but you two may want to stop and get a burger, here is some money," Tony gave us a ten-dollar bill each.

"Leslie, when Daniel says it is time to leave, you will leave. Is that understood?"

"Yes, Dad."

"OK, kids go and have fun. If anything happens let us know."

We left the house, and Leslie was giving me instructions how to get to the party. We were driving on Pacific Coast Highway when she asked me to pull over into a gas station and park on the side like we needed to put air in the tires. She got out of the car and told me to wait, she needed to use the restroom in the gas station. I waited for five minutes and when she came back to the car, she was wearing a tiny mini skirt that sat below her belly button and a sleeveless t-shirt that had been cut to expose the rest of her stomach. It looked like she had taken off her bra. She had left her hair loose and changed the lip gloss for a fuchsia lipstick. Leslie had left the house looking like a sweet fifteen-year-old girl, and when she got out of the gas station, she looked like a twenty-year-old looking for trouble. The clothes she had taken off were bundled up under her arm.

"Daniel, you are not going to tell my parents about this, are you? Now let's go to the party."

I didn't reply. I wasn't planning to tell them. I could have turned around and taken her back to the house, but I had my selfish reasons. I wanted to meet people. I didn't talk on our way to the party, I only listened to her instructions. Before we got the house it hit me—Megan must have said she was not feeling well to avoid dealing with her little sister.

"Park behind that green pickup truck. We will walk the last block," Leslie instructed me.

"Leslie, I don't know what is happening here. Your father told us to get back to your house no later than ten. Regardless of how late the party ends, we are leaving at 9:15."

"Don't worry Daniel, the party will be over by then," Leslie answered without looking at me because she was applying more lipstick while she admired herself in the near view mirror.

We got out of the car and started walking towards a cul-de-sac. She led the way to the house at the end of the dead-end street. The house was white, and it had seen its glory years. The paint of the facade was peeling, the shrubs in the front yard were untrimmed. We didn't go through the front door; Leslie opened the side door. You could hear voices coming from the backyard.

"There is my baby!" a tall guy exclaimed. He was wearing a yellow t-shirt, blue jeans, and dirty white sport shoes. He was drinking from a red plastic cup; I had the suspicion it wasn't water.

Leslie walked toward him moving her body slowly. He

met her halfway and lifted her off her feet in an embrace. He put her down and they kissed.

"Hey everybody, this is Daniel. He works for my dad and today he is my chaperone," Leslie informed the small group that could be caring less about our arrival. There were two girls and four guys, all of them looked a little older than Leslie. I just waved my hand to the crowd; some smiled while others continued whatever they were doing before our arrival.

"Hi Daniel, thank you for bringing my girl, and don't worry about returning her to her old man on time. Make yourself at home, the beers are there. There is food over on the table," said the guy holding Leslie by the waist. He didn't say his name but was polite enough to point at the red cooler with the drinks, and the paper grocery bags on top of a wood table that was falling apart, half painted and chipped on one corner.

"Thanks," I said.

The two went inside the house, and I stayed outside. I didn't know if there were more people in there or why they ran inside. I sat on one of the plastic chairs and looked around. The rest of the guests were holding beers. I got up to look at the contents of the red cooler that I found under a peach tree. Between the bottles of beer there were four lonely orange sodas. I went to the table to check the food in the grocery bags: one had bags of hamburger buns, a ketchup bottle, a mustard bottle, and pickle-relish jar. The other bag had trays of patties ready to throw on the grill. But the grill was cold. A bag of unopened charcoal was next to it, laying on the cement.

The door of the house opened and a girl about Leslie's age came out holding a pack of paper plates, a roll of paper towels, and barbecue cooking utensils.

"Hi! You must be Daniel. I'm Cynthia, Walter's cousin."

"Hi Cynthia. Who is Walter?" I inquired.

"Leslie's friend, boyfriend or whatever. The tall guy. Daniel, could you help me with the grill? Because the hamburgers are not going to prepare themselves."

"Sure thing," I said happy to do something instead of trying to make conversation with the other guests.

Cynthia smiled, went inside the house and left me getting the grill ready. Everybody else just continued talking. Soon the grill was ready and had glowing red charcoals, it was ready to go. I thought about going inside the house, but I didn't want to see what Leslie was doing. I decided to put the patties on. Cynthia came back to bring a spoon for the relish and turned around to go back inside. I was invisible to the rest of the guests until the smell of grilled meat reached their nostrils. One guy stood up and asked me if I needed help. I think he wanted to be the first in line to get his hands on a plain hamburger. I thought Cynthia was going to bring lettuce, tomatoes and maybe onions for the hamburgers, but she didn't. The other guests got up as soon as they saw me putting the grilled patties on a paper plate. I got a few thanks for grilling the meat, and the others just smiled before going back to their seats with their plain hamburgers. I put the second package of patties on the fire because there wasn't anything left on the plate, and I wanted to eat.

Standing there flipping the patties, I thought about asking Miss Ally if I could use the grill at my place. In the weeks I had been living there, the grill never had seen the embers of charcoal since a great rib-eye has been cooked. It was in a corner of the backyard just collecting dust. I didn't have money to barbecue every night, but I could eat a steak once per week and still be able to buy my supply of canned goods for the rest of the week. A steak once a week was going to be a real treat and something to look forward to.

The other guests got up for seconds. I had learned my lesson and put aside three patties for myself. I was taking a break from cooking. I was going to eat, and if somebody wanted more burgers, they had to take over flipping the patties.

I was finishing my last burger when Cynthia came out of the house and approached the grill.

"You didn't save me one!" She pointed with her left hand to the empty, soggy paper plate where the cooked patties had been.

"There are still more patties in the bag," I replied. It was not that there was no food to eat, it just needed to be prepared.

"I don't like to use the grill. The smoke bothers my eyes." She stood in front of my chair with her arms crossed over her chest.

"OK, I will cook them for you. How many do you want?"

"Just two. I will be back."

"You better be back because somebody else may eat them," I recommended.

Cynthia smiled and went inside the house, just to reappear in a minute with two red plastic cups.

"Here," she handed me a cup.

"What is it?" I inquired.

"Punch with vodka."

"I can't drink since I am driving. But thank you."

"Fine, more for me," Cynthia rejoiced and poured the contents of the cups into one.

Walter and Leslie came out of the house. The lipstick on her mouth was gone. Her face was flushed—glowing. Walter had his arm around her shoulders, and they walked towards the grill. I thought they were going to ask me to keep barbecuing, but Leslie informed me it was time to go. I didn't understand—we hardly had been there two hours, and it was not even eight o'clock. Walter and Leslie kissed one last time. I handed over the spatula to Cynthia, who didn't look too thrilled. Leslie and I exited just like we came in—through the side yard of the house. We walked in silence to the car. As we left the neighborhood behind, Leslie started talking.

"There was no point in staying any longer. Walter has to go to work. I don't care to mingle with his friends or relatives."

"I see."

"Soon I will have my own car. I will be able to drive myself wherever I want to go and I'll see Walter as often as I want. Don't worry, this is the last time you will ever have to drive me."

"I wasn't thinking that I was going to become your chaperone. I didn't have anything else to do today, that is the only reason I said OK when your father asked me," I told her.

"Stop in the next fast-food restaurant that you see. I need to change, and I am hungry." She didn't bother to say please. It was a word missing from her vocabulary.

"Okay. Are you going to invite Walter and Cynthia to your birthday party?"

I was curious what she was going to say. Because I had a feeling that her parents didn't know Walter existed.

"I'm not having a party. Instead, my parents are buying me a car."

Interesting. Leslie was foregoing her big sweet sixteen party for the freedom of having her own wheels. A decision driven by her infatuation with Walter. I wondered how long it was going to take for her parents to put an end to it. Sooner or later, they would learn about his existence, but it wasn't going to be that night.

I took the youngest of the Westfields back to her house. She looked just as she did when I picked her up. Tony thanked me for taking his daughter to the birthday party. I said goodnight, took my bicycle, and headed back to my place. I promised myself that this was the last time I was going to help the Westfield family with a task that was not related to the mortuary.

I wasn't scheduled to go to the mortuary on Sunday, but nobody was in that morning. Tony was gone and Frank couldn't be reached. Esther got a first-call, and I was selected and available. I took my bicycle and pedaled as fast as I could; in a few minutes I was running into the office to get the paperwork from Esther.

"Daniel, you were flying, really moving. Are you riding your bicycle recklessly?" she asked this in a motherly tone.

"No Esther, I was careful. There was no traffic; I was lucky and got all green lights, plus now I know the best route to work."

She just smiled and handed me the orders. "Well, there is a client waiting for you in the ER, I wrote down all the instructions. You know what to do."

"Yes, I do."

"Great." Esther turned around and went upstairs while I got the keys to the vehicle.

I could smell the breakfast she was preparing, and I ignored the aroma as I walked out. I took the station wagon with all the seats down, and a gurney in the back. I drove to RFK and went in through the emergency room entrance as instructed, pulling the gurney behind me.

I showed my request to a petite young nurse, and I went straight to the ER with the gurney. There was a table in the center of the room. It was stainless steel and sat atop a pedestal. It was sort of dish-like—concave with a broad lip around the edges so no fluids could spill out. It had holes, or perforations to drain away any fluids. On top of the table was a woman of about sixty years. She had grayish brown hair that was curly and somewhat short. Her mouth was agape and her blue eyes open. The expression on her face was one of both surprise and terror. She was wearing a night gown with a bathrobe over it. The bathrobe was opened, away from her chest.

I pulled the gurney parallel to the table and brought it up to an equal level. The lady was warm to the touch and all bodily orifices had been relaxed—sphincters had failed to operate. I removed the pall from the gurney and dragged the body across, strapped it down and replaced the pall.

By the time I had returned to the mortuary, Frank was back. I wheeled the body in. I had seemingly become accustomed to the foul, acrid stench, whereas Frank had not.

"Good heavens, where did you find this body?" he exclaimed as soon as I rolled the gurney next to the cooling table and as the smell overwhelmed the area.

"The hospital. I picked it up as instructed," I muttered and slipped away. I had a lot to learn.

Frank was left with the task of cleaning the gurney and all the rest. He was the mortician.

CHAPTER 13

GARDENING AND CASKETS

FIRST WEEK OF AUGUST 1982

AUGUST STARTED with a lot of surprises. The first one was when I arrived at the funeral home on Monday morning and Tony asked me to help Friday, Saturday, and Sunday nights because Esther was going to go and visit her sister who was ill. I would have preferred to have the morning shift but that was reserved for Gabriel, the guy that helped in the Torrance mortuary. Esther had told me that it was the last mortuary Tony had acquired, and the smallest. She also shared information about Gabriel—he was in his twenties, was expecting his first son or daughter. His vocation was to work in a mortuary and his goal was to replace Frank as the embalmer. I only had seen Gabriel twice, he was easy-going and friendly, he didn't speak a lot, but more importantly he was not like Terry.

The event of the day was to go with Frank to remove a body from a private home. Until then I only had gone to institutions to pick up bodies: the morgue, hospitals, and nursing homes. Frank kept saying that it was different to go to an institution for a body than to go to someone's home. The houses were not designed to make the process easy. Frank explained to me that the removal of a body from a house could include an obstacle course because people died in the least accessible places, or some had so many things obstructing the way, or the layout of the house made it difficult to maneuver. Those were some of the reasons why two people were always sent to pick up a body from a private residence. Most of the visits to homes were not as easy as pushing the stretcher down a ramp: you had to navigate stairs, pick up people from the floor, take them out of bathtubs—the list of obstacles you could encounter in a house was long. For these reasons house calls were more expensive than removing the deceased from a hospital or nursing home. The other aspect of house visits was that the family members were present when the body was to be taken away. Most of the time it was an emotionally charged moment for the family to see their loved one leave the home for the last time, and horizontally. In the institutions it was uncommon to see the relatives, except for rare occasions such as hospice or nursing home. One time Frank went for the body of lady that was a hundred years old, and her eighty years old son was in the same nursing home. When we went to morgues, hospitals, and nursing homes, the usual individuals we interacted with were staff accustomed to our presence.

That Monday we received a call before 8:00 a.m. to schedule our visit to the residence of Mr. Hillstone. We could have gone at once to the house, but his daughter asked us not to arrive until 10:30 because she had things to do before our arrival. To go for the body later was not a big deal. Some people don't change their routine even after a loved one has died under the same roof; some because they can't change their routine, others because they don't want to. The daughter of Mr. Hillstone seemed to have something to do before having to see her father leave the house for the last time.

At ten o'clock, Frank and I left in the van to go and

remove the body. Mr. Hillstone had died in the early morning, and because was under the supervision of the family doctor we could go to pick him up directly.

"Daniel, I haven't told you, but it is time you know," Frank started talking as we were leaving the parking lot. "Sometimes when we remove a body just after a few hours have passed since their death, the corpse still can make sounds or even move."

"Move?"

"Yes, because there are still nervous signals traveling through the body. Don't be surprised if you hear noises or if it seems like the body is breathing, these are the gases escaping. Once I saw the hand of a woman move, and I have heard so many noises that I have lost count of the times."

"Frank, why didn't you tell me before?"

"Because you haven't gone alone to remove a body, and because I thought about telling you, but I kept forgetting to. I'm starting to forget things. I'm tired. I'm telling Tony that I want to retire.

"Frank, he is going to convince you to stay," I said.

"Like he did to you?"

"Yes, even if I didn't need too much convincing. You know, I don't want to go back to the farm and be helping my father from sunup until sundown."

"Daniel, sooner or later you need to think and decide what you want to do. The way I see your situation, you are young and want to live close to the beach where young people spend their time. But tell me, since you started working, how many days have you been to the beach? It's your life, but be careful that you don't end up working three jobs only to eat and pay the rent, and without time to go to the beach or sleep. All my life I have worked in mortuaries. I can't ask our clients if they did everything they wanted to do during their lifetimes, but I am sure most of them would say no. You are only eighteen years old; it seems you have a lot of years ahead, but remember, we don't know how many years we will live. You have seen it firsthand. You have seen the bodies of children that didn't even celebrate a birthday with two digits."

"I'm not going to do this all my life, Frank. I don't want to eat canned food for the rest of my days."

"You see, not everything is greener on the other side of the fence, or in your case, on the other side of the country. A warm home meal prepared by your mother after a long day working is priceless. The spaghetti and meatballs from a can never will be able to replace a plate of a hearty home cooked meal."

"Frank, maybe you are a better salesman than Tony. I think you are trying to convince me to go back to the farm."

"Daniel, I am just making small talk. First, I need to convince myself about leaving this job," Frank said with a smile, driving calmly.

I noticed that when we drove on the surface streets, he didn't clench the wheel like he did when we drove on the freeway. There he clutched the wheel like his life depended on it.

Soon we arrived at Hillstone residence. The house was a one-level home. There were only two steps from the garden to the front door. Frank liked that. In front of the house there was a large bin like the ones used during construction or remodeling where all the debris is collected. It looked as if Mr. Hillstone was remodeling his place. We rang the doorbell and a woman in her fifties opened the door. She came out of the house quickly and closed the door behind her abruptly as if she was trying to hide something.

"Good morning, my name is Emily. It's going to be easier if you take my father through the back door," she said.

"Good morning Emily, we regret the loss of your father. My name is Frank, and this is Daniel. Please show us where your father is."

We followed the daughter of the deceased to the back yard. On our way we met a man with a wheelbarrow full of cans, newspapers, and magazines. Right behind him was a man carrying two buckets full of stuff. The patio looked more like a dumping ground than a backyard. There were all kinds of garden furniture, several lawnmowers, two or three grills, empty pots, and miscellaneous debris. A toilet complemented the display of junk piled everywhere, occupying every square foot of a decent sized backyard. Frank turned to see me and without a word I knew that he didn't like what we were seeing. The woman informed us that her father was a hoarder before we entered.

"I didn't want you to come for my father earlier because I needed to move things out of the house for you, to be able to take him out." She started crying, and between sobs she said, "I'm so embarrassed about what you are going to see, but he wouldn't change."

"Miss, don't worry. Could you please show us where he is," Frank replied calmly to the woman that was drying her tears with a ball of tissue paper that she took out of the pocket of her dress.

I felt awful because I had thought she was inconsiderate. I assumed she left the body of her father lying there for hours because she had things to do. It turned out that what she had to do was to make our job easier, trying to clear a path through the rubbish so we didn't have to climb over it.

Never in my life I have seen so much trash and junk piled up in a house than what I saw that day. The back door opened to the kitchen that was a disaster. There were dishes every-where, every surface had piles of plates, pans, bowls, empty coffee cans. The faucet of the sink was hidden by all the dirty dishes. The linoleum floor was covered with spots. It was not in days that it hadn't been mopped, not even months, it looked like it had been years. The air in the house felt dense and the smells were bad as we made our way to the bedroom where the body of Mr. Hillstone waited for us. He died on a recliner in what one day had been a bedroom, a bedroom that had become a storage room—trash, clothing, lamps, magazines stacked up to three feet high. Luggage and bags were some of the discernible items in the room. On top of the bed, on the left side were piles of clothing, towels, and blankets. Only a piece of the mattress could be seen on the right side of the bed, a piece of mattress without a sheet and with stains. It was the only surface free of clutter, maybe it was the place where Mr. Hillstone slept. The only light in the room was from the lamps. One didn't have a shade, and the other had a shade that was ripped. The window covers were thick and barely let the sunlight in. To get close to the window and open the curtains, first you had to climb over clothes, bags, and luggage. The closet was doorless. In one section there were garments hanging, and in the other, shoes stored in one of those plastic organizers—a noble effort of the departed to organize his belongings.

"The last few weeks my father preferred to sleep in the recliner because it was easier to get up at night," Emily stated.

"Miss, if you prefer to wait outside while we get your father," said Frank as he approached the body.

"Yes, I will be on the patio," she replied.

As soon as Frank was sure that Emily went out of the house, Frank shook his head, crossed his arms, and looked around. Then he asked me to help him to move Mr. Hillstone to the gurney. After having picked up a few bodies from nursing homes and hospices, I knew that sometimes the bodies were not clean after the sphincters loosened and let out the contents of the bladder and bowels. Mr. Hillstone was no exception.

With the body on the gurney covered with the pall, we navigated the route to the kitchen. From a room that was a full of things like the bedroom of Mr. Hillstone, a little dog emerged. The poor dog needed a haircut and a bath. It looked like an old dirty mop, its hair had become clumps of oil, dandruff, and dirt. It started to follow us, crying because we were taking his master.

"Lipton go back in," Emily said to the little dog trying to follow us. "Come here Lipton, you can't go with them." She bent over to take the unkempt pet in her arms.

We continued to the street. Frank asked me to put the body in the van while he went to talk with Emily. Mr. Hillstone was going to be cremated without any ceremony or viewing so there was no need to ask his daughter for clothing. While I was waiting for Frank, I wondered what the daughter of Mr. Hillstone was going to do with the ashes: to spread them somewhere, leave them in the urn, or to put them with the rest of her father's possessions and send them to the landfill with everything that he had accumulated during his lifetime.

"Let's go Daniel," said Frank and we got in the van. "This is a clear example of somebody who couldn't let anything go. Everything that entered that house never left, it was there forever."

"I have never seen a house like that," I said, somewhat astonished.

"And that is after they already had removed things for us to be able to enter."

"Why didn't his daughter do something about it?" I asked.

"Because it's difficult for a hoarder to change. It was his life and he wanted to live surrounded by junk and filth. Daniel. Every trip to a house to pick up a body is unique. You get to see the nice, the bad and the ugly. And this removal is somewhere between the bad and ugly categories, I can't decide.

———

The first Wednesday of the month Miss Ally lost her gardener. She asked me if I wanted to take over the responsibilities of pruning the trees, cutting the grass, and taking care of the flower beds of her properties. I accepted right away because it was a guaranteed number of hours per month. What I wasn't expecting was to meet some of the tenants. And I wasn't prepared to deal with Miss Angela Williams. She was a lady in her seventies with a mood that was far from angelic. She was always angry, and her little house was one of seven units in a multi-unit property that Miss Ally had in the city of Lomita.

On Wednesday I accepted the offer and on Thursday in the afternoon I found myself driving with Miss Ally to the property. She went with me to show me each one of the rentals, and the one in Lomita was the first. She said that it was also time for her to go and inspect the exterior of her properties. I think she also wanted to check my driving skills because she was going to let me use her truck, given that I could not transport the lawnmower and the gardening tools on my bicycle. Plus, the distances between her house and the different properties were not just a few blocks, but miles.

I just had unloaded the lawnmower from the truck, and I was ready to start when I felt the presence of somebody behind me.

"And who are you? Where is the man that usually comes in the morning to cut the grass?" This was asked by the old lady without even saying "Hi."

"He doesn't work for Miss Ally anymore. I will be taking care of the grass, the trees and the garden," I responded.

"Now Ally sends her lovers to cut the grass," scoffed the woman as poisonously as she could, while she studied me from head to toe.

"Angie, good afternoon, how are you doing today?" said Ally, breaking the tension.

"Ah, Allison what a surprise to honor us with your presence."

"Angie, you know that I come now and then to check on things and inspect the property. And you have my phone number and always can call me if you need something. You are one of my longest tenants and the most punctual with the rent."

"Maybe when you stopped by, I was not feeling well, and I didn't see you."

"Angie, Daniel is going to come to cut the grass, he is the new gardener. Also, he's going to help with the small miscellaneous jobs needed on the property."

"Well now that he is here, I need help changing a light in the kitchen."

"Daniel, you cut the grass while I help Angie," Ally rescued me.

That was the first time I spoke with Angie, but not the last time. During the weeks I helped with the property it was obvious that she was lonely, and she needed somebody to talk with. But it didn't help that she wasn't friendly at all. This was worsened when she had an arthritic flare-up. But I felt bad for her, and I always made an effort to at least listen to her while I cut the grass, trimmed the bushes, or planted flowers. She followed me around the property regularly. She didn't ask if she could hang out with me while I worked. She was like a piece of gum that got stuck on your shoe. I saw her smile once or twice. Each time she stopped smiling and returned to her stern expression when she realized that her lips could move and give her a gentle and caring look.

Miss Ally had ten rental properties. They were located in Torrance, Lomita, Hermosa Beach and Redondo Beach. Four of the ten were two houses on a lot. The other six were properties of four to eight units. I had guaranteed between eighty and one hundred hours per month taking care of the gardening. I had a steady income, but like Frank said, I had less free time. What I liked about being Miss Ally's gardener was the flexibility—she didn't care if I went to cut the grass in the morning or in the afternoon. Her only request was that I didn't show up before eight in the morning and not later than six in the evening, out of consideration for the tenants.

On Friday I got to the mortuary to spend the night because Esther wasn't there. Gabriel was waiting for me to arrive. Frank was in the prep room tidying up.

"Hey Daniel, hopefully you will have better luck than I did. We only had one call today and it was a wrong number."

"Gabriel, I don't know if I will have better luck. I just want the night to be peaceful."

"Me too," said Frank when he came out of his realm—his office, as he called the prep room. "I need a few days to rest, hopefully nobody dies over the weekend. Tuesday or Wednesday they can start dropping dead."

"Well Daniel, consider this your home until tomorrow morning. If you need something, here is my phone number if you can't reach Tony."

"Thank you, Gabriel, I hope I don't need to call you." Gabriel smiled and left.

"He is a good kid," said Frank.

"Yes, I prefer to work with Gabriel than with Terry."

"You are not the only one," Frank said as he briefly put his hand on my shoulder on the way to the kitchen. Frank didn't like to talk about the other employees, but it was obvious that Terry was not one of his favorite people in the world.

I went up to the apartment that Esther occupied. She had showed me the room where I was going to be spending the nights while she was gone for the weekend. She told me I could use the kitchen if I wanted to prepare something for supper or breakfast. This for me was quite a luxury, having a real stove and a real kitchen. The place was simple, but it was welcoming. It had a living room, a dining room, and two bedrooms. There was no laundry room; the washer and dryer were one of those combos that are stacked, and they were behind a closet next to the kitchen. The bedrooms were big, and each had its own full bathroom with a shower and bathtub.

"Daniel, I'm leaving, I locked all the doors," Frank informed me from the bottom of the stairs.

"Thank you, Frank, see you on Monday."

"Yes, if I don't quit before Monday," Frank muttered before closing the door.

I was alone in the mortuary, sitting in the living room ready to see what I could find to watch on television. Until that moment I hadn't thought too much about spending the night in that somber place. I must confess that when you were in the apartment, you easily forgot where you were. Frank told me that a funeral home was one of the safest places to be because there were only corpses, lifeless bodies. He said I should only be worried about the living. My responsibility those nights was to answer the phone.

While I was watching the TV I wondered that if there was a spare bedroom in the apartment, why didn't Tony let me use it while I fixed the room over Miss Ally's garage. Later I also discovered that the mortuary in Torrance also had a spare bedroom. I was starting to agree with Jimmy that Tony was inconsiderate leaving me with all my earthly possessions at Miss Ally's while it was a mess, and not in condition for somebody to spend the night. I was learning.

After I watched a movie and ate chicken and biscuits that I prepared in the oven, I was ready to read or find something else to watch when I received a call.

"Westfield Mortuary," I answered the phone at once. Tony and Esther stressed that the phone needed to be answered as soon as it rang.

"Are you open?" asked a man.

"Yes, we are always open. How can I help you?"

Nobody answered, I only listened to the dial tone. The man had hung up.

It was almost midnight when the doorbell rang waking me up. I had fallen asleep on the sofa watching a movie. I ran downstairs as fast as I could with my eyes half closed. Without thinking, I opened the door. There were two guys, one tall with blonde hair, the other one was stocky and had brown hair.

"Good night, we need a coffin. The cheapest you have," said the tall one.

"Good night. A coffin?" I mumbled; my brain was not awake.

"Yes, a casket, a coffin, a box where you put the dead," said the other one in all seriousness.

"Well, if you want to see the models we have and chose one…"

Nobody had told me what to do if somebody wanted to buy a casket, even if Tony had explained to me everything about the different levels and their characteristics.

I took them to the display room, and I pointed to the least expensive.

"This one is perfect; how much it is?" the guy with the brown hair asked. I turned around to look for the price list.

"Look here is the price," said the tall blonde guy, and at once he took a wad of bills from his pocket. "Here is for the casket and here is a little more for waking you up at this hour. Let's go." The blonde signaled his friend to take the other side of the box.

They left the room before I could check the price or count the money. I was left standing in the middle of the display room with the price list in one hand and the bills in the other. I counted the money as fast as I could and I thought they had given me one hundred dollars more, but I was not sure because the two least expensive models were quite similar.

They didn't give me time to call Tony to confirm the price or to bring a cart to help them carry the coffin; they left almost running. They loaded it in the back of a pickup truck that was parked on the street, and as soon they got in the cab they peeled out, the sound of the tires against the pavement and their laughs echoed down the desolate street.

I closed the door to the display room, and on the floor there was a little piece of paper with the price of the casket. I tried to find a place to put the money, but I couldn't find where to leave it. I decided to take it to the bedroom. Based on my calculations they had left me twenty dollars if the price on the paper was the correct one. Without thinking too much about my sale, I went to bed.

"Daniel, wake up, I need to talk with you now!" Tony was knocking on the door of the bedroom.

"Tony, good morning," I said opening the door half asleep. I didn't know what time it was but deduced it was early because it seemed like the sun was just rising.

"It isn't a good morning. My day started with a call from the Chief of Police to tell me that one of my caskets ended up on the beach. What did you do, Daniel? To whom did you give the casket?

"To nobody."

"Don't lie to me. To nobody? There is one coffin missing from the display room. Did they steal it? Were you drinking last night?

"It isn't there because I sold it."

"What? I told you to answer the phone. I didn't tell you to sell caskets. Where did you get the idea to sell one? Caskets are only sold to the clients that have a corpse to put in it."

"I didn't know."

"You should have called me."

"I didn't have time; they paid in cash and ran out of here."

"How much did you charge them?" Tony's expression had changed from anger to wonderment.

"The price that was in the casket," I replied.

"Where is the money?" Tony extended his hand asking for the money.

I went back to the bedroom to get the bills, which I handed over to Tony. He counted them right away and smiled.

"Don't sell a coffin ever again. Am I clear? We were lucky that they only wanted it for a gag, for a bachelor party or a birthday party. It was found full of empty beer cans and liquor bottles. Maybe the police are going to want to talk with you, but probably they may not even go to investigate because the casket was not stolen. The only crime that the kids committed was to leave trash on the beach."

"Tony, I am sorry, it will not happen again. Did they pay more?"

"Yes, a little more." Tony turned around and left to go back home.

When Esther came back and learned about my sale, she explained that the coffin had the incorrect price. She was putting labels with the prices in the caskets in a discrete place so that we could tell the price to the clients without looking at the price list. She was going to put the price in the casket situated above the one the jokers took, when she got the call that her sister was ill, and she left the price on the cheapest casket. This confirmed that I was right. The buyers paid one hundred dollars more than normal and an extra twenty in a tip for having woken me up. The tip I gave to Tony while I was half asleep. Frank thought the whole thing was hilarious when I told him what had happened.

"Daniel, I believe you are a better salesman than Tony, you even sell caskets for the living, and at exorbitant prices."

"It's not funny, I didn't know. I thought Tony was going to fire me."

"Fire you? After having made a hefty added profit of one hundred and twenty dollars for doing nothing? The only reason he was upset was because the chief of police called him, and woke him up. Don't worry. Always keep in mind that this is a business, and Tony is a businessman. This is not a charity."

I learned my lesson not to do anything else that I was not instructed to do by Tony on the days I was taking care of the night shift. I only had to answer the phones. But to this day I always wonder if it was my apprentice luck, or if somebody told those jokers that I was there and most likely would sell them the coffin because I was new to the business.

CHAPTER 14
PHILLIP'S PARTY

SECOND WEEK OF AUGUST 1982

JIMMY JONES CAME BACK from his family vacation with a cast, due to a severely sprained ankle. He jumped from a rock while walking on a trail on the Central Coast and one hour later his foot didn't fit into his shoe. After a trip to the local hospital, he limped out of there with crutches and a cast to make sure his ankle was immobilized, giving him a better chance to heal quickly.

Somehow Jimmy had only been back in town since Tuesday, and by Thursday he already had seen Eve, Val's cousin, somewhere. She told him that Valerie hadn't been on the beach since she hurt her finger. Also, Eve invited Jimmy to Phil's annual wild birthday party on Saturday. She told him I also was invited, and that Valerie was going to be there.

It was Saturday at last, a welcome break after working at the mortuary almost every day, and running around helping Miss Ally with her properties. It seemed as if that week people were dropping dead or regularly clogging their sinks and toilets, but I was free to do whatever I wanted by Saturday noon.

There hadn't been any customers literally dropping off, and Gabriel had asked Tony if he could have some extra hours now that his wife was due any moment. He wanted to get a little more money to help him pay the extra expenses for the baby. Gabriel was a cool guy, but in the last week he could not stop talking about how his life had changed since the pregnancy was confirmed, and the thought that there was going to be a little human being depending on him. He himself had been depending on his parents until three years ago when he decided to drop out of college, get married, and work as an assistant accountant for a year. Then he went to work for Tony in the new mortuary. I was wondering what he was going to be telling us when the baby arrived, if he really thought his life had changed. I was waiting to listen to him telling us that the baby didn't stop crying all night long. I was two years old when Daisy was born and one of my few memories from her arrival was that she cried all the time. My mom was always running to check on the baby, feeding Daisy, changing Daisy, everything was Daisy, Daisy. The best time of the day was when Paul and I ran out of the house to play and left our screaming baby sister in the house with my mother. Frank said that parenthood was getting to Gabriel's nerves. I was glad Gabriel was around though. What mattered was that I was free to go to the party.

Jimmy told me to be at his place at five in order to get to Phillip's house fashionably late. I still didn't understand how being there an hour late could be considered fashionable. I guessed that when Phil's parties went past midnight, arriving at six would be considered early. I think Jimmy just wanted to sneak into the party and avoid people looking at his leg and having to reply to the questions of how he got the cast, which he told me was in the most boring way. He didn't consider it a badge of summer fun, like when other guys got scratches or bruises because they were skateboarding, skiing, surfing, or playing volleyball. So, we were going to be fashionably late.

I was looking forward to going to a rich house in the hills of Palos Verdes. Jimmy had told me that Phillip's house was outrageous and that there were going to be plenty of college girls there. It had turned out to be a hot day and I was looking forward to the pool at Phillip's house, and not just to cool down, but because The Palos Verdes Mermaid was going to be there.

———

"Are you ready for *the* summer party of 1982, a party that you will remember the rest of the year?" asked Jimmy as I closed the door of the sky-blue Impala—his mother's car that I had been entrusted with as Jimmy's chauffeur for the afternoon.

"You know I'm ready," I said. "You have been talking about it non-stop—the house, the view, the girls, the food, and the drinks. The most anticipated summer party of the year."

"Well, Phillip is the envy of most people. His parents let him have a wild party once per year, the first was when he was 18. In the eyes of his French mother, he was of legal age to drink. Rumors are that he had been drinking wine since he was in elementary school, not like getting drunk, but he was served a small glass of red wine on special occasions. Who knows, those are the rumors. He was smart not to destroy the house with his first party and be grounded forever. Then when he was 19, the party was mild like his first, but when he turned twenty, things got interesting. All of a sudden, he became an eligible bachelor and any girl over sixteen started to look at him as a prized catch. You see, Phillip was skinny and tall, and then something happened after he turned nineteen because he started to put on some serious muscle, and now he has groupies. He turned twenty-one a few weeks ago and everybody is expecting this party to be his big celebration," Jimmy explained all this to me.

"Jimmy, how do you know so much about his parties if this is the first one you are attending?" I asked him since he talked like he had been to every single one of Phil's parties.

"Eve told me the other day," he responded.

"Then tell me, did she inform you what is going to be happening this year at Phillip's summer bash?"

"Maybe a girl will come out of a cake."

"Did she really say that? I thought that was for bachelor parties."

"Danny boy, you don't need to get married to have a cake delivered with a girl in it. No, Eve didn't say that there was going to be a girl in a cake, but she did say that Phillip had something big planned."

"Can you eat the cake, or it is a fake cake?" I asked.

"Some of them, I guess."

Jimmy told me what streets to take; it was a simple route and a route that stayed near the water. First, we went to Valley Drive and took a right on Manhattan Beach Boulevard down to the pier, turned left on Manhattan Avenue and kept going until we merged with Hermosa Avenue, then there was a quick left on Herondo Street to reach Catalina Avenue and then to the Esplanade. After that we took one of the Palos Verdes Drives. As soon as we got to the neighborhoods with smaller streets and surrounded by trees, Jimmy stopped explaining the street names or the area. He was concentrating on telling me to go left or right. I knew we were close to the party when we saw a group of girls walking with gifts, and the street was packed with cars.

"Danny, you don't mind dropping me off in front of the house and finding a place to park, do you? I don't want to walk too much with these crutches."

"Not at all. What type of chauffeur you think I am? I should had worn white gloves and a hat to make it official," I quipped.

"Hey, look, they have parking there. Wow, this is a serious party." Jimmy pointed to the empty lot just few doors down from Phillip's house. It had been converted into a parking lot for the party, with several valet parking attendants and all.

I gave the keys to a guy a bit on the heavy-set side and that looked like he was in his forties, "You guys have fun in there. Just remember that one of you needs to be sober in order to get your keys back."

"He will be sober," said Jimmy, pointing to me.

"Yes, we don't want him breaking the other leg," I said to the guy.

"It is not broken," clarified Jimmy.

"Hey Jimmy, we didn't bring a gift. We are empty handed," I just thought of it.

"We are okay. Eve said Phillip doesn't like gifts. The only gifts he likes are the ones that his parents give him to spoil him rotten, like the keys to that silver Porsche," Jimmy said this pointing to the German car parked next to the four-door garage.

"No way!" I exclaimed.

We walked slowly towards the residence; he was being careful with the crutches.

"Danny boy, while I get to drive my mom's car, he gets a brand-new car. That's life, some people are really fortunate."

"And I get to drive the family tractor. Now and then, once in a blue moon my dad will let me use the truck, but mostly it's off limits."

"Come on let's get in and find a place for me to sit."

We were greeted at the door by a butler. The place was just like Jimmy had described it based on what Eve told him. It was a beautiful big house with an open floor plan. As you entered, there were these columns that look like marble. Later I was told they *were* marble, the finest brought from Europe. A dining room was to the right, a living room to the left. Two semi-spiral staircases framed the entrance which led you to an open space with a floor that was polished and looked like an area for one of those elaborate dancing balls. At the end of the ballroom there was glass from floor to ceiling. It appeared that there was nothing beyond it, just the blue sea. Exiting the house there were wide steps taking you to a terrace where the pool was, and the pool house with glass sliding doors. Inside there was a bar and a kitchen. Beyond the pool there was grass and garden furniture.

"Jimmy Jones, what the hell happened to you?" asked Phillip, looking at us with his blue piercing eyes as we were getting close to the pool.

"A sprained ankle."

"Jimmy, Jimmy," said Phillip.

"Hey Phillip, what do you have prepared for this party? I told Danny, this is the summer bash of the year."

"Jimmy, I hope you didn't set Danny's expectations too high. But I will tell you a little secret, I have a surprise that should be arriving at any minute," said Phillip looking at his significant wristwatch.

"A girl in a cake?" I blurted out.

"Why did I not think of that? That would have been awesome. Next year I will do that. You guys enjoy the party. You know what, follow me."

Phillip took us to the pool house and opened the side of the big room that was not utilized. On the other side there was a bartender preparing drinks for the guests. There was a small couch and two chaise lounges in hot pink.

"This is my mother's favorite furniture. Usually it is off limits, but given your condition you can sit here comfortably, just don't get too wild. When you leave make sure to close the door; most of the people coming to the party know not to mess with my mom's stuff, otherwise they will never be invited back to this house, nor their parents to any of my mom's events."

"Thanks Phillip!" Jimmy said and was pleased.

"You are welcome, enjoy the party."

Our gracious host left to mingle with the rest of the guests. The group of girls that we saw on our way in surrounded him. They gave him the boxes which he put on a table with other gifts. I left Jimmy sitting there very comfortable and content, and I went to fetch snacks and a beer for him. There was a guy serving beer from a keg. We sat in the pool house seeing people coming and going, there was no sign yet of Val or Eve.

It was an amazing house, with a big pool. There was enough food to feed an army and there was beer and booze to make any young adult happy. The music was good, but not too loud because the neighbors could complain and put an end to the fun. I didn't see why Jimmy said that it was going to be the party of the year. But everything changed in an instant. I still remember clearly when I altered my opinion about the party. After almost an hour of sitting there munching away on appetizers and people-watching every-thing changed when *she* arrived. I was ready to take a bite of a little sandwich when *she* made an entrance; just walking through the door and down the patio like she owned the place. Her gaze was hidden under enormous black sunglasses. The sheer silk blouse allowed one to see the shoulder pads and the changes in the flesh tones of her chest, showcasing her perky nipples. She scanned the area to find Phillip, who rushed to greet her as soon as he sensed her presence.

She didn't move when he spotted her. It was like she sent him a signal without talking or moving, telling him "I am here, come to me." He gave her a hug and kiss on the cheek. She held his face in her hands and gave him a passionate kiss, while everybody became still and stopped talking, letting the sound of the music be heard through the open space. Phillip gave her a mischievous smile. I thought that for my next birthday I wanted a birthday kiss just like that. She was wearing red stilettos and a black miniskirt. Phillip introduced the distracting beauty to some, while the two made their way around the pool. She was holding his arm, and he was enjoying it; it was obvious she had triggered a reaction in him. Some of the girls looked at her with disdain. I thought more than one was trying to figure out how she could stop a party just by walking in and captivate the birthday boy, as if she had put a spell on him. But it was not just the way she walked; she knew how to make an entrance. In my case she had my attention as soon as I saw the red stilettos, and the sheer silk blouse.

Phil and his guest reached the umbrella with an empty chair that Phil had saved for her. She sat and took off her heals, carefully putting them under the table, and then she undid her miniskirt and let it slide down. She was wearing a white thong. Jimmy told me they were the bathing bottoms of choice in Brazil, one interesting fact that Jimmy seemed to know. She was not leaving too much to the imagination by wearing the thong. Everybody was waiting to see if she was going to take off the camisole, but instead she walked over the grass to look at the vastness of the Pacific Ocean and the region of the Queen's Necklace—this is what the locals call the view from Palos Verdes, curving around the beach cities to Malibu and beyond when things are lit up in the evening.

There with the gentle breeze playing with her hair, she unbuttoned one by one the buttons of the camisole that had kept her bare skin hidden from all the curious and eager eyes that had been following her, waiting for the right moment, fantasizing for the last few minutes since she made her entrance. She turned around when Phillip said something, and shook her head in response, like saying no. There was only one button holding together the front of the blouse and she was going to undo it when she turned again to face the ocean. You could see by the way the two sides of the camisole were flying with the breeze that all the buttons were undone. She put her hands to her head and started running her fingers through her hair, following the contour of her scalp, and then reaching the bottom of the neck, lifting her face to the sky. The camisole was wide open; the only one that could see the front was Phillip and his friends near him. They had seen every one of her movements. Then she put her arms down and let the camisole slide down from her shoulders down to her arms. Phillip stopped it from reaching the ground, not without caressing her bare back in the rescue. She turned around knowing that there was an attentive audience. She took off her sunglasses and looked around almost as if saying to everybody: *I am looking at you.* All this while keeping a straight posture almost pushing forward her chest, tantalizing everybody who only could dream of kissing her skin. Then she walked to the pool in a way that seemed practiced, in her diminutive bottom, the little triangle in front being precariously held by two thin strings tied at her hips.

"Danny, stop staring," Jimmy said as if he hadn't been also looking with abandon.

"It's not like I'm the only one looking. She lives for the attention. Do you know who she is?"

"No, no idea. I never have seen her until today. Maybe she is visiting, she could be one of Phillip's cousins."

"Really. My cousins don't kiss me like she kissed Phillip. Lucky him."

"Hey Danny, there is Val and Eve. They must have arrived when you were not paying attention. Go and say hi, don't be shy," Jimmy urged me.

"Ha, look who is talking about being shy."

"Danny boy, look at me, I can hardly move with this cast. I promised my mother that I wasn't going to make it worse. I'm just going to keep looking around from this magnificent hot pink chair. Go on, go and say 'Hi.' You know she is just waiting for you to go."

Jimmy moved his hand in a way that indicated he had said enough, and I should get going. I made my way to the hors d'oeuvre table as Jimmy referred to the table with the appetizers. Valerie and Eve were each getting a plate with morsels of food.

"Hi Valerie, hey Eve!"

"Hi Daniel!" said Valerie.

"Hey Dan, where is Jimmy?" Eve asked.

"He is over there, making sure he stays off his foot."

"I'm going to say hello!" Eve said, heading to the pool house.

"What do you think of the show that Bridgette just gave?" asked Valerie looking towards the pool.

"You know her?"

"Know her, no. But she is the daughter of one of my mom's friends from the club. Let's say that she left her home at the request of her parents after not changing her ways. She got in trouble with more than one of the wives in the area."

"What do you mean?"

"She likes older men, married men, and discretion is not in her vocabulary."

Talking with Valerie was easy. I didn't want the summer to end because she was going to go to Stanford soon. Even if I stayed in Manhattan Beach for the long run, I knew I was going to become just part of her summer memories. Memories that were going to blend with the memories of the rest of her summers. Jimmy told me that by Thanksgiving most people attending college had dropped their sweethearts from home, calling that first Thanksgiving the "turkey drop." We only had spoken a few times; I was far from being in the sweetheart category.

As the minutes passed, other girls took off their bikini tops, triggered by the alcohol lowering their inhibitions, meeting Bridgette's challenge, or trying to capture a bit of the attention away from Bridgette, which she had monopolized since her arrival. Valerie smiled every time a bikini top came off. She was wearing a blue summer dress. When I asked her if she was going to get in the pool, she answered she didn't enjoy getting in pools just for fun after spending long hours in the pool training. When she wanted to have fun in the water she favored the ocean. She preferred the salt in the ocean water versus the chlorine from the pool.

Eve and Val left the party before 8:00 p.m.; Val's parents stopped by to pick them up since they had a reservation for dinner at Admiral Risty, a seafood restaurant. Before they left, we agreed to get together on Wednesday to go for a shake and a hamburger. It was the last day we could go out before Jimmy, Val, and Eve went away to college.

Close to nine Jimmy and I left. Jimmy was getting tired of sitting on the garden furniture, and I had lost interest in the party after Valerie left. Even if it was entertaining to see what was happening—couples making out, some disappearing to go inside the house while others went looking for a dark spot in the backyard. Jimmy was smiling silly after having a drink with a little umbrella. Because I had been entrusted with the Impala of Mrs. Jones and her precious son, I only had my share of sugary water, like my mother called sodas. There were a few guests so drunk that they were passed out. One of them ended up against a tree, he was totally out of it, and snoring.

I didn't know how some of those kids got away it, my father wouldn't have allowed it. Jimmy said some of those kids were old enough to drink and nobody was going to care. For others, their parents may have been in a constant state of stupor not to notice their son or daughter arriving home smiling silly and smelling like a distillery.

We got out of the magnificent house and made our way down from Palos Verdes. I enjoyed the drive to Manhattan Beach taking the route close to the ocean. When we arrived at Jimmy's house, I could see the lights in the Westfield residence were on. My days in that house seemed so distant, like years had passed even if it only had been a few weeks. After helping Jimmy to the door of his house, I took my bicycle from the side of the place and went back to reality, to the room on top of the garage of Miss Ally. I had Wednesday to look forward to, to see Val one last time.

CHAPTER 15
GOODBYES

I HAD BEEN WAITING for Wednesday to arrive to meet Eve and Val for dinner and to hang out as planned. I rode my bicycle to Jimmy's house and once again I was entrusted with the blue Impala. We arrived a little early to the dinner because Jimmy wanted to take his time walking with the crutches. To our surprise, Val and Eve were parking as we entered the parking lot. Eve walked with Jimmy while Val and I went in first and got a table. Val looked beautiful, she was wearing a white blouse and a yellow skirt. There was no need for elaborate make-up or overworked hair.

My dinner companions were excited and talking about their impending departures, how they were looking forward to meeting their roommates, what classes they were taking, and the activities each school had planned for their arrival. All the things I was not going to experience. Even if I decided to go to college, I didn't expect my college experience would be similar to theirs. They were going to premier institutions. Jimmy and Val had scholarships, Eve didn't but she was going to a private exclusive school. I was listening, trying to share their happiness, but the truth was that I wasn't happy. Jimmy, my only friend was leaving. The rest of the acquaintances I had made during my weeks in Manhattan also were leaving, and the girl I liked was going away within days without knowing that I liked her a lot.

Val was sitting next to me and after having finished her hamburger, she was eating her French fries slowly, dipping one fry at a time in the into the ketchup. She bit half of the fry then dipped what was left in the ketchup.

"Tell me Daniel, have you decided how long are you staying?" she asked, looking at the few French fries left on her plate.

"No, I haven't. I would like to spend the winter here. It would be the first time in my life to experience a winter without snow."

"Then if you stay, let's get together when I come back," she turned to look at me and said with a smile.

"Yes, Dan, we can meet here with Eve and Val and talk about what happened in Manhattan while we were away," Jimmy said with a big smile.

"OK, I will stay just to report to you any news, and of course to enjoy the sunshine," I said this while my mind was racing. Thrilled about Val's positive response.

We were laughing and were ready to ask for dessert when Val went to the restroom. Eve, Jimmy, and I were in charge of deciding what to have and to surprise her. We requested a slice of chocolate cake. We were recounting Phillip's party when Eve and Jimmy's smiles disappeared.

"What happened?" Eve asked when she saw Val coming from the restroom followed by Katie.

Val sat next to me, and Katie had in her hand an empty glass.

"Sorry Val, I didn't see you. It's just soda; it will not leave a stain on your clothes," Katie said with a twisted smile on her face.

"Miss please go back to your table," our waitress instructed to Katie while Val kept ignoring her.

"OK, I just wanted to make sure my friend knew it was an accident."

"Katie, I'm not your friend, *we* aren't your friends, and you know it wasn't an accident," Val said.

Katie turned around and went back to her table while our waitress followed her with her eyes. She must have been there when we arrived, and we didn't notice her.

"Sorry guys but I want to go home, I don't want to be around Katie, and I want to get out of these clothes full of cherry coke and syrup," Val said.

"What happened?" I asked.

"She just stood up from her table and spilled the soda on me."

"What is *wrong* with her?" Jimmy asked.

"She used to live in Palos Verdes with her father before he remarried. After the wedding, she went to live with her mother. That is how she ended up in Manhattan Beach, and she doesn't like it," Eve explained.

"What is not to like?" I inquired.

"Well, she really wanted to go to the most exclusive high school in Palos Verdes and Los Angeles. When she moved in with her mother those dreams evaporated. Her father's new wife wasn't going to accept the exorbitant expense to keep spoiling the rotten egg as she calls Katie. Let's say that she loathes anybody who lives in Palos Verdes. And Val sitting next to you just made her lose her marbles," Eve added.

"Eve let's go, sorry Jimmy and Daniel for ending our dinner like this."

"Don't worry Val, it's not your fault."

"Are you leaving?" the waitress asked, bringing us an enormous slice of chocolate cake with four forks.

"Yes, there are bad vibes after the incident," Jimmy said.

"I understand. Let me put the cake in a container to go and I will bring you the check."

We nodded, and the motherly looking woman took the cake and came back right away with a box and the bill.

"Sweetie, I have removed your meal, we are sorry that this happened to you."

"Thank you!" said Val.

We paid and got out of the place. We gave the cake to Val and Eve even if Jimmy and I wanted to devour the whole slice, but as the gentlemen that we were, we gave it to the girls.

"Daniel, I hope to see you when I come back, I want to hear all your stories from the mortuary. Take care," Val said and we hugged. I gave her a kiss on the cheek. She smiled and walked away to get in Eve's car.

"Now what?" Jimmy said.

"Now we get out of here. I don't want to see Katie because I'm furious that she ruined our double date."

"I never thought of this outing as a double date," said Jimmy as he tried to walk faster with the crutches.

"Jimmy, Jimmy."

"I don't want to go home yet. Let's go to the pier."

"Are you going to be able to walk all the way to the end of the pier?"

"Maybe, maybe not, but at least I want to go and see it before I leave tomorrow. I know my mother is going to say no if I ask her to drive me there. She is getting all nervous about the trip to Massachusetts to drop me off."

"OK, then to the pier it is."

We parked as close as we could. That night destiny had for us one more surprise. We were walking down to the pier when out of a side street, Todd and his friends appeared.

"Hey, hey! What do we have here? If it is not Jimmy and Daniel *'The Junior Undertaker.'* Yeah, Jimmy and his loyal sidekick!"

I didn't react to the freshly minted nickname that Todd had given me. He saw me during a funeral, and of course he had to find something to say to be annoying.

"Todd what do you want?" I said and was tired of Todd always making his stupid comments.

"Yes, Todd what do you want?" Jimmy uttered and Todd's friends chuckled.

Todd got closer to Jimmy and pushed his shoulder as if to make him lose his balance. Jimmy was trying to balance his weight on the crutches, avoiding at all costs putting weight on his sprained ankle.

"Hey Jimmy, I told you to stay away from the beach. I see you are in a precarious position; you could end up hurting your other foot." Todd laughed and kept pushing Jimmy's shoulder while the other hooligans smiled.

Jimmy for the first time kept eye contact with Todd and Todd was not taking it well. I was thinking what our options were; given that they were four and we were two, plus Jimmy was injured. I saw there were people coming out of a restaurant. I considered if I needed to yell to get their attention but before I could open my mouth, I heard a voice behind me.

"Hello, Todd and friends. What are you kids doing on the street at this hour? Your mothers should be worried about you. Don't you guys have a curfew?"

"Hi Jack, we were leaving," one of Todd's buddies said and the other two just nodded in agreement and started walking away.

"Todd, you are staying here. We need to have a little chat," Jack said as he put his hand on Todd's chest.

"Jack, I must go," Todd said, but Jack moved in front of him. Todd's friends keep walking, they didn't turn back or wait for their buddy.

"Todd, are you learning anything in school these days? Or were you expelled once again? You can address me as 'Sir.' You do not get to call me Jack."

"Yes, Sir," Todd replied without looking at Jack. It was amazing to see that all his bravado had disappeared in an instant.

"What did you say, Todd? I didn't hear you. I didn't see your mouth move, maybe because you were looking at the ground. Look eye to eye when somebody is talking to you. What did you say?"

"Yes, Sir," Todd responded this time looking at Jack. I thought that Todd was shaking, maybe it was just my wishful thinking.

"That's better. You know what the problem with you is? Your parents. They should have sent you a long time ago into the army. Instead, they spoil you, they put up with your shenanigans. I think I will have a talk with your father and give him my opinion about your poor behavior with the members of this community. Anyway, say good night to Jimmy and Daniel because you and I are going to have a talk by the pier," Jack said putting his arm around Todd's shoulders. Jack was taller than Todd by two or three inches.

"I really need to go," Todd said in a quavering voice.

"I don't think so. You didn't look in a hurry when I arrived, you were really enjoying talking with my friends. See you guys," Jack said as he nodded to us.

"See you, Jack.!" I said smiling. I was pleased that finally Todd had found his match.

"Goodnight Jack." Jimmy said.

We turned around and went back to the parking lot. Jimmy didn't want to go to the pier knowing that Jack was taking Todd to the sand to have a talk.

We could hear that Jack said to Todd—"We are going to the beach, your territory. First lesson Todd: the beach is a public space."

We stood at the top of the street, and we saw Jack and Todd going onto the sand. We couldn't see anything else. I learned in the coming days that Todd had been mean with

Lori who was Jack's best friend's younger sister. She was almost like a member of his family. I didn't see Jack after that night; Lori said that his time off was up, and he had to go back to Asia to do whatever he was doing for the government. A few weeks later I saw Todd one more time, and when he saw me, he crossed the street so as to not meet me face-to-face on the sidewalk.

Years later when I spoke with Jimmy, he said that he had seen Jack at a funeral for one of his friends who had died in a military training accident. Jack was wearing a military uniform and had several ribbons on his chest. Jimmy said that he spoke briefly with him and asked him what happened with Todd that night. Jack replied: "Jimmy, there are boys that will never grow up and will be completely forgotten. Todd is one of them. Stop thinking about him, stop wasting the power of your brilliant mind on Todd."

What was for sure was that Todd's dad got transferred by the end of 1982, and nobody knew anything else about the family after they left. Jimmy learned the news when he returned home for his first Christmas vacation from MIT.

CHAPTER 16
GLORIA

FOURTH WEEK OF AUGUST 1982

I HAD BEEN ASKED by Tony to be at the funeral home at 2:00 p.m. on the last Wednesday of August. I needed to prepare the viewing area for a rosary. The family had asked to have a viewing that extended beyond the rosary. For people that couldn't make it to the 6:00 p.m. rosary, they could stop and pay their respects prior at the funeral service on Thursday. The deceased was the matriarch of a wealthy family in the area, Mrs. Elaine Milton. Tony said that the family was old school.

I learned with every day that passed that Tony Westfield didn't do anything if there wasn't something in it that would help his business. He understood personal relations, but he also understood that every funeral was an opportunity to showcase his services to potential customers and the relatives of potential customers. For example, he went with Frank and I to the removal of Mrs. Milton. Of course, he drove in his big black spotless sedan while Frank and I drove the van. Somehow, he knew the kids of the deceased; he mingled with them while Frank and I removed the body. Then he had been personally supervising every detail for the vigil, the ceremony, and the burial. Usually, he let Esther run with most of the details, but for this one he had rolled up his sleeves and was making sure everything was perfect. In addition to the deceased being a prominent member of the community, it was expected that the last series of social events saying farewell to Mrs. Milton were going to be attended by members of her club. And most of them were ladies her age.

I was arranging the chairs in the viewing room when I heard the chime of the front door. I went to see who had entered the reception area when a statuesque brunette wearing a short tight red skirt was walking towards the hallway. Her shoes matched the color of her skirt; they were two inches high. I thought that I would like to see two extra inches on those shoes.

"Excuse me, may I help you!" I greeted her.

"No, but I came to help. I haven't seen you before. I'm Gloria," the brunette exclaimed, holding a little tote and smiling.

I was ready to introduce myself when Frank showed up.

"Gloria, Gloria there you are. Mrs. Milton is waiting for you," said Frank as he moved his hands, exasperated, pointing at the prep room. Tony's heavy investment in this client had increased everybody's stress levels. Everybody was jumpy.

"Frank, it's not like she is going to get up and go somewhere. Is she?" Gloria replied with a certain sassiness.

"No, that is true. But I was expecting you half an hour ago."

"I called and told Esther that I was running late in the salon," Gloria said as she followed Frank to the prep room. Within a minute Frank returned and sat in the viewing area.

"Frank, what does Gloria do here?" I asked.

"Gloria makes the dead look alive. Mostly women. I take care of the men and women that don't ask for big up do. The first time I told Tony I was leaving, he asked me what I wanted in order for me to stay longer. I told him one of my conditions, and not negotiable, was that I didn't want to do any more elaborate hair and make-up jobs aside from what was normal. For complicated cases and special requests, he needed to find somebody else to do it. Oh gosh, it is almost seven years ago since I had my first conversation with Tony about me leaving. Sometimes, I think I am going to die here. But what else am I going to do, sit at home and watch TV all day long? In the mortuaries at least I get to see people, though I know most of them are dead people. I like to think I am contributing to giving a loved one their last good-bye. Anyway, there was no way I was going to be dealing with Mrs. Milton's hair and make-up. You saw the pictures; she looked like she came out of one of those popular TV shows with the big hair," Frank said as he gesticulated with his hands.

"Frank, how long have you been doing this?" I inquired.

"Oh, since my early twenties. I'm turning seventy in December. I guess that will make it at least forty-five years. I'm going outside. If Gloria finishes before I come in, please tell her I am in the back."

"I will," I said as Frank got up from the chair and slowly made his way to the back exit and the parking lot. There were orange trees planted at the edge of the property and a bench between the trees. I noticed that Frank spent most of his free time sitting there. He didn't read, he just sat there looking to the sky or with his lost gaze, looking at the parking lot payment. I wondered if he was pondering whether if he should retire, or if he was reviving memories of his life outside the prep room.

I had finished taking care of the details that Tony had assigned to me. He was expected to arrive in any moment to be ready for the main event of the day, not before verifying that everything was perfect to receive the family members and friends of Mrs. Elaine Milton—the chairs, the flowers, the lighting, the carpet, and the bathrooms had to be perfect.

Tony told me the chairs were to be arranged properly, and if I needed to take out the measuring tape to ensure it, Esther had one. He asked me to change two lightbulbs that were of different intensity from the rest. I had to check the flowers and remove any dead petals or leaves, and review that they looked symmetrical from every angle. I replenished the hand soap and put new rolls of toilet paper in the restrooms after I had cleaned them diligently. After having walked around twice making sure everything was as Tony expected, I was sitting at the receptionist desk, reading a book, when Gloria came out of the prep room.

"Hey, I think Frank interrupted you when you were ready to tell me your name," she said as she looked at me intensely while biting her lower lip.

"Hi, Frank is in the back," I said without giving her my name.

"I know where Frank is, but I don't know your name. Or don't you have one? Should I decide what I want to call you?" she said this as she approached the desk, putting her hand on it, resting her weight on her arm and leaning forward.

"I'm Daniel," I said, a bit nervous.

"Well, it's nice to meet you, Daniel. It's nice to see *younger* blood here. Maybe next time we can chat, and you can tell me your story. I want to know how you ended up here. Before I go, I need to get Frank's approval. But I must say, I believe she looks better than when she was alive. Nice meeting you Daniel."

She turned around and walked down the hallway, her ponytail was swinging with each sultry step. I couldn't help noticing her top. It was a sleeveless simple blouse, you could see through, just enough to give you an idea that she was wearing a lace bra. Her legs were long, tan, and the muscles well-defined. You could see she really stayed fit.

"Nice meeting you Gloria," were the only words that came out of my mouth. Sure, I wanted to tell her my story and I wanted to hear hers.

Esther came down from her apartment and looked at me. I must have appeared entranced.

"Daniel don't let yourself get mesmerized by some red shoes. She is a hardworking girl; I will give her that. But I would be lying if I said she is a nice girl. She is decent but can be complicated. She is more of a woman than a girl and is at least five years older than you, which at your age is an eternity. Don't get yourself head over heels for her."

"Esther but I only said hi!"

"I'm pretty sure you did, but I am also sure that she already created a whirlwind of emotions with the batting of her eyelashes and the swaying of her hips. I'm sure that your mother, the good Mrs. Smith, would agree entirely with what I just told you."

"Esther, OK, thank you for the advice," I muttered.

She went to her office. It was too late; I was looking forward to the next time Gloria was called to the mortuary.

SEPTEMBER 1982

TONY OFFERED me the use of his phone so I could call home to talk with my parents, but I had just put it off. I didn't want to call and hear my mom asking me if I was going to be back soon. I guess somewhere in my head I had started to question my decision to stay longer. Since I had become Miss Ally's gardener and my few acquaintances had left for college, I felt consumed by work. Quickly my days had become a routine from the mortuary to the lawnmower, from the mortuary to the neighborhood store to get more canned goods. At the rate I was going I was going to need a new can opener. Clearly, I had to change my eating habits. I was hoping Esther would need to go somewhere, and that I would be called back to help with the night shift and then cook something decent using the stove.

While I was not going to call my family, I decided to send a letter to my mother instead of picking up the phone at the mortuary. After all, she never received a letter from my brother. At least I could give her a moment of happiness in receiving a letter from her youngest son.

I took the pad of yellow paper that Tony told me to keep, and I sat at the little table that Miss Ally gave me to decorate my room. I wrote:

September 2nd, 1982

Dear Mother,

I hope everything is well.

I am settled in my room that Tony found for me. Miss Ally, my landlady is a kind woman, she gave me a good deal in exchange for fixing up the room. I'm sure you would like her.

I have discovered I'm a decent handyman and gardener. I help Miss Ally take care of the rental properties she owns. I do small projects, cut the grass, and trim bushes.

Working for Tony I have discovered a world of which I was not aware of. What happens when people die and how the circumstances of the death can affect how the bodies are handled is something new. I must tell you I have seen dead children and that is something I will never get used to seeing. Naively, I always thought everybody died old, as an adult. There is so much death that is due to violence or accidents; it is a big city after all. Frank and Esther, my coworkers in the mortuary, are nice people. I enjoy working with them.

My friends have left for college, I will try to make some more.

Please give my regards to Father and to Daisy. I hope Daisy is not too angry because I haven't returned. I'm not going to lie; I don't know when I will be back. But I promise to call or write you soon.

Your loving son,

Daniel

P.S. Mom, I miss your cooking.

I took the letter and my bicycle, and I went to the post office. On my way back I got close to the sand. It didn't feel the same. It seemed so far away from when I met the group from PV, when Megan was introducing me to her friends. It felt an eternity since I had been to Venice with Jimmy. But it only had been weeks. I rode back to my place; I was tempted to splurge and get a hamburger, but instead I decided to go to my room and have a can of chili with few slices of bread and then go to sleep. I needed to be at the mortuary by nine.

I arrived at the mortuary and saw Frank's car was already there. Then as soon as I entered the building I went to the to the prep room and there lying on the slab was a man who undergone a full autopsy, his head was propped up on the head block—this is made of rubber and could be described as a rectangle of firm rubber, red in color, with each long side having a scooped out sort of semi-circular area where the neck or head would rest upon.

I was startled and had to really take a good look to figure out the situation. This was new to me and somewhat fascinating. The top of the man's skull had been removed. The skull had been cut cleanly and neatly around the circumference of the head.

The body cavity was open, and the brain was located there, in a plastic bag—tucked away, like giblets inside a turkey.

The reminder of the man's head—resting on the block—had a curtain of skin that dangled down with gravity and had delicate waves of folding almost like a drapery. Stranger still, and new to me was the interior of the cranium.

The brain being removed left these perfectly formed what could be described as shallow cups, which were almost plastic-like in appearance and seemed to sit upon perfectly formed squat "posts." This was the area at the base of the brain.

I was studying the corpse when Frank entered the prep

room with a cup of coffee in hand. "Hey Sport!" Frank said as he put the cup on the counter with his shaky hand. He seemed full of energy.

"Good morning, Frank!" I greeted him as my gaze returned to see the body.

"Daniel, if you are wondering how we are going to put back together this puzzle, don't worry. The family has opted for a closed casket. After Tony explained the condition of the body, they agreed to having a closed casket funeral. Let's get the casket. C'mon Daniel let's get moving."

We were closing the casket when Esther walked into the prep room.

"Are you guys almost done? Tony wants you to meet him in Palos Verdes. We have a high-profile client."

"Tell me, is it a female or male?" Frank asked.

"Female."

"Ah, one more in less than a week. Get ready Daniel, Tony is going to want everything perfect."

I smiled. While Frank wasn't too excited in having a high-profile client, it meant that Gloria was going to be called to help with the body.

"Then, what do I tell the boss?" asked Esther while she scratched her head with a pencil.

"Tell him we will be able to leave in fifteen minutes," Frank responded.

We set out for PV, both of us clad in dark suits, as was the norm.

We arrived at the property. The house was bigger than Phillip's place and there was household staff everywhere you looked—taking care of the grounds, dusting all over, placing flower arrangements. When we were shown to the living room, there was Tony talking with the son of the deceased, who looked agitated. We moved into the large living room. In a leather chair next to the sofa where Tony was sitting, the lawyer of Mrs. Rose Evans sat emotionless with his hands resting on the arms of the chair. Tony had a nice leather portfolio with the forms and paperwork needed to be completed to take care of the body and for the service. Later we learned that Mrs. Rose Evans had two sons: one that lived in Palos Verdes and the other in New York. They were more enemies than brothers and her lawyer was there to explain how she had left instructions to have two funerals—one in Los Angeles and one in New York. The matriarch knew that her sons were not willing to be under the same roof, even for her funeral, and in order to avoid any public drama during her last event, she opted for two funerals. In addition, her relatives and friends were scattered all over the country. Her final wish was to be buried somewhere in New York next to her husband.

"Gentlemen, Frank and Daniel have arrived; we can start with the transportation of your mother to our facility and get her ready for the funeral," Tony said, and the lawyer looked relieved. It seemed he had enough of what Mrs. Evans' son was saying.

There was an almost royal staircase to the second floor. I was concerned if the body was upstairs; I was okay with it, but I knew it was getting harder for Frank to do the more physical removals. We all followed the grieving son to the back, and out to a magnificent backyard with flowers and trees everywhere, it seemed like an enchanted garden. On one side of the enormous backyard there was a guest house that had been serving as Mrs. Evans' dwelling place. A nurse was sitting on a bench outside the guest house. She got up quickly to open the door of the place and the door to the room of Rose Evans. There on the bed and propped up on cushions and pillows was the lifeless body of an elderly woman. Her mouth was slightly open. There was a tank of oxygen next to the bed and a medical device that had been unplugged.

Tony explained what we were going to do and asked everybody to leave if they wished. The son and the lawyer exited the premises, but the nurse stayed. When we had secured Mrs. Evans on the gurney, the nurse took a travel bag from the closet and handed it over to Tony. It had three outfits to choose from and recent pictures of the old woman. She said the Evans matriarch couldn't make her mind up on which one she wanted to be buried in. She had opted to leave it to the professionals to decide, based on her complexion after death. She also wanted her make-up to look like it did when she applied it.

Back in the mortuary I left Frank with Mrs. Evans to start preparing her. She was going to be embalmed, given that she needed to be presentable for her two funerals, one on the West Coast and the other on the East Coast. She would be flown from Los Angeles to New York.

I was in the kitchen talking with Esther who was refilling her cup of coffee when Frank came in wearing his plastic apron and with gloves on his hands.

"I know that look, and the answer is no. Daniel, you are going to need to help Frank." Esther said.

"Help to do what?"

Until that moment my involvement with helping Frank had been going to collect bodies, dress them and put them in the casket.

"You will see," Esther said.

"Daniel could you please help me massage Mrs. Evans."

"What? Why? But she is dead," I choked the words out.

"Yes Daniel, she is dead and because she is dead cold, rigor mortis has set in. The body sat there for hours waiting for the lawyer to deal with the two grieving disgruntled sons. Come on Daniel, I need you to help me massage her arms and legs to continue with her preparation."

Reluctantly, I followed Frank. I had been told that I needed to help with miscellaneous stuff. I guessed that this was one of those miscellaneous tasks. I had seen Frank embalm a body, but I never had seen him massage a body.

Either he already had done it, or it was not always required based on how long the body had been sitting around.

I went into the prep room and just as Frank had said, I only needed to massage Mrs. Evans' legs while Frank massaged her arms. After Frank was satisfied with the results, I was excused. I left and went to wash my hands. I had seen an embalming, and I was not eager to see another. A bit later Frank called me to help dress Mrs. Evans with one of the outfits that we were given. Underwear and all, and not one of my favorite tasks. Esther helped us choose the ensemble. Then it was time for Gloria to arrive to give Mrs. Rose Evans the final touches. I still had one more hour at the mortuary and I was hoping Gloria would be there before it was time for me to go home.

The back door opened and there was Gloria, wearing tight white jeans and a dark blue silk blouse. Her hair was again in a ponytail and her shoes were black heels.

"Hey Daniel, are you going to tell me all about yourself?"

"Hi Gloria. Sure." I tried to sound casual and hide my excitement.

"Well, why don't you keep me company while I do my thing?" she said as she opened the door to the prep room. I followed her as if I were on a leash.

"Frankie, what do we have here?"

Frank explained to Gloria who her customer was, showed her a few pictures, and then she got to work. As usual, Frank left the prep room to go and sit on one of the benches in the parking lot.

Gloria started talking and working, with her eyes focused on Mrs. Evans. She asked me where I was from and how I got the job in the mortuary. It was a real interrogation. I kept talking even though I was somewhat shy, and I wasn't too forthcoming with information or skilled at making conversation with people I just had met. But I wanted to talk with

Gloria, and if talking to her was going to be by way of an interrogation, I didn't care.

Gloria was done giving life to Mrs. Evans and making her hair look like she had just come out of the beauty parlor.

"Daniel, before I check with Frank to get his approval on the makeup and hair, do you have any plans for Labor Day weekend?" Gloria asked while she was putting her kit away.

"No, I don't," I said, my mind racing.

"Good. Would you like to go to a party?"

"Sure," I replied as nonchalantly as I could. I didn't have any plans and hadn't been told I was scheduled to work the weekend. I wasn't going to pass up an invitation to a party.

"Then stop by my place on Sunday around five, here is the address."

Gloria took out a little piece of paper from one of the pockets of her white jeans, and then went to look for Frank. I put the paper in my wallet carefully and left the prep room, it was almost time for me to go home.

I was sitting at the receptionist desk when Gloria was ready to leave after getting the OK from Frank, but Tony stopped her. I could only hear them whispering in the kitchen, then she giggled, came out of the kitchen, and went out by the back door. Tony went to his office, and I went to ask Frank if he needed anything before leaving.

"Hey Frank, it is almost time for me to go. Do you need me to help you with anything?"

"Daniel, we are done for the day. Rose Evans is ready to be displayed like an Egyptian mummy."

"Why like an Egyptian mummy?"

"You know how they take those mummies from museum to museum to be part of a temporary exhibition? Well, this lady is going to have a viewing and a service here and then she will be flown across the country to have another funeral in New York. All because her kids can't get along and because they have money for these elaborate funerals on both coasts.

Daniel, sometimes death is easier when there are no riches and family dramas involved.

"Daniel, you can go, I don't need anything, go and enjoy the rest of the day."

I left. I was not going to be able to enjoy the rest of the day until I was done helping Miss Ally with one of her properties. By the time I was free from my responsibilities as handyman and gardener, it was time to have dinner, shower and go to bed. But the little paper in my wallet kept making me smile, knowing that I was going to see Gloria.

Sunday arrived quickly; it was time to go to the party. I had searched in the map book that was in Miss Ally's truck, and Gloria's place was on the other side of Manhattan Beach in an area called El Porto. It seemed far from where I lived, but on my bicycle I was there in less than fifteen minutes. I got to the place—it was a two-story apartment. I knocked on the door and a blonde wearing a short bath robe opened it.

"Hi, I am looking for Gloria."

"Hi there! Gloria, a cute guy is looking for you!" the blonde screamed up the stairs while she leaned against the side of the door, sliding her arm as if to stretch it. The robe opened a little letting me see that she was not wearing a top. She didn't say a word, she just kept looking at me smiling. I turned to see the ocean down the street.

"Hi Daniel, was it difficult to park?" Gloria inquired.

"Gloria, the handsome one arrived on his bicycle," the blonde said, and she turned around and went upstairs.

"Hi Gloria, I don't have a car," I said, almost with a touch of pride.

"Good for you, don't get one, they are just money pits. Come-on we will take my car, you can leave your bicycle in here."

I stepped into what was the living room, dining room, and kitchen area. Then we went around the property to where the open garage was. Gloria took her Mustang out and I got in.

We drove to El Segundo where the party was; it was my first time driving around El Segundo. Soon we were parking in front of a white house. You could hear the music from the street. We walked directly to the back yard where there were several tables set with paper tablecloths, paper plates, plastic cups, and disposable utensils. People were mingling; everybody seemed to know Gloria. She introduced me to everyone, and I couldn't keep up with the names. The party was a real planned barbecue, not like the one that I went to when chaperoning Lesley. I indulged in a beer. I was not driving, and nobody was asking me if I was old enough to drink. After we ate, we stayed there for a while chatting, then Gloria got close to me and asked me if I wanted to get out of there and walk on the beach. Of course I said yes.

We went back to her place to park her car; the lights of her apartment were off, and we started walking down to the beach. There was still some sunset glow in the sky as we headed towards the water. I learned she shared the apartment with two flight attendants—Wendy, the blonde that opened the door and Rachel, a redhead. Gloria didn't talk too much about them, and I didn't ask too much. I learned Gloria was from California, Northern California and she moved to Los Angeles just four years ago. She wanted to work in the film industry doing make up, but she couldn't get in and she didn't like living close to where the studios are located. She preferred the beach lifestyle.

"Daniel, let's go back to my place, maybe Wendy and Rachel are there with some friends. When they are around there is never a dull moment."

We walked up the street and the lights were on, they were back. As soon as Gloria opened the door you could hear the laughs. I was properly introduced to Rachel and Wendy and to their friends. Rachel was sitting next to Peter, a pilot. I learned later that he was not her boyfriend but her lover. He was married and spent every night he could with Rachel.

There was also Joanna, a neighbor of theirs with her boyfriend Rick.

"Daniel, would you like a drink or to smoke with me?" Wendy said as she approached me with a handmade cigarette.

"I will have a drink. I don't smoke."

"You don't know what you're missing."

She turned around and put ice in a plastic cup, poured vodka and a splash of orange juice and gave it to me without saying a word. Then she went out to the balcony to smoke.

I went and sat on the couch next to Gloria. Everybody was having a good time. Laughing, drinking. Rachel got up and searched through a stack of records until she found the one she was looking for.

"Gloria, it is time for your song," Rachel said as she put the turntable needle down on the disc of black vinyl.

"Oh no, no, I don't want to dance," Gloria said.

The music started and it was the song by The Doors, "Gloria."

"Really? Come on dancing queen," Wendy said, pulling Gloria off the couch.

"Daniel, this is going to get fun," Peter said while he got up to get a beer.

Wendy, Rachel, Joanna and Gloria started dancing while we guys just watched them follow the tempo of the music with their bodies; it was like they were getting into some type of trance; I know *I* was mesmerized by Gloria's movements. The song ended.

"Let's dance it one more time, but this time you guys dance with us," Rachel said trying to catch her breath.

"I hate to be a party pooper, but we need to go," Joanna said.

"It is too early for you two to go," protested Wendy.

"We are spending tomorrow with my family and need to get on the road early," Rick said holding Joanna by the waist.

They made their exit and as soon as the door closed, Rachel started playing the song again. Peter refused to get up and dance. I joined the girls; they were surrounding me while I was giving it my best. Then Gloria got close to me and Rachel went and straddled Pete; she started to move to the rhythm of the song while Pete just sat back and enjoyed the show Rachel was giving him. I was sandwiched between Gloria and Wendy for a bit, then Wendy lost interest and went to join Rachel and Pete.

Gloria said in a whisper "would you like to go upstairs to be alone with me?" I nodded and she took my hand. I turned around and Wendy had taken off her top and was standing behind Rachel helping her remove hers.

We almost ran upstairs and went into the last door of the narrow hallway, to Gloria's room. We got in and closed the door. She looked at me and started to unbutton her blouse. She had undone the second button, and by instinct I took her in my arms and found her lips. I started to kiss her gently, but she returned the kiss passionately and she started to touch me.

"Daniel, are we going too fast for you?" Gloria asked while she had her hands on my body.

"No, it is just that..." I looked away from her.

"What? Tell me Daniel."

"I haven't been with somebody."

"Are you a virgin?" Gloria said stepping back.

Gloria's stepping back shocked me and my heart sank for an instant. In my mind everything unraveled. I righted myself quickly though and responded.

"Yes, but I want to continue if you don't mind."

"Are you sure, because there is no turned back," Gloria said as she got closer.

"Yes, I am sure. I have never been so sure."

"I don't mind at all, come here Daniel, I will show you," she looked wild and her nostrils flared.

"Just I didn't come prepared."

"Don't worry about that. I am. Then you are sure you want this?" she asked as she started to touch me again.

"Yes, I do want this," I said as I took her face in my hands and started to kiss her.

The next day for the first time I woke up next to somebody. I had lost my virginity in the expert hands and mouth of Gloria. It had been a long night. When I opened my eyes, it was almost nine. I laid there looking at her. She seemed so peaceful and so innocent, but she didn't have an ounce of innocence. When she woke up, she wanted more, as did I. Around eleven we went down to the kitchen and prepared scrambled eggs. In the dining room there were pieces of clothing from Wendy, Rachel and Peter. Wendy was the first to join us; she went to the living room and picked up all the evidence from the night before. I left without seeing Peter or Rachel.

I rode back on my strand cruiser to Miss Ally's; I felt as if I was in heaven. It was a dream-like feeling of placid contentedness. Gloria said that she wanted to see me soon, and naturally I said yes. I was going to stop by her place on Wednesday after work. She told me she didn't care if I arrived late, she was going to be waiting for me and be "ready." That was the first time I went to her place after work, the first time I spent the night there in the middle of the week, and the first time I slept only a few hours just to get up at 6:30, run to my place, shower, change, and get to the mortuary by 8:00.

If I was not in the mortuary or taking care of something for Miss Ally, I was with Gloria. She consumed all my free time. She became my obsession, and I became hers. She liked saying she was my teacher, and I needed daily lessons. I was an eager student wanting to get an "A."

Soon September was coming to an end. I had spent so

many nights at Gloria's that Miss Ally asked me if I was planning to move out because she hardly saw me spending the night over the garage. I told her I had a girlfriend, and I was not planning on moving out.

I felt I was in heaven; September had been the best month so far, and thanks to Gloria. But was she really my girlfriend?

CHAPTER 18
PURGATORY

FIRST HALF OF OCTOBER

IT WAS Friday and the first day of October. I was in the mortuary waiting for Gabriel, we were going to pick up a body from the airport. While easily one person could do the job, Tony wanted me to see what needed to be done. Frank had not been feeling that well the last two weeks of September and I was suspecting he was going to retire at any moment. Maybe this was the reason that Gabriel was spending more time in our location and Tony was spending less time in the mortuary. Esther had said in passing that Tony was working on a deal to get a fourth location; she hinted that soon there could be a full-time job for me. I just smiled regarding her comment. The truth was that since I had met Gloria, the only thought in my mind was when I could get to her house and be with her.

Gabriel said he has going to be there at 10:00 and it was 9:30. I had time to daydream about my upcoming trip to Catalina Island with Gloria. We had planned to go on Sunday and spend the day on the island. She said it was a nice place to get away from the city. Mostly we spent our time together at her place under the sheets. Only a few times did we go to the beach or to have a bite close to my house. I was discovering how difficult it was to do everything you want with somebody when both people work. I started to daydream about my upcoming trip, but it didn't last because Gabriel arrived early, he was there at a quarter to ten.

"Good morning! Is everybody here?" Gabriel greeted me, seeming enthusiastic.

"Good morning, Gabriel. Yes, Esther is here, and Tony hasn't arrived yet. Frank you know is not feeling well, but he said he will be in by the time we get back from the airport."

"Cool, well let's get going."

As soon as we rolled out of the parking lot, I asked Gabriel, "How many more weeks until the baby arrives?" It was better just to get the talk about the baby over with.

"Just three, but I feel like it could happen at any moment. The good thing is my mother-in-law is arriving next week to be at home with my wife in case the baby decides to arrive early."

"Well, that is good. Gabriel, who are we picking up from the airport?"

"Tony said it was a trust fund baby."

"A trust fund baby? Like a newborn?"

"No, the cadaver is not a newborn, it's a guy in his twenties. He is somebody that was lucky enough to have his parents or a wealthy relative leave him a significant bank account that was providing money to him."

"Well, I don't think he was lucky. First, he lost a loved one to get the money and now he himself is dead."

"I see your point," said Gabriel, and then he didn't say a word until we got to the airport.

We went to the cargo terminal, and the process was more or less what I had been told—it was like picking up any other package that had been flown into Los Angeles Airport. Soon we were back in the mortuary. Gabriel had to get back to his location and I had to bring in the body by myself. Frank was sitting at the receptionist desk reading the newspaper. It was the first time I saw him sitting there.

"Hey Frank, how are you doing? I got you a customer."

"Daniel, I am better, but truly considering resigning soon."

I heard Frank, and for the first time I didn't question him, nor did I start joking about how Tony would convince him to stay. He looked tired, there was a certain melancholy in his eyes. I kept rolling the cardboard encased package we picked up to the prep room. Frank folded the paper and put it under his arm, got up slowly and made his way to his office.

We removed the cardboard shipping case revealing a basic blue coffin.

"Well let's see what we have here," Frank said as he was ready to open the casket.

"Tony said it was a trust fund baby," I informed him, and Frank chuckled at my comment.

"Dear boy, what we have here is the mangled and partially burned body of a spoiled kid that died in a crash on a road in Italy while spending the money left by one of his wealthy relatives."

Frank opened the casket, and I was not prepared to see what I saw. There was a thick clear plastic bag containing a heavily disfigured body. The poor fellow was pretty thoroughly burnt. There were patches of unburnt flesh which still retained a flesh tone, but the rest of the body was charred. It was black; like chicken that was left on the grill for too long and the flames got to it. The worst part was the liquid. The thin, watery bodily fluid—and there was a lot of it—sloshed back and forth as we moved the casket around. I looked away; I didn't want to study it too much beyond standard morbid curiosity.

"Oh, yeah, he died in a bad car crash and then the car

started to burn. The good thing is that with a crash like that you die on impact, there is no suffering when the flames start."

Frank just talked matter-of-factly about what the poor soul in the casket must have gone through. I didn't want to know or imagine how the trust fund baby died; it was going to be bad enough to try to forget what I had seen.

"Frank, then a trust fund baby is a rich kid?" I asked, trying to change the conversation as Frank was closing the casket.

"Yes, it is a kid who is lucky or unlucky to have a hefty bank account that will be supplying him or her with a periodic stipend, and sometimes the amount is such that it could be for the rest of their lives. That is if they don't end up crashing in a fast car somewhere in Europe, like this bloke."

"Oh, I see."

I thought if I ever was that fortunate, I was not going to be reckless. Of course, I knew too well that I wasn't getting a trust fund, ever. None of my relatives had riches. I left the prep room and soon it was time to get to my second job before going to Gloria's.

When I got back to my room, there was an envelope under the door. There was writing on the envelope: "Dan, Gloria left this note for you. Miss Ally." I ripped open the envelop right away.

"Daniel,

Our trip to Catalina Island will need to wait. Something came up. I won't be able to see you until Wednesday. Come over for dinner.
Gloria"

Like that she had cancelled our Sunday day trip. I was disappointed, I didn't realize I would be more disappointed a few days later, and not because I didn't have weekend plans. I survived Saturday and Sunday. For the first time in weeks, I was able to go to the beach. I even decided to splurge and went to have a sit-down meal. On my way back I stopped at the little convenience store and bought a six-pack. How did I manage to buy beer if I was not even nineteen? Well, a few days earlier Gloria and I went into the convenience store and when we were leaving, Gloria said that the cashier was mesmerized with me, and added, "I'll bet she will even sell you booze." I laughed at her comment. She didn't like that, and she pulled out a bill and dared me to go and buy some beer. She said, "Get a six-pack, it's on me."

I went back in and took the six-pack. The clerk smiled when she saw me. I said that we had forgotten the most important item, and then I complemented her on her eyeglasses. I handed the twenty over and she took it with a big smile. Gloria was waiting in the car and the only thing she said was "You don't get it do you? You are tall, strong, hand-some, and young. You are a prince-charming for girls like her."

I didn't like how she said, "girls like her." The cashier looked like she was a nice young lady, she had always treated me well. I didn't even know why I bought the six-pack; I didn't have a refrigerator. I drank only one beer, and I was taking the rest to Gloria's house on Wednesday for dinner.

Wednesday arrived and that day I didn't have to go to the mortuary in the morning, plus I couldn't take care of the gardening for Miss Ally since she had taken the truck to the mechanic. I decided to explore a bit on my strand cruiser, to see what I could discover riding around. I was heading south on PCH when I saw Gloria's car parked in a motel. I knew it was Gloria's car because it had a minor dent and a scratch near the back tire on the driver's side. I got off my bicycle and walked into the parking lot to take a closer look. Yes, it was hers. My biggest surprise was not that it was her car, but that the gleaming black sedan of Tony Westfield was a few cars down. I approached the black sedan, and I saw that his leather portfolio was under his jacket on the back seat. I didn't need any other confirmation, but I didn't want to believe it. How could it be that Gloria and Tony were meeting in the early morning in a motel? Why would they be so obvious?

I got on my bicycle and continued riding south. I lost track of the cars; it was like I was in a trance. I had tunnel vision. Now and then the rush of a car buzzing by brought me back to reality. For a section I rode on the sidewalks until a lady walking a dog screamed at me "You, get off the sidewalk." I was furious, my mind was full of questions and thoughts of Tony and Gloria. I was almost hit by a bus pulling away from a stop. The bus driver honked and screamed at me to pay attention to his signals. Without realizing it I had reached Hawthorne Boulevard. I knew I was far from my place, and I turned around. I was numbed, and everything seemed to be moving in slow motion. I couldn't believe that Mr. Anthony Westfield, the perfect husband, the wonderful father, and the outstanding member of the community was cheating with the makeup artist of the dead. I was wondering how long they had been doing it. Did Gloria spend time with him during the day and then spend the night with me? Was Tony the reason she cancelled our trip to Catalina? Did Tony know about she and I?

I got home and Miss Ally had returned from the mechanic. I asked if it was OK for me to go and take care of the gardening at the Torrance property. She said yes. I went and tried to take as much time as I could. I was trying to calm down, pushing the lawnmower thinking, but it wasn't working. When I got to my room, I didn't shower. Lately Gloria liked seeing me arrive to her place full of dirt and sweat from working; she found it sexy. I took my backpack with a change of clothes since the last few times I had gone from her house directly to the mortuary. I didn't want to change anything, I had decided to play it cool, not to ask, and see how she behaved. I was naïve in thinking that somehow she would all of a sudden confess her rendezvous with Tony.

It was time to go to Gloria's house. I took my bicycle, and I rode as fast as I could. I wanted to know, I wanted to arrive and ask her, but then I also wanted to see how long she was going to keep lying. I arrived sweating and hyperventilating, knocked on the door, and there she was, all smiles.

"Hey lover, you look like you had a hard day at work. I hope you saved something for me," Gloria said and kissed me on the mouth. I tried to return the kiss, but the thought of Tony Westfield having kissed her lips few hours earlier made my stomach turn.

"Hey Gloria, how was your day?" I asked, knowing I was going to get a bunch of lies.

"Oh, as usual some perms, a few haircuts and a bride trying out makeup and hair styles."

"Wow, you get a lot done in a day." I tried not to sound sarcastic, but it did.

"I do. You know this apartment is not cheap, even with Wendy and Rachel. By the way, they are flying. They won't be back until the day after tomorrow. We have the place to ourselves. Every corner of this place for the two of us," she said as she was getting her hands under my t-shirt.

"How about dinner first, I didn't have lunch."

She looked at me and then she pointed to the bags with take-out. Gloria didn't cook too much, and that night wasn't the exception. She bought some Thai food that she had picked up on her way from the salon or wherever she was. She wasn't pleased about me stopping her advances; she was used to getting what she wanted, but that day I wasn't planning to let her have it.

"Why don't you take a shower before dinner?" she recommended.

"OK, I'll be back."

I took my backpack and went to her bedroom. I entered the bathroom and was ready to take off my clothes when I noticed two toothbrushes. It always had been only one. I opened the medicine cabinet and there was a men's deodorant, shaving cream, razors, and men's cologne. I hadn't seen those items there before. Was Tony now spending the night here and had his own things? I took the toothbrush and decided to confront her, there was no point in waiting for her to say something.

"Gloria!" I said as I started going down the stairs.

"Daniel why are you not taking a shower?"

"Because I want to know, why is Tony Westfield's stuff in your bathroom?" I was holding the toothbrush in front of her face. She turned pale, put her back against the wall and crossed her arms.

"That isn't Tony's toothbrush, it's my boyfriend's toothbrush."

She turned red and tears started running down her checks. Somehow, I knew they were not tears of sorrow or remorse. They were tears that she had been caught. I didn't say a thing.

"How do you know about Tony?" she asked looking away.

"Wow Gloria, with how many men do you share the bed? Are we more than three? You know what? Don't tell me. You know why? Because I have the feeling that you will not tell the truth anyway."

"Daniel how do you know about Tony?"

"Does it matter? What difference does it make?"

"Did he say something?"

"You are more concerned about how I learned about Tony, than about me discovering you were sleeping with him and that you have a boyfriend? I wouldn't be surprised if you also sleep with Wendy's and Rachel's friends."

She didn't say anything. I wanted her to say I'm sorry or

something, but she just stood there fuming like it was my fault. I let the toothbrush fall from my hand and ran upstairs to take my bag. When I came back, she was sitting on the last step of the stairs facing the door. When she heard me coming down, she started to talk without facing me.

"When I met you, I was not with my boyfriend. We had parted ways and decided to be apart for a while. He just came back, and we were going to give it another try. Tony happened a few days after you and I spent the night for the first time."

I listened to what she said, and I didn't see the point to keep asking questions or wait to see if she was going to say more. I was done with the whole thing, and I didn't want to be her boy toy, one of many men in her life. It was obvious that she didn't have plans for telling me about the boyfriend coming back. She wanted me to stay that night, maybe on the same sheets that he had already slept upon. I took my bicycle, and I opened the door.

"Gloria, until this morning I thought you were the best thing that had happened to me since I arrived. Now I regret that first night I spent here. You are just lies."

"I never said that I was your girlfriend or that we were exclusive," she said defiantly.

"But you never said we were *not* exclusive, and you never asked me if I was okay with not being exclusive. Next time you and Tony go to a motel, maybe go far from work and far from people that know you. Goodbye Gloria."

I exited and closed the door behind me. She opened the door and screamed "You would still be a virgin if it wasn't for me!" I kept riding downhill towards the water and I ignored her comment. When I got to the strand, I rode my bicycle slowly. What was the rush? I felt that if I slowed down, the breeze was going to take every memory of her away, but it didn't. I got to my room and went straight to the shower and stood there numb under the hot water.

I couldn't fall asleep, I was tossing and turning all that night. The moon wasn't full, but I felt as if its light was illuminating my room and not letting me sleep. But it wasn't the moon, it was Gloria and the realization of who she really was. With my eyes half opened I saw the five beers sitting on the floor, the beers I was planning to take to her place but didn't. I got up and gulped down the first one while standing, then took the tape recorder I had picked up in a secondhand store and turned on the radio. I searched for a station until I found one with a mix of pop and rock. I sat on the bed and started to drink the second beer, and then the third one.

I woke up with empty beer cans on the bed. It was almost nine and I was expected to be at the mortuary at nine; the place I would have preferred not to set foot in for the rest of my life. But I had to go and work, even if I felt like disappearing from Manhattan Beach. Then I thought if I did go and leave town, Gloria would win. But most likely she wouldn't care what happened to me and she would already have somebody else to keep her entertained. I got dressed, ran out the door and rode to the mortuary as fast as I could. In my half-asleep state and feeling drowsy, I was experiencing my first hangover. I was late by ten minutes, but it wasn't a big deal. Only Esther was there. I said good morning without showing my face in her office and then went to get a cup of coffee. I needed something to settle my stomach. She walked into the break room.

"What happened to you?" inquired Esther while she looked at me knowingly.

"Nothing, why?"

"You didn't comb your hair, you never show up late, and your t-shirt is inside out. You also smell like a bar."

The woman had a highly tuned sense of smell, that was one of the reasons she didn't like going into the prep room, she complained that the embalming fluid smell stayed in her nostrils for hours.

"I woke-up late," I said and turned around.

"Well, it is good the boss is not going to be here today, he is going to a funeral directors' conference in Las Vegas. He said he told me earlier, but I don't think he did. I think it was a last-minute thing, or his wife wants to go to Vegas."

I thought, sure, Pam dragging Tony to Las Vegas, or maybe he went with Gloria to gamble. After all, he was already gambling his reputation for that pair of red high heel shoes.

"Good morning! What the hell happened to you?" Frank said.

"That was the same thing I asked Daniel, but he insists that nothing happened. It looks like he has a major hangover."

"Daniel, go and comb your hair and put your t-shirt on properly," Frank said in a fatherly tone of voice.

I walked out of the break room, and I went to the restroom. They were right, I looked pale and my face looked like I had aged overnight. It didn't help that my hair was a total mop. I tried to comb it with my fingers but had a few rebel spots that kept getting out of place and I had to wet my head to control things. I went back to the break room to get my cup of coffee.

In the prep room a new body had been brought in and I wanted to take a look just out of curiosity.

I learned that a trocar in the mortuary business in a sword-like instrument about two feet long. It is chromed and shaped to have a handle at one end so it can be easily gripped. The other end is pointed and sharp but is hollow like a syringe, so that fluid can flow through. The whole thing is hollow in this regard and has an area at the base where a rubber hose can be attached.

The hose runs to the sink in the prep room. The sink has a vertical column where water can be run through from the top. There is a narrowing of this pipe about midway down.

Here a tube protrudes, and the hose from the trocar is attached there. Running water through the tube creates suction at the narrow throat of the pipe. This is the Venturi principle, and the system works similar to how a carburetor operates.

This I found interesting and thought I'd give the trocar a try—it is used to remove fluids from the major organs in the body cavity of the deceased.

Frank explained to me what I needed to do. I plunged the trocar into the stomach of the man. It took more effort than I anticipated, and I jammed it in. The water in the sink had been turned on and the suction was there. I probed and searched for vital organs. The system made a sucking and slurping sound. I pulled the trocar in and out. As I hit the liver, or maybe a lung, a gout of bloody fluid spouted down into the sink through the bottom of the vertical pipe. I kept going and searched for the fellow's heart, and upon puncturing it, a near solid red burst of fluid shot into the sink. I continued this for some time, enjoying it a bit. I seemed to have removed most of the fluid from this fellow's body cavity and felt a touch of pride. We turned the water off and I withdrew the trocar.

Friday, I didn't need to go to the mortuary, so I could work all day doing gardening and getting a unit ready at the Lomita property; the tenant had left it in bad shape. At least somebody was going to be happy to see me—Angie.

The day went fast, maybe because there was a lot of work to do and Angie stopped by while I was painting. She stood around talking about her family, the changes in the area, and more. She didn't mind at all that I just grunted now and then in response to her comments.

On my way back to Manhattan I stopped by the neighborhood store. I thought it was a good idea to have something stronger at home, like vodka. The sweet young lady was at the cash register, it was going to be easy to buy the liquor.

"Hey, how are you doing?" I said as a greeting, trying to be casual.

I had put first on the cashier counter the cans of food I was planning to eat in the coming days, some fruit, a bag of ice, orange juice, and lastly two bottles of vodka.

"I am okay, it looks like you are going to a party, or having one," she said.

Yes, it was going to be a pity party, but I didn't tell her.

"Are you studying to be a doctor?" I asked. She had a big biology book next to the register.

"No, I'm studying nursing at the community college, maybe one day I'll go to med school. But for now, I help my aunt here while I am not going to classes."

"Ah, school and work, that's a good idea."

"It's cheaper, too."

I handed over the money to pay the amount that the register was showing after the nurse-to-be had entered the price of the bottles of vodka.

I began the healing process, trying to blot out any and all thinking of Gloria. I spent Saturday drinking and sleeping; it seemed wise to me avoid a hangover at all costs, just by continuing to drink. I remember only having a can of chili the whole day. On Sunday I took my towel, my bicycle, and the bottle of orange juice with half of the contents being vodka, to the beach. I believed the spirits were going to wash away the memories of my time with Gloria and somehow elevate my mood. But they didn't, and the only thing that happened was that I made a fool of myself when I returned to Miss Ally's. She was working in her garden and looked great; she was a beautiful woman. She was wearing tight stretch shorts and a tank top; it was a hot day even if summer had ended.

"Hi Daniel, so soon back from the beach?"

"Yes, got bored."

"Sometimes it can be boring and more so on the windy days," she said as she kept pruning a camellia bush.

"Ally, you are gorgeous," I said with my slurred speech while I reached and touched her bare shoulder.

Miss Ally took my hand and pushed it away. "Don't touch me like that, Daniel. Are you drunk? Have you been drinking? And remember, for you I'm Miss Ally, not Ally."

I stepped back with my gaze down. I had made a drunken mistake. "Yes, I drank some vodka."

"Well, if you drink or not, it is not my problem. You need to behave properly while you live in this property. I don't know what happened to you, but I have a feeling that it has to do with that woman."

I listened and just looked away and stood there. Then finally I said, "Miss Ally I am sorry!" And I started to walk to my room.

"Daniel!"

"Yes?" I stopped, trying to keep my balance.

"We will talk when you sober up. Until you decide to stop drinking, I would prefer that you don't drive the truck."

"OK."

I collapsed on the bed and woke up when it was dark. I ate some slices of wheat bread, and I had a drink from the second bottle of vodka to wash it down. I had stored the vodka and the orange juice in an old cooler that I found while cleaning one of the properties of Miss Ally. There was no ice left in it, only chilled water. I took the dripping bottle, and it was half gone, I took another drink and went back to sleep. I didn't open my eyes until noon when Miss Ally was knocking at my door. She was not alone, Frank was there.

"Just a second," I said as I was trying to get up. My head was spinning, and I couldn't get my leg into the jeans. Finally, I unlocked the door and opened it an inch for them to come in, I dragged myself back to bed.

"Daniel, you look like you are in bad shape," said Frank describing the obvious.

"There is no point saying good afternoon to you. I will be back with some strong coffee," Miss Ally said, leaving me there with Frank standing in the middle of the room and looking around at the mess I had.

"May I sit down?" he asked taking the chair by the table.

"Sure."

"Daniel, what is happening? If you don't want to talk, then just tell me and I will go."

"Did Tony send you?" I asked.

"No, he doesn't know you didn't show up for work. Esther called the phone number in your records and Ally said you were not doing well. Then I decided to come on my lunch hour to check on you. Given how you looked on Thursday, Esther and I agreed that I should pay you a visit."

"Thanks Frank."

"Then what happened, Daniel?"

I looked around, and I decided to tell Frank the truth. I needed to talk with somebody, and he was the closest to a friend I had. I also I thought that, given his age, he could impart some advice.

Miss Ally came back with a pot of coffee and cups. She asked if I wanted her to go and I told her she could stay. I already had made a fool of myself the day before, so what else did I have to lose?

They listened; they asked a few questions, and I felt a little better even if my body was hurting after having drank almost two bottles of vodka and hardly eaten in the last two days.

"Daniel, you can't go on a path of self-destruction based on how you feel about Gloria, what you lived with her, how she treated you the last time you saw her, and the rest. And unless you quit your job at the mortuary, you are going to have to see Tony sooner or later. I don't think he knows you know, and I highly doubt she is going to tell him," Frank advised.

"Frank is right. You are young and this is just one experience in your life. Daniel, there is romance, love, passion and lust waiting for you out there. It seems she didn't want the same thing you wanted. Regarding Tony, even if he knows, I highly doubt that he will say anything. He can't come down from the pedestal that he and Pam have built," Ally said.

"I am sorry how I behaved yesterday; you can understand..." I trailed off.

"Apology accepted. Get some rest, eat something, drink plenty of water and sleep. There is a reason why the saying *sleep it off* exists," Ally continued, "Frank, nice meeting you. You two finish talking, I need to take care of some errands."

"Ally thank you for the hospitality," Frank replied.

Miss Ally took the empty coffee pot and the cups and left us there.

"OK champ, let's go to lunch, after all it's my lunch hour."

"Frank, you are going to be late."

"Late for what? I already took care of the customer we had over the weekend, and there isn't too much to do today. Plus, the boss is not coming back until tomorrow. Come on, take a shower and let's go out and have some lunch, my treat. But before you shower and change, let's pick up some of the mess you have here."

Frank looked around the room. The trash can was overflowing, the empty cans of beer had rolled in different directions, I had dirty clothing scattered all over. It didn't happen in the last few days, it started to happen since I meet Gloria and I became consumed by my relationship with her.

I got off the bed, and I took an empty paper grocery bag and collected everything that needed to go to the trash bin. Frank sat there supervising. When he said, "let's pick up," he didn't mean it literally, he was there for moral support only. I got to the bottle of vodka that still had some left and I went to the bathroom sink and poured out the last drop of it.

"Daniel, I am proud of you for getting rid of what was left in the bottle. I have seen too many lifeless bodies pass through the prep room due only to alcohol. I had friends that kept the nearly empty bottle because there was only one or two shots left, and later those few ounces were the first of many more. It may be a good idea to stay away from the booze for a while, maybe until you turn twenty-one. I'll take that bag; I will be waiting for you in the front."

"OK, thank you Frank, I'll be there shortly."

I decided to rip the sheets from the bed and wash them. I wanted that night to have a fresh bed for a fresh start the next day. I ran to put them in the washer and emptied the trashcan. When I came out of the bathroom, I felt I stepped into a new reality. It was interesting the difference that a little tiding up and a shower could make.

I found Miss Ally and Frank sitting on the hanging bench on the porch of Miss Ally's house. They discovered that Frank knew some members of her family.

Frank and I went to The Star café, and while it wasn't easy to eat at the beginning, I felt a little better bite after bite. Frank asked if I wanted to go to the mortuary and work the hours that I should have worked in the morning. I wasn't too sure, but I figured it couldn't be worse than what I had lived through the last four days. It was better to go and get it over with. I asked Frank not to tell Esther about things. I told her a condensed version of what happened but withheld the names. I thought it was not my place to be advertising that Tony Westfield was having an affair, and I didn't want Esther giving killer looks to Gloria if she ever showed up again. Frank told me I could be assured he was not going to say a thing, because it wasn't his story to tell. We completed some minor tasks and wrapped up.

"Well, are you ready to get out of here?" Frank asked.

"Yes, let's go. Esther, see you tomorrow."

"Daniel, take care. Remember time takes care of every-thing, and I am expert in that after all the heartbreaks I have had during my youth. I am sure I also caused a few, too. One day at a time, dear and don't worry, I won't tell Tony about today," Esther said.

"I appreciate it, thank you."

Frank dropped me off, and walking to the garage to pick up my laundry it felt as if I had left a long time ago. I found that Miss Ally had dried my sheets, and they were folded on top of the dryer. I guessed all was forgiven and we were OK. I went and finished cleaning my room, ate a can of soup and called it a day. Like Esther said, "Don't let the actions of that heartless woman destroy your life; only you can do that."

CHAPTER 19
HALLOWEEN PARTY

DEAD COLD

IT WAS SATURDAY OCTOBER 23, when I saw again the PV group. Call me sentimental, but I didn't feel at home if I wasn't going to the section of the beach where I meet the PV group, and where I used to go to with Jimmy. It just seemed like a familiar place, and those days I needed familiarity. It wasn't the best day to be at the beach, the sky had an orange yellow hue due to the smoke from the brush fires; the smoke was blown out over the ocean by the offshore Santa Ana winds. I was sitting looking at the water when I recognized some voices behind me. A group of girls and guys barefoot were running toward the hard sand, the women wearing lavender bridesmaid dresses and the men, beige khakis and white shirts. It was Val, Eve, Phillip, and other people I hadn't seen before. I got up ready to greet them.

"Daniel!" Val exclaimed.

"Hey dude!" Phillip patted me on the back.

"Hi Dan, what a surprise!" Eve said.

"Hi guys, what are you doing here?"

"One of our cousins got married and we are here for the

wedding. And Val was gracious enough to honor us with her presence," Eve said.

"Stop it Eve, I have training and tons of homework. She is giving me a hard time because I haven't been home until today. It's not the same driving from Palo Alto than it is from downtown LA," Valerie explained.

"Tell us, how are you doing?" Eve asked.

"I'm doing great, I am working, trying to keep myself out of trouble," I said.

I wasn't going to tell them how many experiences I had since they left, nor that there were days I wasn't doing that well at all. But it was the truth, I was keeping myself busy. I discovered this was the best way to forget Gloria.

"Daniel, talking about trouble, I am having a Halloween party on the thirtieth. Come over and bring friends," Phillip told me.

"Yes, Daniel you can ride with me. Valerie isn't going to come to that party because she will be studying and swimming. I will be staying at my parent's place that weekend. Come over at 6:00," Eve said.

"OK, I'll be there."

"Come on ladies, we are needed," Phillip said.

The photographer wanted to start taking the pictures of the wedding party. The bride was arriving with the groom and some of the guests. After the pictures were taken, Valerie held hands with a guy that was carrying her shoes. She turned around before leaving and waved goodbye. It was the last time I saw that beautiful smile.

I stayed there a little longer. I was happy for Val, she looked great. I had something to look forward to: a well-stocked Halloween party at Phillips, but I was going to do my best to stay away from the booze. Maybe I would make some new friends.

I had been working as much as I could with Miss Ally. She had a long list she put together after visiting all the properties. I was expecting to have a busy first week in November because she was going to have three vacancies, which meant more things for me to do. At the mortuary, Tony was spending more time in his new location, fixing it, introducing himself to the places that could send him business, and making sure it was running how he wanted to run it. It had worked well for me not seeing him around that much. Gloria hadn't been called either, because nobody needed her services or else because Frank was doing the make-up. Esther was right, I was feeling better already. I wasn't as angry as before and I didn't think of her that much.

———

Eve said as an introduction, "Girls, this is Daniel, the Invisible Man!"

"Hi! Hello! Hi Daniel!" the group answered.

Eve had invited some of her sorority sisters to the party. They were dressed as a cheerleader squad. Esther came up with the idea that I could dress like The Invisible Man. She told me all about the movie. I was wearing black gloves, a dark sport coat, fedora, and very dark sunglasses.

"Daniel, are we going to get to see your face?" one of Eve's friends asked.

"He is handsome," Eve said without even giving me time to answer.

"It's not fair; I want to see," a feisty petite girl with dark short hair and honey-colored eyes said. She got in front of me trying to part the gauze that I had wrapped around my head and neck.

"You will need to wait, I will show you, my eyes." I removed my sunglasses.

"I like them, I want to see more."

"Come on girls and guy, let's get in the car," Eve said.

"Are we going to fit? I asked, we were seven.

"Yes, you are invisible, remember." Eve said.

"I volunteer to sit on Daniel's lap," said the feisty one, and she was serious. She said this as she got on top of me.

On the way to Phillip's house everybody was laughing and talking. Soon we were arriving and there weren't as many cars as there had been for Phillip's birthday party. But inside, the party had started, and the smaller crowd seemed animated and in a festive mood. There were all types of Halloween costumes from clowns to astronauts, people wearing costumes inspired from movies like *Indiana Jones*, *Saturday Night Fever* and *E.T.*; plus, the classics like vampire, ghost, cowboy, nurse, fireman, naughty student, and all the others were also seen. And then there were two or three that didn't bother to wear something different than their regular garb. I was the only Invisible Man. The host was dressed as a Roman Emperor.

I found wearing the costume helped me overcome my shyness. I joined for a while a group of girls that were dancing. More than one tried to remove the gauze wrapping to see my face. I talked with some of Phillip's teammates from his water polo team and met more of Phillip's and Val's relatives; they had a big family. When I got hungry, I took a plate with as much food I could put on it and went to find a spot where I could eat without people seeing me parting the bandages a bit. I wanted to keep my identity secret to the end. I tried staying away from the booze, but I drank some blue punch that had a high concentration of liquor; you didn't realize how much until shortly after finishing the first cup. There was a sign next to it that said "LETHAL." I should have known, but that didn't stop me from having a second cup. I started to feel a little tipsy and decided that I didn't want to end up like the chap that was snoring with his back against the tree during Phillip's birthday bash.

I walked around and found Eve; she was animatedly talking with one of Phillip's teammates. The rest of the cheerleaders were scattered around dancing; one was swimming. I needed a break from the party though it looked like we were not leaving anytime soon. I had to wait, even if I was ready to leave. I decided to get outside the house for a little air and just walk and check out the houses on the street, when I saw a tall pixie coming out of the party walking to her car. I didn't recognize her at first because she was wearing a masquerade mask and because she was wearing a tiny dress this time.

"Hey Invisible Man, are you leaving?" she asked as she got closer, not trying to remove the bandages from my face like the other girls.

The way she walked reminded me of somebody, but I couldn't put my finger on who, or from where.

"Not yet, I need to wait for my ride," I answered.

"Well, I could give you a ride, I am going to a friend's house in Redondo Beach to continue with the Halloween weekend celebration. Would you like to join me? I will give you a ride but first you need to show me your face. That is the price to take you down the hill."

"The Invisible Man can't reveal his identity," I said staying in character.

"Come on!" she persisted.

"Only if you show me yours," I responded.

"Invisible Man, you are not in a position to negotiate, I am a fairy. I can grant a wish or two, plus I have the car keys," she said as she jingled her key ring in front of me.

"OK, but let me tell my friends I am getting a ride."

It must have been the punch or being intrigued by the mysterious woman that I thought it was a good idea to get a ride to Redondo Beach at night and be dropped off who knows where.

"Well, it seems that you are a decent guy, not everybody goes and tells their friends that they are leaving with me." She got closer and straightened the lapels of my jacket.

I ran back inside, and I had to tell one of the cheerleaders that I was leaving because I couldn't find Eve. When I asked if they had seen Eve, one of her sorority sisters pointed to the second story of the house. I ran out and the pixie was smoking a cigarette, with her back against the driver's door.

"OK, Invisible Man, come here and let me see if I know you." She dropped what was left of the cigarette and stepped on it to put it out.

She removed the sunglasses, then the fedora hat and then gently she started unwrapping the gauze. She stepped back when she saw my face without the costume.

"Oh, you are just a kid. I think I have seen you somewhere, but I don't know where. What is your name?"

"Daniel Smith."

"No, I don't know you," she stated.

"Maybe if you let me see your face, I could tell you if I know you. The way you walk reminds me of somebody, but I don't remember who."

"OK, I will let you see my face just because I am curious if we have met before. My name is Bridgette."

"The topless girl in the last party!" I blurted with excitement.

She was reaching to undo her mask, but when she heard what I said she stopped. "Yes, that was me. Let me see, ah, now I remember, you were one of the kids Phillip had let use his mother's cabana. Were you the one with the broken leg?"

"No, that was my friend Jimmy. It was not broken, he had a sprained ankle."

"OK, Daniel let's get in the car."

"And your mask?"

"There is no need to take it off, you know who I am."

We started driving downhill through the winding streets.

"Daniel, how do you know Phillip?

"I met one of his cousins at the beach and he invited my friend and I to his birthday party. How about you?"

"Let's just say Phillip happened to show up one afternoon

unexpectedly when his father thought nobody else was going to be home. I was walking out of the house when Phillip arrived. He knew who I was and the two of us made a deal."

"A deal?"

"Yes, a deal. His silence in return for a performance during his birthday party. I showed up for the end of the bargain, and he didn't tell his mother about my being there alone with his father."

I recalled what Eve and Val had said about Brigette—that she liked older men, married men.

"And today was part of the deal with Phillip?

"No. Phillip and I are on good terms. He invited me and I came. It's always good to have friends like him, and to be introduced to people like him. What school are you attending?"

"I don't go to school; I work in a mortuary and do handyman work, and gardening."

"Wow, a hard-working kid. That's a nice surprise, most of the kids in the party don't know how to earn a living, they have been spoon-fed since they were born."

"And you were not?" I said without thinking, but I knew she was from the hill.

"I like your direct style. Until I was sixteen, I was a spoiled girl, then things started to change at home and my parents kept up the appearance of having money while their bank accounts were dryer than the LA river. When I was seventeen, I started to figure out things, making a plan. At eighteen, I knew how I wanted to live my life, who I wanted to be with, and at the same time I could be making money doing something I enjoy immensely."

I didn't ask anything else. Soon we were parking in an apartment building two blocks from the water. I followed Bridgette to a unit that had the door open. There was so much smoke from everybody puffing that you could see it swirling around. The attendees were clad in costumes a bit different from the PV crowd, they were less elaborate and most of the girls were wearing sexy costumes, skimpy, sexy outfits.

"Hey, there is my pixie. Bridgette, I thought you were working tonight," the tall guy said. He was dressed as a construction worker and had muscles like a body builder. He lifted Bridgette from the ground effortlessly, and she put her legs around his waist.

"You know Mark, I work when I want. I'm allowed to have a day off. Mark, this is Daniel."

"Hey man, make yourself at home."

"Daniel is a good working kid," Bridgette added.

"Cool, there are beers over there and snacks in the kitchen," Mark said as he motioned with his arm.

"Thanks!" I said loudly because with the music and everybody talking, you couldn't hear a thing.

Mark took Bridgette's hand and pushed through people to make it to a corner of the crowded living room. They went to talk with a couple. I went to the kitchen and there was a display of cookies and brownies. I didn't see any snacks, just desserts. I took a large brownie; it tasted a little different from the ones my mother baked, I thought they may have been from a mix or from the store. The crowd didn't seem like they cooked from scratch. I took a second bite, and I didn't care for the flavor, but I ate the whole thing since I was hungry. I also pocketed a good-sized cookie.

I walked around saying "Hi" to people and making small talk. It could not have been more than thirty minutes when things turned interesting. A door of one of the bedrooms opened and a girl half-dressed came out searching for Mark. He rushed to the room and just as quickly as he went in, two guys came out carrying a guy that was passed out and it looked like foam was coming out of his mouth. The girl was running behind them trying to put on a denim jacket.

"Don't ever set foot on my place again if you don't know how to control your intake," screamed Mark.

Everybody was silent.

As soon as they walked out of the door, everybody continued enjoying the party as if nothing had happened. I started to feel lightheaded and felt I needed some air. I walked out of the apartment and saw a woman wearing a little red riding hood outfit on the sidewalk smoking a cigarette. I went and talked to her.

"Hey, taking a break from the party?"

"Yes, I needed some fresh air. I'm tired of all this drama, every party is the same. Who did you come with, I haven't seen you," she asked.

"I came with Mark's girlfriend, Bridgette."

She stopped smoking and let the smoke out of her lungs at once, in a hurry. "I'm Mark's girlfriend. Bridgette is just his *friend*, but I am starting to doubt that."

"Bridgette gave me a ride from a party in PV. I don't really know her," I said quickly in case there was bad blood between them. I didn't want her to think I was also Bridgette's friend.

"Yeah, you don't look like one of her *friends.*"

"What happened to those guys?"

"What always happens at Mark's parties, they mixed stuff; or they had too much booze, pills, brownies, and the rest."

"Brownies? What's in the brownies?"

"You know, some herb. Don't tell me you never have tried a *brownie?*"

"No. That is why it tasted differently."

"Yes, don't worry you will feel back to normal in no time."

"Have you eaten one of the brownies?" I asked. She didn't look like she had been drinking or eating brownies.

"No, I am three months sober. I'm tired of all this. I arrived in Los Angeles with a dream of becoming a singer, and I ended up partying way too much and finally discovered I can't even sing. Maybe if I had played an instrument, I could have had a better chance to succeed in the entertainment industry. Now I work in a medical office as an assistant. My next move is to leave this, get out of this cycle of party life that I don't enjoy anymore." She pointed with what was left of the cigarette to the condo complex.

"Is the guy they dragged out of there going to be fine?" I asked.

"I hope. Usually, they just drop them outside the ER, or a fire station, and then they run away. A few weeks later they are all back here doing the same thing."

"Wow, what type of friends are they?"

"I don't know where Bridgette found you, but you are kind of innocent, that is cute. Do you want to go and get a soda? There are no more sodas left. I don't think there were any to start with. There is a little market around the corner."

"OK," I said, putting my hands in my pockets and following her.

"Isn't it fitting?" she said as we passed Bridgette's car.

"What?"

"That Bridgette's car is an Escort, just like her."

When I heard the word escort, everything that Bridgette had said made sense. I thought she only liked old guys, but she had made a business out of her preference. Before I could say anything, Mark came out looking for Little Red Riding Hood.

"Hey babe, where are you going? I've been looking for you."

"I guess, I should go back in. See you!" she said resignedly and returned to the wild party.

"Thanks guys, I'm going to get going."

Mark and his girlfriend waved, and I kept walking. I was turning the corner when I saw a cobalt blue sports car going at a ridiculous speed. The driver had ignored a four-way stop sign. Luckily nobody was crossing the street, but seconds later I heard squealing tires trying to grip the payment, and the sounds of the brakes trying to stop the car. Then there was the sound of a hard impact. Even in my jumbled mind I thought the blue car had hit another car. I thought about turning around to head towards the beach and start walking back to Manhattan via the streets closer to the water, but instead I kept walking towards the intersection where the sound of the brakes had come. As I got closer, I could see people coming out of the apartment buildings and houses nearby. They were running towards the crash. I kept walking; I was within a block from the accident. Some people were running back into their houses to call for help, others were surrounding the car. There was a teenager screaming with her hands to her face. A few young kids came out of their houses just to be taken back in by their parents trying to prevent them from having a memory of gore and death. I could see that the car had lost control in the intersection after hitting a white car. Somebody was saying that the sports car ignored the stop sign and hit the white car hard enough to spin it around.

I stood there looking at the scene. I was still very wasted. My brain was affected by the brownie and the cups of the lethal punch at Phillip's party. I was getting closer and closer to the epicenter of the commotion. The scene was unreal. A few people couldn't take the scene, and they went back inside. An ambulance was driving by when they saw the accident, and stopped to help, or maybe by luck they were close by and got the call. I was sure the ambulance had arrived without the sirens or the lights on. Somehow, they managed to get the driver out of the car. The other body was mangled inside the car; it had taken all the impact against a cement light pole. One of the paramedics made a signal that the passenger was gone.

I was in the front row seeing how they were trying to stabilize the driver. He was unconscious for what to me seemed like a few minutes, but then again, my sense of time and space was affected. I thought the individual was going to make it. They had ripped open his t-shirt, there was blood on one of his hands. The guy could not be older than twenty-five. In an instant, things changed. He was turning pale every second that went by, he looked like he was sweating profusely. His face glistened with sweat. He was pale, like marble. There was no color at all to the lifeless waxen face. They kept pounding away regardless. One of the paramedics said, "we are losing him." It seemed their efforts intensified; they were still trying to resuscitate him, just in case.

The firemen and the police arrived. Two firemen ran to check on the people in the white car. They seemed okay, shaken but okay. The police started putting flares around the area; they didn't have to tell people to step back, we had kept our distance even if I got as close as I could.

More ambulances arrived, there were so many lights flashing. A fireman took a white sheet to cover the passenger side of the car and after a few minutes there were blood stains on the sheet. I stood there wondering if those bodies would be heading to one of Tony's mortuaries or if I was going to go and pick them up from the hospital or the morgue. I was not feeling well at the sight of the lifeless bloodied body in the mangled car. And the dead driver lying on the ground was getting to me. But at the same time, it was exciting. A woman started crying and a few people started praying while the paramedics persisted, still giving the young victim CPR. Finally, they looked at each other and they put a sheet on top of him. He was very dead, dead cold.

As the paramedic stood up, the crowd was in complete silence. Some stood there shocked from having seen somebody die in front of their eyes. Others turned around and headed back to their residences.

The air seemed damper and cooler, a somber breeze took over the place. Death had passed through, leaving pain and a chill behind.

I started walking. I had seen death pass in front of me.

There was a bus stop on the next corner, and I sat there resting my spinning head in my hands. I got onto the next bus that came to a hissing stop. I thought that wherever the bus was going was fine with me, I wanted to be away from the accident scene as soon as possible.

I leaned my head against the window. Only few people were riding the bus at that hour. The bus driver asked me if I had seen the accident. I said "No, but it seemed a car was going too fast. At least they only killed themselves."

The driver nodded his head in agreement and said, "Good, they were asking for it." He didn't sugar-coat his opinion about the recklessness. I was sure he had seen his share of speeding cars.

The lights of the street were glowing block after block until the bus arrived in San Pedro, close to the Port of Los Angeles.

"Where are you going, man?" the bus driver asked me when there was only me and one other guy in the back of the bus.

"To Manhattan Beach," I said.

"Manhattan Beach? You took the wrong bus. You needed to be on the other side of the street. At this hour there are no more buses leaving from here in that direction. You are going to have to either go back walking or take a bus to downtown L.A. and then the route that takes you near the airport. You should have asked me! Look here comes the bus for downtown." The driver took the radio and told the driver of the downtown bus that he had a passenger for him. "Brother, I usually I don't do this, but I don't want to leave you stranded in the middle of nowhere. He will take you to downtown and tell you what to do."

"Thank you!" Luckily, I still had enough money on me to pay the fare. I stepped off and the bus pulled away, groaning as its motor revved.

I ran across the street. I didn't wait for the proper way, there was no traffic. I got on this new bus.

"Carl tells me you are lost, that you want to go to Manhattan Beach. I am going to take you to a stop. You will need to take two or three buses depending on the morning schedule."

"Thank you, I appreciate it," I said truthfully.

There were just a handful of people; I sat in the first seat close to the driver. I didn't want to miss my exit, but it was miles and miles before we got to the stop. I dozed once or twice. We crossed paths with two or three vehicles with sirens and flashing lights; one was a highway patrol. Later an ambulance and a firetruck shot by. Every flashing light reminded me the crash scene and the lifeless body on the pavement.

"Hey kid, this is the stop. I am going to drop you off. You need to take the next bus going in that direction. Stay there, don't move because this area is sketchy. Good luck kid."

I was still really smashed. The high seemed to be long lasting. I got out of the bus, there were some old buildings and warehouses mainly. I didn't have any idea where I was. But if I took a bus in the direction the bus driver said, I was going to be heading towards the ocean and that to me sounded like the right direction. I sat there for a while. It was quiet, and it felt cooler. I didn't know if it was the temperature, or the hangover from the shock of seeing somebody die. I was hoping the bus wasn't going to take too long to come by, but it did take a long time.

Then I saw three guys walking on the other side of the street. I was hoping they were going to go into one of the buildings. Or if they were passing by, just to ignore my presence. But they didn't. They crossed the street and walked straight towards the bus stop.

"Hey kid! What is a kid with a nice jacket doing here?"

"Yeah, were you in a wedding and got lost?"

"I am waiting for the bus," I said as forthrightly as I could.

They laughed and got closer.

"Boy, you may need to wait until sunrise for the bus. By the way, can you spare us some cash?"

I didn't see the point in arguing and took the few bills and coins I had in my pocket and gave them to them. I had left the wallet in my room; not that my wallet had more money in it.

"Are you kidding me? A kid like you should be carrying plenty more cash."

"That is all the money I have."

The shorter of the guys, signaled the other two to search me. They pulled at my jacket; they got their hands into the pockets of my jeans.

"What have we here? A bandage, and a pair of glasses. Oops!" The taller said while he dropped the glasses and stepped on them.

"Hey, hey, he may be needing these bandages, let's not toss them," said the short one.

Without any warning, the tallest punched me in the face. I fell and they were ready to start kicking me when flashing lights illuminated the street and the loud banging of a metal pipe against a trash can broke the silence of the night. A scream could be heard just around the corner. The guys started to run. My head was spinning—I could see an older man dragging a pipe, approaching me and a tow truck pulling over. A guy with tattooed arms stepped out of the truck.

"Hey, are you okay, are you okay?" the old man said. He looked like he lived on the streets and was shaking constantly.

"Yes," I said as I was trying to get up.

"Come on, you can't stay lying there," the tow truck driver said as he helped me to stand up.

"Nice, nice jacket kid. I made them run, and fast. They, they were afraid," the old man stuttered on as he did a little dance.

"What a hell are you doing *here*?" the tow truck driver asked.

"I took the wrong bus, and I was waiting for another to take me to the airport. I need to get back to Manhattan."

"Manhattan Beach, I want to go to Manhattan Beach," the old man cackled.

"Look, I can take you to a bus stop closer to the airport, and in a better area. Or you can stay here, they may come back, and you will not be as lucky. You were lucky they didn't take out their blades."

"I would appreciate it sir," I said, still bewildered.

"Hey kid, do you have money for a warm meal, a, a hot meal?" mustered the old man.

"No, those guys cleaned me out. But here, you can have my coat. Thank you for helping me."

I took off my coat and handed it to the old guy and extended my hand to give him a handshake. He smiled, showing the few teeth, he had left.

The tow truck driver went to his rig, brought back a banana, and something wrapped in a tin foil. "Here, good man, a homemade burrito."

"Thank you, thank you. Good night!" replied the old guy. He had already put my coat on and settled into it. It was too big for him, but you could see it made him feel much better. He put the burrito and the banana in the pockets of the jacket, dragged the metal pipe behind him and disappeared, turning the corner.

"OK. My name is Ricardo, let's get out of here."

"I'm Daniel. Thanks for your help."

We got in the truck, started driving, and got on the freeway almost right away. I learned Ricardo was coming back from dropping a car in Pico Rivera and was heading back to Santa Monica. He was happy to have somebody to talk with and I was happy I was getting closer to the part of the city I was familiar with. My cheekbone was hurting;

Ricardo recommended putting a steak on it and then eating it. We laughed.

Then he got off the freeway, and I don't know where he dropped me off, but it was a nicer part of town. I only had to wait five minutes for a bus to get there. It seemed the sky was changing color, the darkness was getting lighter. The bus arrived and the driver let me ride for free when I told him I was just mugged. He told me the closest he was going to where I wanted to get to was to the corner of Sepulveda and Imperial. I told him that was perfect. I didn't care if I had to walk. Soon we were passing the airport. I could see a plane taking off, and at that moment I decided it was time to go back home. I got off the bus and I felt relief by stepping on a sidewalk and setting my foot in El Segundo.

CHAPTER 20
GET UP AND GET OUT

I DECIDED to walk the last four miles to my place at Miss Ally's. Four miles—almost the same distance from the site of the accident to my place. I could have walked them easily; instead, I took a bus to nowhere and ended up having the detour of my life.

After taking a bus without any destination in mind, and experiencing Los Angeles in a way I hadn't expected, I was ready to get to my bed and sleep all day Sunday. I was tired. The sleepless night, the encounter with the three ruffians, and seeing somebody die up-close had taken a toll on me.

Without a jacket over my shoulders, I felt the cold of the early morning, at least that was what I thought. But now I think it may have been the hangover kicking in, and the sleepless night that was affecting my body temperature. After all, it was Southern California where the mornings are not cold. I was ready to collapse on the next bus bench if somebody had offered me two or three newspapers or a nice cardboard box for warmth.

It was almost 7:00 a.m. I was walking south along Sepulveda in El Segundo. It looked like a ghost town; it was desolate at that hour on a Sunday morning. Everybody that was usually there getting to work in one of the aerospace companies or at the air force base was comfortably sleeping at home. I felt like I had stepped in into an episode of the *Twilight Zone*, like I was the only one left on the face of the earth. With my hands in the pockets of my jeans, the collar of my shirt up, trying to keep the breeze from reaching my throat, and maybe a bruise on my face, I just kept putting one foot in front of the other.

I remember passing a pancake house that was already open. I wanted so bad to go in and rest and have a hot coffee, but I didn't have money. I looked inside and there were airport workers in one booth laughing, a police officer at another table with a big stack of pancakes in front of him. I kept walking. Why prolong my return to Miss Ally. I was standing shivering, waiting for the light to change to cross the street when I heard somebody behind me.

"Hey buddy, rough night?"

It was the attendant of the gas station on the corner where I was waiting to cross the street. I shook my head, I felt like my whole body was shaking.

"How about a cup of coffee?"

"You bet. Thanks!"

"OK, follow me," said the guy with a broom in his hand.

I had missed that he was sweeping. I followed him to the little store area of the gas station. He was heavily built, wearing a uniform and a baseball cap with the logo of the gas station. There was a red flannel hanging from the back pocket of his pants. He wore glasses with significant power—the lenses were thick. The sign on the door still said closed, but the door was already opened. The aroma of fresh brewed coffee impregnated the small space, it felt warm in there.

"Here you go. My name is John," he said pointing at the name on his uniform.

"Thank you, John, my name is Daniel."

The cup of coffee immediately warmed my hands. I felt I

could easily make it to my bed and tomorrow think how I was going to get back to my parents' farm.

"Hey, too much partying last night? Or do you work at the airport?"

"Yes and no."

John gave me a look, trying to discern if he should keep the conversation going, or just ask me to take the coffee and head out, so he could finish sweeping around the gas pumps. I thought, better to give an answer with more words, after all, he just had showed me some kindness by offering me a cup of hot coffee that I desperately needed.

"No, I don't work at the airport. Last night was a hell of a night. I could have gone from Redondo to Manhattan where I am staying, but instead, I took a bus to San Pedro and then one to somewhere in downtown L.A. Three guys took my money and punched me in the face. A homeless guy and a tow truck driver rescued me from the thieves, and I got a ride to a bus stop from the tow truck driver. Then a bus left me on the corner of Imperial Highway and Sepulveda. And all this after seeing people die."

"Die?"

"Yes, somebody going too fast, running lights and ignoring stops. One died with the impact, the other died on the pavement. He was dead cold. Pale. Lifeless. Standing there, for some reason, I saw the last four months of my life shoot by in front of my eyes. The stupor caused by the spirits and a big brownie from the two crazy Halloween parties I attended lasted quite a while. I walked and I sat at a bus stop to try to make sense of what I had just seen and what I have been doing here in California, when a bus stopped, and I just got on it. Then I got robbed in downtown Los Angeles, and here I am."

"Hey Daniel, you did have a hell of a night. I was wondering about the bruise on your face. Just put a steak on it. It will help, and if doesn't you can eat it. Would you like a donut? They are from yesterday, but they are still good. I like to pick them up from Randy's Donuts on my way here."

"Yes, I'll have one. Thanks John."

"You look like a good kid. Go home and get a good day's rest. Tomorrow everything will be fine." John took the broom, and I knew it was time for me to keep walking.

"Yes, tomorrow will be a new day. Thanks, this was what I needed for the last few miles that separate me from my bed."

There was a gentle knock on the door. I saw the alarm clock and it was almost five in the afternoon. I had slept almost ten hours. There was one more knock on the door, this time harder.

"Daniel, are you OK?" It was Miss Ally.

"Yes, Miss Ally. Just a second." I got up trying to find my jeans and putting them on as quickly as I could.

"Hi Miss Ally!"

"Oh, what happened to *you*?" She looked at me and looked at the room.

"I went to two parties last night…"

"No, no what happened, you have a bruise on your face."

"I was robbed, it's a long story. I'm ready to go home."

"Wow, that's interesting. Are you seriously planning on leaving?"

"Yes, I want to get out of here soon."

"Well, if you are up to it, would you like to join me to have some Mexican food in El Segundo?"

I hesitated, I didn't want to spend money now that I had decided I wanted to get home. I was going to need every single penny.

"Daniel, I am inviting you."

"OK, thank you, Miss Ally. I just need a moment to make myself presentable," I said.

"Yes, I would not like to be seen with an eighteen-year-old

that looks like a hobo, or a wild rockstar after a night of debauchery. If somebody knows about rock stars and debauchery, it's me, but that was long time ago. Those were the days of just waking up in some hotel on the Sunset strip, sometimes in a suite, sometimes in the most dilapidated room of Hollywood. Never mind. Enough of my stories. Get ready," Ally said.

It was the first time that Miss Ally had shared something about her life with me. Suddenly her personality had changed from the serious landlord lady to a happy and funny auntie. And just like that, my landlady turned around with the flair of an old grand dame of the silent movie era, and went down the steps, crossing the patio between her house and the garage.

I got ready, and in fifteen minutes I was knocking on her front door, in my Sunday finest to go have Mexican food.

"There you are, looking like a distinguished young gentleman." There was a mischievous smile on her lips.

She stepped out of the door and made sure it was locked. She had her wallet and a key ring that I hadn't seen before. We took her truck and went to a little Mexican place on Main Street, called La Paz, which meant The Peace. I liked the name because I needed some peace and tranquility after Saturday night.

Between guacamole, flautas and fajitas I told Miss Ally everything that had happened. She listened to my story attentively.

"Tell me Daniel, do you really want to leave Manhattan Beach and go back to Wisconsin?"

"Yes, I don't think the city is for me."

"I understand you, I enjoy immensely the ocean breeze and I don't know if I will ever be able to live away from the ocean. But I do know I don't want to live forever in the city. Sometimes we must do things that we don't really want, because in the long run they are better for us."

"Miss Ally, you are not planning to move from Manhattan, are you?"

"No. Well, not tomorrow, but for a while I have been considering if I want to spend all my adult years here in the concrete jungle. I want to live in a smaller place where I don't have to drive miles and miles to get out of town and get to unspoiled nature."

"Do you want to move near a forest?"

"Not necessarily. What made you say that?"

"You are talking about wanting to be close to nature. I thought you may want to be close to trees and wild animals."

"No, I don't want to be *that* close to nature. But now that you mention trees, one of the places I'd like to move to is the Central Coast. There are so many small communities near the water and surrounded by trees. Yes, I can see myself walking on a crisp foggy morning listening to the waves crash on the shore, then going to a little local market, getting my produce, and having a picnic under the canopy of a tree. You know, if William Randolph Hearst built his castle there, I will build my beach shack and enjoy the same scenery he did."

"Sounds like you have a plan, Miss Ally. But wouldn't you be alone, away from your friends?" I asked.

"For true friendship there is no distance. Half of the people you think are friends are just acquaintances; they wouldn't move a finger to help, or be with you in a time of need. I have closer friends from my childhood in North Dakota. Most of these women here are witches that just want your friendship because of your connections."

"I see. Then when you are planning to make your big move, Miss Ally?"

"Oh, I don't know. Next spring I will go exploring the Central Coast."

"Would you like something else?" the waitress asked. She had the check ready.

"No, just the check, please," Ally responded.

"Then when are you leaving, Daniel?"

"Maybe in two weeks. Tomorrow I am telling Tony. I have seen enough of Los Angeles; I have met people and have had so many things happen in the last four months, but I feel it's time to go home and figure out what I want to do with my life. I can't be here just drifting day after day, waiting for something to happen."

"Well, I have an idea for you to get back."

She paid the check, and we got out of the restaurant, but instead of going back to the truck we started walking down the street until we stopped in front of a hobby shop. Miss Ally unlocked the gate that opened to a narrow pathway leading to the back of the property. We crossed a patio and then she opened the door to a garage. Inside the garage there was an old black Chrysler Imperial.

"Daniel if you are serious about leaving town, you can leave in this car, it will be yours."

"Miss Ally this is too much, I can't accept."

"Daniel, I'm going to tell you a story. This car belonged to my best friend. When she died, she left the car to me. I haven't driven it since the day I drove it to park it here. She was a happy and talented woman. She was trying to get into acting, but she met a man and fell in love. He ended up being married. She got depressed, started drinking and one day she mixed the alcohol with pills and never woke up. She was pregnant. If she were alive, her kid would have been a few years older than you. You don't know it, but I worked in Hollywood for a while. In my years there I saw so many people ready to leave one day, and the next day they were back in their routine. I know people that made it out of town just to turn back and give it *one more try*. And guess what, years later they are still here trying. They had become part of the unsatisfied Angelenos that never have found what they came looking for. Some, they may have already forgotten what brought them to Los Angeles. If you are serious about leaving, the car is yours. This car could have driven away my friend with her unborn child. Now, this car can drive you away from all this."

Miss Ally's voice broke down when she said "my friend and her unborn child," then she smiled and showed me the keys to the car.

———

The twelve days before my departure went fast. On Monday, November 1st I told Tony I was giving my notice—the thirteenth was going to be my last day at the mortuary. He didn't react, he just said, "fine." He showed some emotion when I asked him for the money for the ticket I didn't use when I changed my plans and stayed. He gave me a look; I didn't back down and I reminded him of his agreement with my parents when he made the call to ask them if I could help with the dogs. He looked around. I knew he wasn't used to somebody trying to negotiate with him, then he said, "fine, Esther will give you a check." I thanked him and walked out of his office smiling.

The following week Frank informed Tony of his intention of not going back to work after Thanksgiving; he was finally retiring.

On my last day at the mortuary, I went with Frank and Esther to have lunch. It was a nice sendoff they gave me. When I walked out of the funeral home for the last time, I knew one thing for sure: I did not want to work in that industry ever again.

Miss Ally had hired a gardener by Tuesday, and I didn't work any days in November doing the yards. She wanted me to focus on getting her vacant apartments ready. She said that way I could enjoy a few afternoons on the beach if I wanted. I went to my favorite place in Manhattan near the pier. I did want to spend more time at the beach.

The last day I went to get ready the remaining empty apartments, I cut two white roses and some red camellias from the garden of the property. I stopped at the little neighborhood market and gave the flowers to the cashier, the one that had sold me the vodka when I wanted to drown myself in liquor. She had a different book next to the register. She smiled when she saw me, and when I handed her the flowers she was overjoyed. I told her I was leaving town, and we wished each other well.

The last Thursday in Manhattan, I asked Miss Ally if I could use her truck to take my bicycle to Jimmy's house. I could have brought it with me if I took it apart, but I was not too much of a bicycle guy back home. I knew my friend would enjoy it more than me.

I drove to Jimmy's place, knocked on the door, and Jimmy's father opened it.

"May I help you?" he said with a newspaper in hand.

"Hi, my name is Daniel. I have this bicycle for Jimmy."

Jimmy's dad looked at me and then at the bicycle. Jimmy's mother came to the door.

"He is bringing something for Albert," Jimmy's dad said to his wife. He smiled and turned around leaving Mrs. Jones to deal with me.

"Hi Daniel, come in."

"Thank you, but I can't. I need to go back to my place. I'm going back home, and I want to give my bicycle to Jimmy."

"I am sure he is going to love it. We wanted to buy him one after his was stolen, but he always said no."

"Mrs. Jones, your husband said Albert, not Jimmy," I queried.

"Ah, you didn't know that Jimmy is Albert James Jones. Since he was a toddler, he didn't like to be called Al or Albert. When he could say his name, he always said that it was Jimmy. Only his father calls him Albert.

"Please give my regards to Jimmy and here is my address back home," I said, handing over a slip of paper.

I said goodbye to Mrs. Jones and walked to the truck. I turned to see the Westfield residence. I didn't intend to say goodbye, but I saw Consuelo leaving and I ran to say hello and goodbye.

"Consuelo, Consuelo!"

"Oh Danny!"

"Consuelo, I'm leaving tomorrow."

"Thank goodness you are leaving. The city is a crazy place, just like this house." She pointed at the Westfield's place and then held my arm, and we walked to the corner.

"It has been weird lately; mister Tony is sleeping in the guest room since the day somebody dropped off a cassette of a rock band called the Windows."

"You mean the Doors?"

"Yes, there was a note with the cassette. Mrs. Pam was furious. I don't know what happened later because I had to leave, but the next day mister Tony was sleeping in the guest room."

I had an inkling of what may have happened, but I was not going to share it with Consuelo.

"Oh Danny, I don't want to work with them anymore, they are always angry, you can feel their bad, bad energy. Leslie has been grounded for a while and she is as miserable as her parents. The doggies and I are happy when nobody is at home. I'm glad you are leaving. Goodbye Daniel, my ride is here."

Consuelo gave me a strong hug, opened the door of the little compact sedan, and left. I didn't know how she got to work, I guess she carpooled. I walked by the Westfield house and turned to look at the window of the guest room, and I smiled. Somehow, I was pleased to know that Tony was in purgatory for his fling with Gloria.

———

I spent my last Friday in Manhattan Beach packing my belongings and cleaning the room. Miss Ally had taken the car to her mechanic, and it was ready for me to drive it home. I sat with a road atlas and traced a route to take, then I talked it over with Miss Ally. She recommended a few places to see on my way back home. She said that if I was going to drive, why not see some landmarks. She insisted that one of my stops be the Grand Canyon in Arizona. I said I wanted to drive through Las Vegas, and she shook her head. She asked me to avoid Las Vegas altogether. She said I should instead stop by The Hoover Dam. I decided to accept the recommendation, and I scratched out Las Vegas from my itinerary. I added the new route: exiting Highway 17 to 164 and then taking 95 toward The Hoover Dam. After that I was going to stop at the Grand Canyon and spend the night there before I headed to a ranch near Santa Fe, New Mexico. Miss Ally had spoken with one of her friends, and he was going to give me work for a week. That way I got more money for gas, and I could split up the long trip. After the week in Santa Fe, I was going to head north to Pueblo, Denver, Nebraska, Iowa, and finally home.

It was Friday night; my backpack and suitcase were by the door. The nonperishable food for the trip was in a supermarket paper bag on the table. Miss Ally had in her refrigerator sandwiches, yogurt, three-bean salad and potato salad that I was going to take in the cooler. My plan was to get up and get out town before sunrise.

Lying on the bed, I looked around the room. It was my last night there. In more or less ten days I was going to be waking up in my room at home, just a few days before Thanksgiving. I was looking forward to spending the holiday with my parents and Daisy. I went to sleep with an image of my family in my mind.

At six I was ready to hit the road. Miss Ally was standing outside her kitchen door.

"Okay Daniel, I will be expecting a call when you get to Santa Fe, and one when you get home. Also, I don't want to see you here in a week, a month, or a year. Go and explore the rest of the world. You already lived in Los Angeles, and once is enough."

"Yes, Miss Ally, and thank you for everything," I choked up a bit.

"Give me back the key to your room. Come here and give me a hug," she said. This time I gave her a significant, full-body hug I felt was due.

I was ready to get in the car when Miss Ally had something else to say. "Daniel, remember you don't have to live by the beach to enjoy the sea breeze."

I smiled and got in the car. I started the motor and slowly drove off Miss Ally's driveway, merging into the first street of many, making my way to the freeway. By 8:00 a.m. I was gaining altitude in the Cajón pass. I had left behind Manhattan Beach, and Los Angeles County. I was a driving a car that I was not expecting to have, with memories of almost five months, new clothes in the trunk, and rolls of films to develop. As the car was slowing down going uphill, I realized that what was most important at that moment was that I was leaving behind Los Angeles alive, and I knew I could make my dreams a reality. I kept driving and I didn't look back.

The End

EPILOGUE

MISS ALLY WAS RIGHT, you always have choices even if it seems you don't. I found opportunities after I left my dreams of living by the beach behind in Los Angeles. I'm not a farmer, and I didn't go to college, but I found my own way in life.

I had time to think during the days I spent on my trip from California to Wisconsin. In the solitude of hours on the open road, I decided I didn't belong in the city, I didn't belong on the farm, and I was going to find something to do. During my time in Manhattan, it became obvious that I like to fix things, I like working with tools. After having spent two weeks on a ranch in New Mexico helping Miss Ally's friend, MJ Roberts, I was certain that farm work wasn't for me, even if I excelled at it. MJ wanted to hire me to help him on one of his ranches—he had two ranches in Texas besides the one in New Mexico. I politely declined and headed home; I had learned my lesson of accepting job offers just to avoid returning home, just because I thought the grass was greener somewhere else than on the farm.

When I got home, my mom came running out of the house to welcome me with tears in her eyes, tears of joy. Daisy punched me on the arm as a greeting and said, "Welcome home, brother!" I ran to the barn to greet my father, and the old man gave me an unexpected hug, it was one of the few times he showed some emotion. He said, "Son, welcome home, it's good you are back."

The next day Mom prepared a feast. After dinner, I presented to my dad half of my earnings. I wanted to help with some of the overdue maintenance; it was not a fortune, but it was something. I clearly remember his face when I handed over the bills. At first, he didn't want to accept them, it took some convincing for the old man to put them in his pocket. I told him it was the least I could do after having left him with all the work for months. My parents were amazed at how much money I made by selling the paintings that Miss Ally had given me. Mother liked the painting I kept, and to this day, it's proudly displayed in her living room.

After a few days, I got back into the rhythm of things on the farm, the waking up early, the working all day non-stop and enjoying the wonderful home cooked meals. For the first time I felt a sense of accomplishment in what I did on the farm, knowing that my efforts helped my family. My efforts benefited us, not somebody else's business.

Carson and Matt were ecstatic when I went to pick them up in my Chrysler Imperial. Carson kept saying, "No way! No way somebody gave you a car!" Matt walked around the car inspecting it. We went out for a burger, and they wanted to know everything about my months in California. I remember the feeling of satisfaction that for the first time I was able to splurge on a burger, fries, soda and a piece of pie, and still have money in my pockets.

I have travelled the world and experienced places I never imagined I would when I was just a kid in the summer of 1982. I didn't win the lottery or get a big bag of money due to an inheritance—no wealthy relatives left me a trust fund. I have worked hard and enjoyed life.

It was the last week of 1982, and I was walking around downtown when I met one of my high school teachers, good old Henry Anderson. He was coming out of the hardware store. He was the auto shop teacher, and he asked me how my first semester at college went. I informed him my absence was not because I went to college but because I had been working in a mortuary in sunny Southern California.

Mr. Anderson listened to the highlights of my brief stay in the Golden State. At the end of our chat, he asked me if I would like to help him rebuild a tractor engine that had been sitting in his barn for a while. I accepted his offer. During the hours I spent with him, he introduced me to the idea of technical careers after I told him I didn't want to be a farmer, and I didn't see myself going to college. He explained I didn't need to go for years to a university to make a decent living. I took his advice and visited a community college and a technical school. Soon I enrolled in a welding program. I took every course I could. Over the years I became certified for underwater welding. I worked on oil rigs for a while, went to Asia and the Middle East; I became a contractor for big construction companies. I got to see countries I never had imagined, like Japan and Kuwait. I spend a few years in Alaska.

If you are wondering what happened to the farm, well, the farm is still there but my cousin Andrew is working it. You see, his father lost their farm after some mishaps and a gambling problem. When my father died, it was clear to me that I wasn't going to go back to the farm, but I didn't want to sell it, a sentiment shared with Mom and Daisy. Yes, even if I didn't want to farm the land, I was attached to it. On the other hand, my brother was eager to get rid of the place, a farm that had been in the family for over a century. Paul sold his share to me; Mother was unhappy about Paul selling it to me instead of just transferring the title to Mom. I believe that was the moment when she realized or accepted how much Paul had changed.

After fifteen years working all over the States and overseas, I decided to go back to my hometown. It was my lucky week when I arrived home because Bill T. was selling his mechanic shop. I never intended to set up a welding shop in town, I was used to working on big projects or underwater. Having just been in town for a few days, I decided to buy his business, it was an ideal situation, I didn't have to build a clientele, I just needed to keep the current customers happy and find ways to gain a few more. I managed the business and took automotive classes to refresh what I had learned in high school and gain knowledge that could help me better manage the business.

After having a steady business, it was time to start a family. I married Mary Lou, who I had only spoken with a few times in high school. She was a down-to-earth and intelligent young lady in high school, and when I came back to town, Mary Lou was still down-to-earth, intelligent, beautiful and single. We have two daughters and two boys; my mother adores them.

Through the years I have kept in touch with Jimmy, or should I say Eddy. I never have called him Eddy or Edward; for me he will always be Jimmy Jones. The Christmas I returned home I received a postcard from Jimmy. I noticed the postcard was thick and after inspecting it I realized there were two postcards. I took a blade and gently separated them. Jimmy had glued a postcard of the Manhattan Beach Pier with a postcard of a suntanned beauty clad in a tiny red bikini and wearing a Santa's hat, lying on the sand with a backdrop of palm trees and the Hollywood sign.

He went to do everything that he said was going to do, and of course in record time. He got a degree on electrical engineering, a masters in aero physics and a doctorate from Caltech in

Pasadena. Once on my way to Asia, I had a long layover, and Jimmy picked me up at the airport to go and have a burger in a fast-food place just a few blocks from the runways. He showed me all the badges he had hanging from his neck, but discreetly hidden in his shirt pocket. When I asked him what he did for a living, he said "If I told you, I would need to kill you. Top-secret." I didn't ask or try to get a little more info. Jimmy got married before I did. I went to his wedding, and I got to see Wendy; she said Pam and Tony divorced, and after the divorce the family moved from Manhattan Beach—Pam had enough of Tony's indiscretions. Megan went to work for NASA. Leslie married a rich kid, and while she became an interior designer, the only house she decorated was her apartment after getting married. Her marital bliss didn't last, and she never recovered from the divorce. Last I heard, she worked for Tony and in a department store, selling rugs.

Miss Ally became a friend of my mother after coming to visit us in the fall of 1983. She decided to take some time off and drive through the country to explore places to retire far away from the city. She found her spot when she met Lucas, a winemaker from the California Central Coast. And until this day she lives between Cambria and Paso Robles in a beautiful house in the middle of the vineyards. How do I know all this? Well, my mom still is in touch with Miss Ally.

Last year when I took the family to Southern California to do all the touristy activities—amusement parks, landmarks and a baseball game—we spent an afternoon with Jimmy and his family. He invited us to a barbecue at his house; he lives in the place he grew up; the house doesn't look like the one I saw when I spent the summer in Manhattan Beach. Jimmy gave it a major facelift; he exclaimed how everything was removed down to the studs, leaving the skeleton as a canvas for an architect to redesign the boring looking house into a modern property in a vibrant beach town. His house was not the only one that looked different. Most of the modest homes had been given a makeover or just torn down. Jimmy mentioned that some call Manhattan the "Beverly Hills of the Beach." Real estate has increased in value and the modest homes I remember have been replaced by mansions. After having eaten, we walked with our families to the beach and crossed the place where Metlox Pottery was. Now there is a shopping center, a hotel and a parking structure there. It was something else to walk down Manhattan Beach Boulevard and see the pier.

As we approached the strand and the salty breeze hit my face, I had flashbacks of those days when I was sitting on the sand thinking that I had found paradise. I smiled, just recalling how I thought I was destined to live there. But my bittersweet first love, seeing the victims from the crash after Phil's party, and the unforgettable memory of being attacked on some desolate street in downtown L.A. put an end to my daydreaming. That eventful night made me face the reality of the big city. But the bad memories faded away as soon as I saw my kids running towards the waves, and my beautiful wife walking on the sand while chatting with Jimmy's wife. Jimmy and I stood by the lifeguard station and reminisced while we looked at the sun disappear over the horizon and jets taking off from Los Angeles International Airport. I was happy to be there and happier still, that I left when I did.

I found happiness away from the alluring golden light of Southern California.

ABOUT THE AUTHOR

Born in Manhattan Beach, CA. Thomas was introduced to the art world at a young age. His father was a painter and sculptor, an artist. Thomas is a writer by vocation and a recovering financial analyst.

He considerers himself fortunate that his first jobs allowed him to travel internationally and participate in projects in Europe and Central America.

While Thomas considers himself a sea creature, he lives in the Arizona high desert.

Visit www.thomaskilcourse.com